RED SHOE DIARIES

Zalman King's

RED SHOE DIARIES

Four on the Floor

Stacey Donovan & Elise D'Haene

BASED ON THE TELEPLAYS

♦ "The Psychiatrist"
written by Nelly Alard

♦ "Four on the Floor"
written by Joelle Bentolila

♦ "Emily's Dance"
written by Richard Baskin

AND THE ORIGINAL STORY

♦ "Sex in the Hamptons: The Writers' Confessions"
written by Stacey Donovan & Elise D'Haene

BERKLEY BOOKS, NEW YORK

THE BERKLEY PUBLISHING GROUP
Published by the Penguin Group
Penguin Group (USA) Inc.
375 Hudson Street, New York, New York 10014, USA
Penguin Group (Canada), 90 Eglinton Avenue East, Suite 700, Toronto, Ontario M4P 2Y3, Canada
(a division of Pearson Penguin Canada Inc.)
Penguin Books Ltd., 80 Strand, London WC2R 0RL, England
Penguin Group Ireland, 25 St. Stephen's Green, Dublin 2, Ireland (a division of Penguin Books Ltd.)
Penguin Goup (Australia), 250 Camberwell Road, Camberwell, Victoria 3124, Australia
(a division of Pearson Australia Group Pty. Ltd.)
Penguin Books India Pvt. Ltd., 11 Community Centre, Panchsheel Park, New Delhi—110 017, India
Penguin Group (NZ), Cnr. Airborne and Rosedale Roads, Albany, Auckland 1310, New Zealand
(a division of Pearson New Zealand Ltd.)
Penguin Books (South Africa) (Pty.) Ltd., 24 Sturdee Avenue, Rosebank, Johannesburg 2196,
South Africa

Penguin Books Ltd., Registered Offices: 80 Strand, London WC2R 0RL, England

This book is an original publication of The Berkley Publishing Group.

This is a work of fiction. Names, characters, places, and incidents either are the product of the authors' imagination or are used fictitiously, and any resemblance to actual persons, living or dead, business establishments, events, or locales is entirely coincidental.

PRINTING HISTORY
Berkley trade paperback edition / August 2005

Library of Congress Cataloging-in-Publication Data

Zalman King's red shoe diaries: Four on the floor / [edited by] Stacey Donovan and Elise D'Haene.—
    Berkley trade pbk. ed.
        p. cm.
    "Based on the teleplays "The psychiatrist," written by Nelly Alard; "Four on the floor," written by Joelle Bentolila; "Emily's dance," written by Richard Baskin; and the original story "Sex in the Hamptons, the writers' confessions," written by Stacey Donovan and Elise D' Haene."
    Contents: The psychiatrist—Four on the floor—Emily's dance—Sex in the Hamptons, the writers' confessions.
    ISBN 0-425-20279-8
        1. Erotic stories, American. I. Title: Four on the floor. II. D'Haene, Elise, 1959– . III. Donovan, Stacey. IV. King, Zalman. V. Red shoe diaries (Television program)

PS648.E7Z347 2005
813'.01083538—dc22   2005045364

PRINTED IN THE UNITED STATES OF AMERICA

10 9 8 7 6 5 4 3 2 1

Contents

◆

WOMEN

Do you keep a diary?
Have you been betrayed?
Have you betrayed another?
Man, 35, wounded and alone,
recovering from loss
of a once in a lifetime love
looking for reasons why.

Send diaries to Red Shoes, P.O. Box 315,
Los Angeles, CA 90203

The
Psychiatrist

♦

JAKE

Stella, tell me. Who do you know who doesn't have a secret? A bone buried somewhere—either in the past, in the closet, in his or her psyche? My guess is there's not a soul alive without some kind of secret—man or dog. In your case, the bones are made of rawhide, and you tend to bury them under my dirty laundry in the loft. As for me, it's as if I'm choking on the secrets Alex left behind, choking on Alex's bones. After countless sleepless nights, I finally stopped asking myself why she did what she did, but that only led me to wonder what it all meant, what secrets themselves really mean.

Do we hide them deep inside because what we ultimately want is to have something that is truly ours, something no one else can take away? Or do our secrets help define us, somehow represent who we actually are? Maybe it's even simpler: Our secrets keep us from being lonely. Nah, I don't buy that either; I bet hoarding secrets makes us even lonelier. And—depending on just how dark they are—our secrets might scare us so much we can't possibly imagine revealing them;

we'll hide inside of ourselves instead, not wanting anyone to encounter our darkest parts.

Yet it occurs to me that being scared might not be such a bad idea. I mean, fear might make us behave in ways we would never otherwise, which ultimately could be a beautiful thing.

Listen to this, Stella. Then you let me know what you think:

♦ ♦ ♦

Dear Red Shoes,

Secrets you can't confess to your mother, shrink, or priest. That line has haunted me. You want to know why? I'll tell you. It's because *I'm* a shrink. A medical doctor. A psychiatrist. Twelve hard years of college, medical school, and residency, just to earn the right to listen to people's secrets all day long. To judge, to advise, to administer, to help.

It's a profession I adore, an honor I strive to live up to. Yet where am I to go with *my* secrets? I can't possibly talk to another psychiatrist. The bedrock of the relationship between psychiatrist and patient is confidentiality, so that is where my loyalty lies in this instance. Yet my question has become terribly urgent, and so I ask you: What happens when the wall between you and your patient comes tumbling down . . . ?

EVELYN

I wish I knew the answer to that. I'd been trying to find it in the crisp autumn air of Paris, the winding streets I'd been roaming obsessively, troubled by the confessions of my patient Linda.

Linda was young, hungry, fresh faced. She was dark-haired,

impulsive, stylish. I was older, moderate, seasoned. I was white-blond, contemplative, classic.

Linda lived on the Right Bank near the Seine with her father, a somewhat recent widower who clearly felt the need to try to control her every move. Because Linda was still pursuing her undergraduate studies, she felt trapped by her father's control—which extended to her sex life. Yielding quite the opposite effect of his intentions, I imagine, his old-fashioned sensibility eventually helped transform the way in which Linda approached dating and relationships.

Because she couldn't bring a date home without her father nearly coming to blows with whomever it was, she quit that activity pretty quickly. Linda replaced it with a purposeful lack of commitment to anyone, which soon led to the birth of anonymity in her sexual relationships. Not wanting to become too serious with anyone during her university scholarship anyway, Linda began to date strangers only instead of the occasional fellow student she'd been involved with initially during her stay in France.

It thrilled her, she explained. Naturally, I thought, being so young with so little experience, her spirit was expansive, adventurous, untainted. Yet because she created a rule that governed her experiences—she would see someone only once—I wondered whether she was becoming truly obsessive.

During our sessions, I soon discovered that when we'd reach psychological material she simply did not want—or was unable—to explore, she'd leap back to what had become a very safe subject matter: the strained relationship at home.

"I had another fight with my father last night," she announced recently. "So I got pissed and I stormed out. I rode around in a cab all night. Until I got this brilliant idea to go to Nice. . . ."

"Nice?" I asked.

"Yeah."

"Why Nice?"

"I don't know, Evelyn. My friend Dominique's from there. So I took the TGV . . . and that's where it happened again."

"Again?"

"I met a man." She paused. "He took my hand . . . and I followed him along the corridor to the very back of the train . . . to the very last compartment. It was empty except for a woman who seemed completely oblivious to us. We made love in the aisle and on a seat near her. How odd is that?"

"Interesting. And again this was a man you'd never seen before? A complete stranger?"

She beamed. "That's what makes it so exciting."

"And very dangerous." Uncharacteristically, I found myself stating the obvious.

"I know. But that's part of the thrill."

Her obvious excitement disturbed me, though I knew instantly I would not have been able to explain why.

"Then what happened?" I pressed.

"Well, turns out the man and woman were together. They asked me if I wanted to join them for bouillabaisse at their hotel in Antibes."

"And?"

"They were staying at that fabulous Hotel du Cap. Of course I went!"

She told me the details of her experience there, and then she stood up.

"Bye, Evelyn. See you next Thursday."

"Linda, please be careful," was my reply.

"I will."

But would she? Was it my own personal inexperience with that kind of impulsive behavior that initially led to my concern? Or was there something else about Linda that I was responding to—something deeper—that I was not yet privy to in myself?

After she left, I saw that her necklace had fallen between the pillows of the sofa. I retrieved it, rolling the colorful stones between my fingers as I ruminated over my troubled reaction to our discussion today. My mind wandered back to my very first session with Linda, when she told me about her first anonymous encounter.

She was approached by two young men while searching for some paperback editions of Proust at a bookseller's outside stall by the Seine. The two students invited her for a drink at a small café on Rue de la Harpe, a medieval street in nearby Place St. Michel where many students spent long hours in philosophical or literary discussion. The pair of young men was interested in art and literature, and because Linda was studying to be a translator, they found they had much to talk about.

As the night wore on, no one wanted to leave. Leo, the bearded, black-haired, quick-witted art historian, eventually suggested that they return to his place for a cognac. Linda, infused with the energy of their nonstop banter about Paris's history and its many luminaries—the poets, the painters, the novelists, and sculptors—readily agreed.

"Fish," as he was called, the lean, somewhat quiet, more somber of the young men, bumped lightly against Linda as they walked. The closer they got to Leo's, the faster they strode, Leo now moving in step with Linda, eventually encircling her shoulders with one of his burly arms. At that point, the trio had begun to sing an old Bob Dylan song called "Simple Twist of Fate" in wobbly French. Fish slipped his arm around her waist as they weaved along the cobblestone streets.

What was happening? Whatever it might be, Linda was game. The idea of being with two men had never even occurred to her, and the fact that they were so different from each other was even more enticing. As Leo fumbled for his keys outside his apartment building, Fish leaned against Linda and kissed her hands, her neck, her lips. She kissed him back hungrily.

Leo grunted in approval as he opened the door to the building, and he then gestured for the two of them to walk ahead of him up the stairs. Linda soon understood why when he reached one hand between her legs and cupped it there as she continued to climb. Leo let out a low whistle.

He was so like his name, Linda told me: big and beefy as a lion, the thick beard framing his face as a mane would frame a lion's. The sounds he emitted were an early indication of the kind of pleased growls that would soon escape him—once he'd watched Fish strip Linda, throw the bedcovers back, and lay her naked across the bed, sideways. From behind her, Leo slid her to the edge of the mattress, her knees in the air, so that Fish could begin to lap at her private mysteries while Leo knelt above her, his leonine penis dangling from its fur like a fleshy spear as he leaned over her and lowered his mouth to her breasts.

Linda reached up to grip Leo's hips, hoping to take his stiff penis into her mouth, but he answered that wish by taking each of her hands with one of his own and pushing them to the bed. She gasped as he held her there, his lips, tongue, and teeth gently teasing each breast until the hidden rope of pleasure between her breasts and her vulva began to tighten and her breath turned ragged. When Fish leaned back and blew long hot breaths against her clitoris, she arched with pleasure. Leo responded by sucking each of her mounds, his beard chafing the tender flesh in a way she had never felt before. Fish ran his fingertips up and down the back of her thighs, making her shiver with pleasure, a feeling that leapt like fire to the aching velvet of her aureoles and made her cry out.

Leo grunted with deep satisfaction as Fish wrapped his lips around Linda's swollen clit and licked lightly. Leo leaned back and lifted her legs straight up so that the bare soles of her feet pointed toward heaven; he held them there while Fish flicked his tongue slowly and Linda started writhing, panting from her own heat.

When she arched back again, Leo bent both of her legs and spread them apart so that she could push against his firm grip as she climaxed. It was like riding the wind, she explained. The orgasm soared through her like a skiff released from its mooring in a sudden gust, and her body bucked ecstatically. She realized where Fish had gotten his nickname: He was quite the expert at swimming through the sea of a woman's desire. Her cries only intensified as his skilled tongue barely lapped her exploding clit, waves of rapture sailing through her.

Above her, Leo groaned, his pleasure obviously deepening as his erect penis pulsed. When Linda reached up with both hands, he finally allowed her to grasp it. She felt its teeming strength and trembled at the idea of his entering her.

Still watching, Fish stood up and began stripping off his clothes. Leo knelt above Linda as she ministered to him.

"Slow at first," he directed, and she obeyed. She watched the one thick vein on the underside of his penis swell as she massaged the flesh; it made her hungry to take him into her mouth. She flipped over and knelt where Fish had been on the floor by the edge of the bed, urging Leo to come closer.

With a growl, he did. As she wrapped her lips around the rosy head of his cock, Leo moaned. She reached around and held his muscular buttocks so that she could anchor herself as she began to suck him. Leo whimpered with pleasure.

She watched as Fish started to touch himself, his sweet, boyish body belying the masculinity of his erect cock. Different from Leo's, it was darker, purplish and lean; Leo's was thicker, hues of pink and rose. Fish's testicles nestled higher than Leo's, and he stepped beside Linda and reached for one of her hands to cup his jewels as his hand slid up and down, squeezing milk from the cock's tip and smearing it over his stiffness.

She sucked Leo faster now. His groans deepened.

"Not yet," he whispered, and he pulled away from her mouth. He slid onto his back and let his legs dangle to the floor, his throbbing penis standing so proud at twelve o'clock she almost leapt on top of it. That was when Fish slipped behind her and Leo reached up with both arms. Fish lifted her by the hips as Leo encircled her ribs with his hands. For a moment Linda was completely suspended in the air. She gasped at her sudden weightlessness and felt the heavenly vulnerability of her throbbing vagina.

As if they had done it a thousand times before, Fish lowered her slowly onto the head of Leo's waiting spear. They both held her there as she gasped again—in anticipation now—and Leo growled playfully as he slid unhurriedly inside of her. From behind, Fish stroked her buttocks until they tingled. She was shivering with delight as Leo held her hips and rose and lowered her onto his massive cock. Her breath was coming hard now as she rode this gentle lion, and her thrill met surprise as she felt the arrival of Fish's cock pressing against the opening of her anus.

Her legs trembled as she realized he wanted to enter her. Could she take it? Lord, having two cocks inside her had never before crossed her mind. As if on cue, she felt Fish's slick tongue tease her dark hole. It was such a strangely sweet feeling she collapsed against Leo, allowing Fish to begin to rim her expertly. He'd circle her hole maddeningly slowly with his tongue before curling his lips around the virginal chasm and lightly sucking as if in slow motion.

Linda moaned as each man found a rhythm. Each time Leo lifted her, Fish would tongue her hole, now and then dipping a slippery finger into that hidden chamber. Then Leo would pull her down, plunging inside and holding her in place so that Fish could part her cheeks and burrow his darting tongue deeper.

For a moment, she thought she would faint—it was just too much. But that was when Fish pulled his mouth away and replaced it with the tip of his cock. Leo slid his hands around her ass and cupped them there as he undulated gently inside of her.

Linda felt she would burst as Fish gripped her hips and glided slowly into her. She wondered how much she could take as he inched tenderly inside, filling her with so much feeling she thought she would explode there and then. Amazing creature that he was, Leo licked one of his thumbs and then began to circle it around her clit, once, twice, and her back arched again. Fish moaned as her ass rose to meet him, and Leo pulsed inside of her as he stroked her clit with one hand and trailed his other lightly along her spine.

Once, twice—his thumb felt like a flame. Four, five circles, and as Fish stiffened against her, ready to burst, Leo came first, a gravelly bellow filling the air. Their bodies locked together, and rapturous tears slid from Linda's eyes as Fish filled her ass, a fierce quivering overtaking him as his cum seeped hotly inside. He still held her hips as he sucked in a fresh mouthful of air and Leo's thumb circled once, twice more.

Linda panted and stiffened suddenly as her climax started to climb through her. Her entire body began to spasm ecstatically as the men held her from above and below, and while Linda was rocked by the delectable waves, she vowed silently to devote herself to a life filled with passion—and passionate strangers.

As I drifted back to reality, I could not help but wonder whether or not Linda would get what she wanted from life. I admit, it was impossible not to get swept up in the intensity of an experience like that. I also have to confess that, as I recalled her story, I found myself splayed across my own sofa before my next patient arrived forty-five minutes later, my skirt hiked up so that one hand was free to plunge into my own wetness while the other teased my swollen clit. With my head dropped back on the sofa's arm and my eyes closed, I did not notice my office door open, nor did I see the person step silently inside.

I breathed hard as I imagined the sensation of two stiff cocks filling me simultaneously. I dragged the necklace across my breasts, the weight of the colorful beads heavy as fingertips, which excited me even more. I let the necklace rest atop the flimsy fabric of the blouse covering my breasts as I reached down and slid my index and middle fingers inside, the very same fingers of my other hand lingering on my clit.

Once, twice, I circled my aching button. Three, four, I fucked myself that many times. Five, six, the number of breaths before I came in a rush, moaning, dripping, my heartbeat hurried.

After the pulsing of my heart eventually slowed down, my eyelids fluttered open. There was Linda, watching me from the doorway, a shy yet rapt smile on her face.

"I came back for the necklace . . ." she began.

I tore it from its perch on my bosom and bolted upright.

". . . but it's my gift to you. See you next week."

I was speechless. She was gone.

I pulled myself together just in time for my next patient's arrival. After the session, the last one of the day, I decided a long walk would help me think things through. How did I feel about Linda watching me? How long had she been there? Obviously I would have to say something about what had just happened at our next session, but I had no idea what. How could I have let it occur?

Had I ever done that in my office before?

There was something about Linda that was really getting under my skin.

I could feel myself blush with each step. What did that smile of hers really mean? Was she turned on by me? Was I jazzed by her? Just as she had never thought of being with two men at once, I had never thought of being with a woman. The truth was, I could not even remember the last time I had sex with a man. Even if I had, would I have the courage today to embark on a sexy rendezvous with a stranger? Two men? A woman?

I found myself staring at my own image in a store window. Tentatively I lifted Linda's necklace to my neck and fastened the clasp from behind. Given what I had done with the accessory earlier, I now imagined it was like strapping on a sex toy, yet this one was visible, proudly displayed, even. Was it the anonymity of a public place that led me to do this? Did I want others to see me? What was I capable of, really?

Mercy—I was the one who needed a shrink.

All night, I tossed and turned. I was tormented by the story Linda told me earlier that day. No matter how I tried, I could not get the man—or the woman—that Linda had met on the train to Nice out of my mind.

He was in his mid-twenties, the younger of the two, Linda said. They might have been ten years apart in age. He had winked at Linda as she made her way to the bar car for some water, a shock of black hair falling over one eye as he peered shyly at her, and then he boldly met her gaze on her way back when she smiled at him. It was then that the train shook and she lost her balance, grabbing the back of a seat to avoid falling. He had leapt up and grasped her free hand. Without a word, she allowed him to squeeze it.

Wearing an expensive black suit, he led her back through several compartments, all the way to the last car of the train. It was completely empty but for a lone woman, an elegant, sharp-featured beauty, her midnight-colored hair settling softly against the edges of her face. Yet she seemed completely oblivious to them, her unwavering gaze locked on the countryside beyond the train window as the train sped toward the coast.

Balancing himself against one of the seats with his back toward the other woman, the man drew Linda closer slowly using both arms. He pulled her near as if in a dance, his lanky arms pressing her against his chest. Though they had not uttered a word to each other, she found herself leaning into him with no hesitation, only excitement. His hands slid to the small of her back as she tipped her head and met his gaze, their lips merely inches from each other's.

His mouth was bow shaped, a dimple deepening each side of his smile. He bent his head and met her lips softly, surprising her. He kissed her with utter tenderness, every so often nibbling her lower lip as his hands began to caress her back, her hips, slowly half-circling her waist and torso, teasing each rib as his fingers gradually rose to her breasts.

It was a challenge to stay balanced as the train barreled across the landscape, but he had stepped carefully when he first embraced her, setting each foot down on the outside of hers so that if she lost her balance, she'd fall against him. She was particularly aware of this as his hands cupped her breasts and he finally parted her lips with his tongue, meeting hers for the first time.

Their breaths quickened as their tongues tasted each other's, and the man's hardening erection now strained against his trousers. Linda swayed a bit as his fingers began to play with her nipples through her blouse. He knew just how to touch her, it seemed. The pressure he exerted between thumb and index finger was so perfectly orchestrated it was as if he had always known what she wanted and had done just that.

She moaned and fell against him as the train jerked, his fingers moving in expert circles that sent pulsing currents through her pelvis, deep into her groin. His tongue moved faster now, exploring the silky tissue beyond her lips, probing her mouth with his small, eager shoot as she reached around and began to stroke his buttocks.

It was his turn to moan as she pressed her pelvis against his, welcoming the sudden rush of adrenaline that accompanied the connection of their genitalia. Still kissing her, his mouth was open as he sighed, and she swallowed the sound as she would the comforting voice of an old friend. She squeezed the cheeks of his ass and ground herself against him harder, her breasts hungry for the continued touch of his fingers.

As if he knew just what she were thinking, he slowly unbuttoned her blouse, tenderly caressing the satin of her black bra before lifting it above her breasts with both hands. She gasped as he cupped each exposed mound in his palms and then lightly kneaded the flesh that had begun to throb from this very unexpected attention. He returned to her nipples after licking the tip of his index finger and slowly circling each aureole with it.

"As big as silver dollars, but worth their weight in gold," he whispered.

His first words to her, in a throaty (was it Italian?) accent, but what could she say in response? She could barely remain standing as he started to drum each nipple with two of his fingers, luscious, steamy currents coursing through her with each beat. She felt her knees about to give as he softly stabbed her mouth with his tongue and did not stop teasing her now aching buds.

As she moaned and began to writhe beneath his touch, he quickened the tempo of his fingertips. They lightly slapped her nipples now, and the faster she breathed, the more his fingers moved. He added pressure then, so that her breasts began to undulate from side to side as he tormented them so enticingly. Her entire torso began to tremble from delight—and her shame in that delight: to be so exposed, so vulnerable, and with a stranger to whom she had not even spoken!

Her breasts bobbed with each breath, the flesh heaving with desire. He finally relented, releasing her aureoles from their spanking and grabbing her to him, crushing her aching bosom against him. She reached for his belt buckle, and he went still for a moment, allowing her to unbuckle it. But then he bent her backward, lowering her onto an empty seat, in full view, Linda realized, of the one woman who sat in their compartment. Yet when Linda glanced in that direction, the woman was still looking intently out the window; he still had his back to her.

With the same certain fingers he had used on her breasts, the man hiked up Linda's skirt over her red panties. He slid a slow thumb over the drenched fabric covering her mound and stopped at her swelling clitoris, pressing against it so softly she trembled from such foreplay—and mounting frustration: He would not let her touch him at all. She stopped trying to as he inched off her scant bottoms, then spread her legs wide as he knelt before her pussy, that same slow thumb roaming up and down her dripping slit. Surprising her, he suddenly dipped a finger into her wet, wanting hole, plowing deep inside as he circled her clit with his maddeningly languorous thumb.

Linda moaned as he began to play her pussy as he had her breasts, such supreme orchestration of touch and pressure she thought she'd come at any instant. Yet just as she'd arch back and begin to peak, he would pull away, mesmerizing her with his mouth on her inner thigh, his tongue dancing across the tender flesh, his fingers taunting the moist pelvic crevice where her leg ended and her torso began.

What was he waiting for, she wondered? Did he want her to beg for it? She realized she still had not said a word and could not even imagine speaking now. Small sounds had been escaping her since he'd lain her down, punctuated by lingering sighs and the occasional need to catch her breath.

Again he seemed to read her mind. His mouth crept from the top of her thigh to her throbbing nest. He dragged his tongue across the flushed tissue and when he found her clitoris, he closed his lips around it. Her eyes tightly shut, she thought she would explode. He lifted his head away from her then, and her eyelids fluttered open. With a smile, he gently parted the lips of her vagina before lowering his head once more and flicking his tongue along her clit with a superb, searing precision.

She shut her eyes again, but something made her open them,

and she caught the gaze of the other woman in the compartment. Stunned, Linda held her penetrating gaze as she felt her deepest being begin to flush. The pent passion that had been trapped inside all the while he had masterfully punished her breasts, legs, hips, now ravaged every nerve ending as she arched back, the orgasm soaring through her. She bucked over and over, her ass slapping the leather seat as the endless groan that escaped her filled the compartment.

When it was over, the woman looked away. He, of course, had not seen this silent exchange, and he seemed quite satisfied by what had just occurred. He stood up then, straddling her sideways as she sat up. He unzipped his trousers, finally freeing his cock.

It was uncut.

She was amazed.

Linda had never seen an uncircumcised penis before. Initially, it both attracted her (its girth, its mystery) and repelled her (its appearance, its unfamiliarity). Yet, when she reached out her hand, she described doing so as if in a dream. It looked like a dark, fleshy stocking covered his hard shaft. It felt like there was a revelation beneath. A little round gape was visible at its tip, and when she teased back the blanket of foreskin, the folds around his cock appeared a deeper red than his pinkish naked spear. That made her feel, she explained, oddly tender. That and the reality of his shaft, glistening and exposed, as if it were so vulnerable it needed the embracing wall of wrinkly flesh around it before her touch. Was it unusually sensitive from being protected all the time? she wondered. She licked her palm and glided the skin back very gently, circling the pink, exposed shaft a breath at a time.

He let out a wanting, teeming sigh.

With one hand on his penis and the other cupping his hefty scrotum, she began to stroke him, taking delight in the fact that each time her hands met at the base, his foreskin had followed. She marveled at the shiny wonder before her, such a combination of testosterone and tenderness.

Besides delicately naked, his exposed cock seemed newborn. Needy, was how she put it.

It throbbed beneath her touch, and Linda intensified her ministering. Each time she stroked upward, she lingered on the exposed head. She sped up; she slowed down. He squirmed with pleasure, one hand in her hair while the other kept balance, gripping the back of a seat.

The train chugged along, and as if in sync, his pelvis rolled forward as his head tipped back. A guttural sound from his throat accompanied the final throb of his cock before it began spurting a shaky stream of milky cum.

Again, she was amazed: The woman across the compartment was smiling at her.

The man withdrew from her touch and slipped his penis back inside his trousers, zipping his pants with a heavy breath. Only then, after leaning down and kissing Linda gently, did he turn and meet the gaze of the other woman in the compartment.

She was still smiling.

What was this all about, Linda wondered as she dressed. Some kind of private game that the two played? Sex in public but only with strangers? Did the woman participate at all or was it only he? Did they take turns performing for the other? How long had they been doing this? How far would they go?

Linda found herself intensely curious.

As if on cue, the train conductor opened the door to their compartment, announcing the train's imminent arrival in Nice.

The woman rose from her seat as the man reached for Linda's hand. Again she allowed him to take it and stood up.

"Will you join us for lunch?" he asked her softly.

"It would be our pleasure," the woman hastened. She shared the same accent as he—yes, Italian. As she came closer, Linda took in the woman's sharp, foxy features, both predatory and protective, jutting forward, but in such a graceful way, before she kissed Linda on both cheeks. Her lower lip was long and full, her upper lip more delicate, the center of it spilling forward seductively. And her kiss was so casual, as if they had known each other forever.

Without hesitation, Linda agreed.

She arrived late for her next session. After not meeting my gaze at first, she finally looked at me.

"So are you one of those women who'd just go with men who won't even look at you?" she asked casually.

I smiled, but I did not answer. Hers was a challenging inquiry, asked with a sharp edge that belied her seeming casualness. The question revealed instead a level of anxiety that I was sure had to do with her seeing me with my hand between my legs after our last session.

"Linda," I began, "we need to talk about what happened the last time you were here. . . ."

She looked at me blankly.

I could feel myself blushing but pressed on. "First of all, I apologize for putting you in such an uncomfortable position. I want to assure you that nothing like that will ever happen again."

"I wasn't uncomfortable," she replied with a shrug. "Hey, what you do in the privacy of your own office is none of my business. I should have knocked on the door and I didn't, so I'm sorry for that. It's history," she said with a smile. "And never mind about what I just asked you about men. I was just wondering. . . ."

Her words faded away as a look of new wonder crossed her face. "You know," she admitted, "I dreamt about you last night."

"Really?" I answered. "Well, what did you dream?"

"I was at the Royal Saint-Honoré Hotel with a man. He was sitting in an armchair just like yours. I was standing there, naked, wanting him to make love to me. But you were there, too, in the doorway. I kept thinking: *What are you doing there watching us?* What do you think that means?"

My mind grappled with my own associations. The reality was, Linda had stood in my doorway a week ago watching me. She'd been fully clothed, of course. In her dream, her nakedness possibly expressed her unbound desire. Why a hotel? Hotels create a certain sense of anonymity—even loneliness—in many of their guests. Who was the man, I wondered, sitting in *my* armchair? Was this Linda's way of wrestling with her own homoerotism? Was I really the object of her desire? Was the dream a study in wish fulfillment? Linda had not mentioned whether I was naked, too. I needed more information.

"I'm not sure, really," I finally responded. "Why the Royal? Did something happen there recently? You want to tell me about it?"

"Well, I went there recently. Just after our last session as a matter of fact."

"Why?"

"I wanted a drink. I heard somewhere that they're not as strict about women going alone into the bar. You know, that sort of thing."

"Is that really why you went there?" I pressed.

"I guess I went out of curiosity. There was a man there . . . a Spanish businessman. Eventually he told me that he often came to Paris and stayed at the Royal because he liked the smell of the roses from across the street in the park."

"You mean the Tuileries Gardens?"

"Right. There were other men at the bar, of course. But he stood out—something about him. Oh, he was gorgeous and sophisticated, all right, but there was something else about him, something . . . mysterious. He certainly had my attention, and he never stopped looking at me. After I finally smiled at him, he came over and put an envelope down in front of me. Then he left the bar."

"He just walked out without a word?"

"Yeah. I waited a minute, but then I opened the envelope. It was full of money along with his room number written on a little card."

"What did you do?" I asked, not at all surprised at Linda's coquettish smile.

"I had another drink, and then I went to his room. He was waiting for me, I could tell. As soon as he opened the door he said—with quite the sexy accent: 'It excites you, doesn't it, that I want to pay for you? That's why you don't do this professionally.'

"'And how do you know that?' I asked him.

"'I pay,' he answered, 'I get to ask the questions. What's your name?'

"'Isabel,' I said.

"'What's your name?' he repeated.

"'Linda,' I told him. I took off my coat and sat down in front of him.

"'Linda,' he echoed. 'That means "pretty" in Spanish. Tell me, Linda, what's your favorite color? And don't tell me red. That's what you tell everyone, but it's not true.'

"'Yellow,' I answered. He was right—red was not my favorite color.

"He nodded. 'Yellow—that's a very simple color. Very honest. That's why I like money. It buys simplicity and honesty. A lot of money buys a lot of simplicity and a lot of honesty. No?'

"He opened his briefcase and took out a stack of currency bills. 'One thousand euros,' he said. He stepped toward me and placed one bill at my feet. 'Will you stand here, by the window?' he asked. I did. He put another bill at my feet. I swear, I was already creaming. . . .

"'Take off your dress,' he said. 'Show me your breasts.' I shivered—there was a slight chill from the window, and my nipples were hard as I pulled my dress down to my waist. I wore a black bra, and I took it off very slowly.

"He put another bill on the floor. 'Turn around,' he ordered. 'Lift up the back of your dress.' As I did, he put another bill on the floor. 'Take off your panties,' he demanded. I felt myself starting to tremble, but I did it; I shimmied out of them and let them fall to the floor.

"He stared at me. 'Drop your dress,' he whispered. As he put another bill on the floor, I realized I was surrounded by money. I let my dress fall into the pile, and I stood there naked except for my stockings and stilettos. It was hard to breathe I was so turned on, my chest heaving. His eyes drank me in. . . .

"'Can you see the reflection of yourself in the window?' he asked.

"'Yes,' I whispered.

"'Are you amazed by what you see?' That I couldn't answer.

"'Men have always tried to capture the beauty of a naked woman,' he went on. 'The ancient Greeks . . . Michelangelo . . . Rubens . . . Rodin . . . But how could you ever contain the heat . . . the scent . . . the luxury of a woman in paint or alabaster? You're beautiful, such a lovely creature . . .' As he talked I slid to the floor—it was just too much. My nipples were hard, my breasts swelling. I didn't intend to touch myself, but I started to, one hand holding each mound, just to calm down, to catch my breath. 'Yes,' he said, 'yes, beautiful.'

"He kept tossing money on the floor so I kept touching myself—eventually I slid my hand between my legs. 'Yes, yes . . . lovely,' he kept saying. God, it was like a lake down there. I didn't know I could get that wet, dripping wet. 'Beautiful . . . lovely. Oh, yes!' he went on.

"It was amazing, to touch myself like that in front of someone—in front of a stranger! I had never done anything like it before. No one had ever watched me like that, showered me with money that way. Unbelievable, but I walked out of there with five thousand euros! Evelyn, you can't imagine what it's like to have a man want you that much. Can you?"

The question was: Could I even speak after hearing that story? Was Linda telling the truth, or was she spouting fantasy? Ultimately, it seemed, this Spanish stranger had paid her to masturbate—the very activity she had recently seen me engage in. Because that experience had occurred mere minutes after that session—for which *she* paid—I believed there was an undeniable parallel between the two situations. My mind scrambled to make sense of it all before I spoke specifically about my thoughts to my patient.

Evelyn, I told myself, *you've been doing this for years. You've heard many stories . . . just not been quite so "involved" in one. Act like a professional!*

Stalling for time, I cleared my throat. "Ah, Linda, I thought that you were going to stop doing things like this."

She stared at me. "Did I say that?"

"You said you would be careful."

"Well, what about my dream? You still haven't told me about it."

Her tone was challenging; what I'd come to expect when she didn't want to talk about something any longer. But switching gears to ask for my thoughts about the dream meant that Linda was seeking something from me, rather than pressing herself to find her own meaning or offering more of her own psyche to herself. To be most effective, a dream should be interpreted by its own dreamer. I searched for a soft way to say this in order not to alienate Linda.

"I think it's okay . . ." I began, "I think it's okay that you're dreaming about me. And that the work we're doing is having an impact. . . ."

But then I felt myself blush at the thought that our "work" had led to Linda's masturbatory session with a stranger. Oddly aroused, my words faded away as sexual energy flushed through me and my clitoris suddenly throbbed.

Linda stared brazenly at me, insistent and uncomprehending.

"You know what I think?" she blurted. "I think you don't have the slightest idea what it is to feel anything. What it is to feel love . . . pain . . . fear . . . even pleasure. You just sit there in your big chair telling people not to do this, not to do that. I mean, you think I don't notice the way you look at me when I tell you about my life? You should be paying me. Hah!"

There it was—*she thought I should be paying her.* My theory was correct.

She leapt up and headed for the door.

"Linda, wait a minute!" I called.

But without another word, she left. If she had stayed, I

wonder whether I would have been able to tell her she was right—I did have a big chair. Yet she was wrong about the rest, wrong about thinking all I did was tell people not to do things. It was my job to help her see things about herself and about what happened in her life, so that she could make the most of her own experience.

At the moment, I questioned my ability to do just that. Had the experience of seeing me masturbate in my office traumatized Linda? Had she made up the Spanish Stranger? It suddenly occurred to me that I could actually walk into the bar at the Royal Saint-Honoré and see if he really existed.

Something else that struck me then was about myself. Linda's experiences were teaching me that casual sexual escapades could be spectacularly sexy. Judging from my level of embarrassment and inarticulateness on the subject, however, I myself was not quite ready.

Is anyone ever ready?

Linda's abrupt exit left me feeling exhausted, so I indulged myself by reclining on the couch for a moment. As I lay there, I recalled what had happened when Linda arrived in Nice. The trio strolled along the promenade that ran parallel to the sea there, a row of long-standing, ornate hotels flanking the curb on the opposite side. It was still warm enough for a bevy of bare-breasted girls to sunbathe on the strip of beach that hugged the water, but traffic was loud, bordering on frantic, and Catarina—the name of the woman who had finally met Linda's gaze on the train—rushed them into a cab. She ordered the driver to take them to Antibes, which was situated between Cannes and Nice.

———

wonder sashaying across her ass as she made her way to chemistry class or French class or anywhere.

There was one boy in particular, who Linda had known since childhood, who was obviously smitten the very first time Olivia walked into homeroom. Mike was the boy that all the girls had swooned over and dreamed about. Until Olivia, he had been oblivious.

Linda remembered the agony. She recalled what it felt like to watch it happen, to see Mike fall for Olivia in exactly the same way she did—completely. It was one thing for she and Olivia to become "best friends." It was quite another to watch her heartfelt love succumb to Mike's charms.

Mike was lucky enough to kiss her.

Linda was unlucky.

Mike got to lie with her in the grassy lawn outside school, let his hand roam beneath her blouse and hesitate there, let his body press against hers.

Linda had come upon them one afternoon doing just this. Though she really did not understand at that moment all it meant, that excruciating instant so influenced a part of her becoming: Why wasn't it her there pressing? Why, though she felt the aching desire for Olivia, did she also know that the expression of those feelings in that particular circumstance would be unwelcome at best?

It unmoored her.

Does anyone ever forget what it's like to love and to be misunderstood? In Linda's situation, what could she have said to her friend other than "I love you"? They certainly expressed that to each other. Further, Linda fell to tears when Olivia presented her with a birthday gift that year: a crew-neck sweater in a forest green, Olivia's favorite color. It was a color Linda never would have chosen, so lush and vibrant, so like Olivia herself.

Linda would sometimes wear the sweater when she saw Olivia; otherwise it lay perfectly folded in a special place in her closet. In fact, it still did, which was an interesting admission, of course. I refrained from surmising too much of it, however, for sometimes young love is truly genderless. When a girl loved a girl or a boy loved a boy in a special, intimate way, it did not necessarily mean that later in life a woman would love a woman or a man a man in a romantic way. Still, from time to time, Linda would crush the sweater against her face, wanting always to be that close to Olivia herself.

No matter how lovely or verdant the sweater might be, wrapping it in her arms never came near to what it felt like just to be near Olivia, to accidentally brush against her, to breathe in her earthy scent, to inhale her voice. To hear Olivia say the sweet things young women whisper to each other when they've entered love together—albeit without touch—still filled her with longing. Their laughter, so sudden and innocent, echoed in her ears.

Nothing had ever been more magical than those moments, and the misery that followed when they faded—into more and more of Mike—was unforgettable.

Linda could do nothing but weep and wrench herself away. She withdrew from her circle of friends and vowed never to fall in love again. The cry of an adolescent in agony, undoubtedly, but the reality was, Linda had not fallen in love since.

Was that to be my fate, too? For the rest of the day, Linda's voice—and her experiences—filled my mind: *You can't imagine what it's like to have a man want you that much. Can you? Are you one of those women who'd just go with men who won't even look at you? I don't think you have the slightest idea what it is to feel anything. I was at the Royal. I heard somewhere that they're not as strict about women going alone into the bar.*

After I left the office, I wandered from boulevard to boulevard—my favorite way to think. Maybe it was the sound of my own feet on the concrete below, convincing me that I was alive. Maybe it was the challenge in Linda's voice or my seeming inability to embrace a new sexuality. Regardless, I vowed to change.

Right now.

A new outfit was essential—something provocative, short and tight. It took three stores to find the perfect black suit. New stilettos were next: the highest heel, the sleekest toe. Finish it off with a steaming bath, fresh hair and makeup, a dose of hope—thanks to my new suit—and I was ready for my appearance at the Royal.

When I walked in, I was greeted by a smoky haze surrounding the sleek wooden bar. There were a few patrons seated on stools—men, of course.

Still wearing my camel-hair coat, I sat down and greeted the bartender in French: *"Bonsoir."*

"Bonsoir, madame," he replied.

I ordered a vodka martini and sipped it slowly. I crossed my legs, already feeling a riveting flush inflame my synapses, silently shirring across the private pond between my legs. I dared not look around too much; I was anxious that Linda's date—or her apparition—would somehow sense I had come specifically to find *him.*

When I put a few bills on the bar to pay for my drink, the bartender said: *"C'est deja arregle, par le monsieur la bas."*

He motioned to the approaching businessman, who had apparently already paid for my martini. Ah, he must be Linda's Spanish Stranger! He was indeed a classically handsome, raven-haired man of sculpted features. Another flush vaulted through my synapses, momentarily causing a deep contraction in the neglected tunnel below my hips. I made myself turn away from him and told the bartender: "Tell the *monsieur* thank you, but no."

Too late—the businessman sat down beside me.

"Good evening," he said.

The thick, deep-throated accent immediately unnerved me.

"Look . . . I'm . . . I'm not what you think," I stammered. My first line—I was that rusty.

He smiled slowly. "And what do you think I think you are? Do I think you're a prostitute? If you are, you're a prostitute trying very hard not to look like one. If you are, can I afford you? Paris is very expensive these days."

"I just came here for a drink," I answered. Mercy, that was flat. And here he was, teeming with wit and oozing testosterone.

"Then let me buy you one," he crooned.

"No, thank you. I . . . I've already had one." I sounded like a schoolgirl. Where had my new dose of hope gone? And my conviction to change?

"There was a time when a woman alone at a bar was considered *la puta*. In your case I'd say you were *la perdita*—the lost one."

He was exactly right; I was so lost at this moment.

The edges of his mouth curled deliciously as he went on. "Listen, I'll pay you a thousand euros if you let me buy you another drink. I'm sorry, I don't mean to insult you."

It was a dizzying proposal, but I could not find any centered part of me with which to respond. "No, it's . . . it's so strange," I blurted. "I mean, why would you do that?"

Come on, Evelyn, don't behave like a psychiatrist now, I chided myself.

"Let me buy you another drink and maybe you'll find out," he answered.

I vowed not to lose this moment, this possibility. "All right," I whispered.

"In my room," he said breathily.

"All right." I surrendered without so much as a smile.

He took my arm and escorted me toward the elevator, murmuring how lovely I was into my ear. When we arrived at his room, he invited me in.

"Take your coat off," he said. "Make yourself comfortable."

I did remove my coat, but I was certainly far from comfortable. I was grateful when he handed me a glass of vodka.

"Now that's a beautiful outfit," he said. "Do you wear it often?"

"No." My voice was flat.

"When you go on a date?" he teased.

"Ah, no, ah . . . I don't really go on . . ." Oh, I sounded like such an idiot! "No . . . hardly ever," I blubbered.

"So it's a special night." He lifted his glass in a toast. "To you," he said.

I froze right there and then. Toasting a stranger? What was I doing? "Ahhh . . . I really think I should be going," I said.

I put my drink on the table and headed for the door. From behind I heard: "I'll give you fifteen hundred euros if you stay."

I turned around to face him. Again, I could not resist him. It was his dark, penetrating eyes. It felt as if they had seen *everything* and yet were still willing, still wanting more.

"And five hundred euros more if you take your jacket off."

I unzipped and removed my jacket. My cheeks tingled with desire, with vulnerability.

"And the skirt . . . five hundred," he went on.

I slipped it off, then froze again. My shame overwhelmed me, taking control of the rest of me. I turned away from him, my arms reaching up to cover myself.

"No! Please, turn around . . . please . . ." he beseeched.

In spite of myself, I did.

"You are beautiful," he proclaimed. "Touch your skin . . . by your shoulder." He smiled, gesturing to his own shoulder, showing me what he wanted.

I tried to give him what he asked, caressing the softest part of my neck. For a moment, that felt okay, maybe I could do this, and I started to unhook my bra. Then I froze once more; he watched me.

"I want you to touch me . . ." I whispered. "I want you to touch me, please. . . ."

His turn to freeze. His mouth flattened into a thin, tense line. "No, please, don't. I can't," he answered.

Mortified, I grabbed my clothes, covering myself as quickly as I could. He wouldn't? He couldn't? What kind of game was this? I didn't understand. But then I remembered that he hadn't touched Linda, either.

"It's not you," he went on. "Listen, it's hard to explain. . . ."

"Never mind," I cut in. "You don't have to."

"Look," he insisted, "there's a certain type of girl I go for, you see. And you're not the type. You're the type I want to go out to dinner with and buy flowers for and bring you home and make love to you. Not *fuck* you. Not fuck you but make love to you."

I was dressed now, heading to the door, wanting to flee my humiliation at putting myself in this situation. Some game, his. But why did it make me feel so small?

"Don't go . . . please . . ." he went on.

He grabbed my arm.

I faced him and blurted: "Look at me. Maybe I want to be fucked. Maybe I want to be paid five thousand euros and walk out of here and never see you again—and not care."

Oh, that felt good beyond reason! I had liberated myself by merely stating my own truth. I yanked my arm away then, but he stopped me—and finally kissed me. I kissed him back.

There I was: not small but big, real, and so alive.

My lips on his literally took my breath away. I did not remember the last time I had kissed a man with such fever, abandon, fervor. Our mouths were ravenous; we seemed never to take our lips fully away from each other's during the long, pungent night.

Ours was the kind of lovemaking that included words, demanded words, and catapulted them into the mere breath of space between us. They were dazzling and unexpected, full of promise and wonder:

"Where have you been?"

"Do you like how I feel?"

"I knew I'd find you."

"Tell me something about yourself that nobody knows."

My heart began to hurt as he touched me. It had been such a long time since I'd felt anything as powerful as this, his hands climbing over me, my body waking as if it had been in a faraway sleep.

And then, his laughter. We swooned in each other's arms standing up for as long as we could. When we started to stumble, his throaty laugh burbled up, melodious, inviting. I could not help but laugh myself. Who was this hunky wonder of a man who had actually paid me to have a drink with him, offered large sums of money so that my clothes would fall away, beckoned me to touch myself, grabbed me in his arms with such beseeching glances?

I thought of him watching Linda, of Linda watching me. And then I forgot those thoughts: How often do you meet someone who makes you feel this way—fresh, playful, pure?

What did he really want?

What did *I* really want? I breathed him in as his hands roamed over my torso, my side, my hips. His touch started at my shoulders, my neck, and traced supple lines across my flesh.

He still had not reached for my breasts, though there they were a mere caress away. I appreciated how he refrained from the obvious.

I was naked; he, of course, was fully clothed. Time to change that, my hands said. They slid off his jacket, letting it fall to the floor. They began to unbutton each pearly circle of his Oxford shirt very slowly. They reached underneath it and roamed across the warm flesh of his belly, his chest, his nipples.

He moaned as I pulled off his shirt completely, my hands racing up and down his naked back. He was exquisite: smooth, burnished skin, his sinewy muscles like small mountains—and I could not wait to climb them!

I crushed my breasts against him. He responded by dragging his fingertips across my shoulders and then descending to my décolletage. The tips of his fingers whispered to my cleavage, the slightest pressure bending me backward slowly so that my breasts were eventually freed, anticipating him, dangling like ripe fruit in the sweet air between us.

All the while, kisses and words:

"Who are you?"

"I've been waiting for you for so long."

"You feel amazing."

"I've missed you so."

He reached down to the floor and lifted the shirt I had just slid off of him. He draped it gently around my shoulders and began to play with my breasts, grasping each one with his entire hand, dragging his fingers in that way of his, from the entire mound to the tip, over and over again.

I gasped, trembling from his insistence, his certainty that he was creating the very response in me that I was in fact experiencing. I knew this from the look in his eyes, the way he watched me each time his fingertips found my nipples.

Our eyes locked together, he began to squeeze my nubs, suddenly, superbly. I cried out. He slipped to one side of me and held me there, one arm around my waist, making me lean against him as the other reached again for my tits, which were stinging in the most glorious way.

Slap, squeeze, slap. The tissue flashed cold with fire. I could barely stand up. I fell into him as he spanked my breasts and crushed my nipples between his thumb and index finger, twisting the helpless nubbles into oblivion before bearing down on them with sudden pressure.

Time, for all I knew, had stopped.

I cried out as he lingered, softly teasing the searing flesh with an edge of pride I could only have imagined before that moment: Would he punish me for my desire? Castigate my pussy as he had my breasts? Would he push me down, lift my legs over his shoulders, and take me quickly? Urge me onto my knees and pump me from behind, making me wail as his rod raced in and out, holding me down so that I had to take all of it, so that he could reach deeper inside of me each time he thrust?

And how much did I want him? I would straddle his face at that instant if he wanted me to, spread my legs as wide as I could and grind my slit against his mouth. I would guide his strong, slippery tongue inside me as if it were his prick climbing in, my ass in the air, his wagging tongue straining to meet me.

I would offer him my asshole, lie flat on my back before rising up so that the handfuls of my cheeks filled the air. I'd balance on my elbows and heels, spread my ass cheeks apart before I swung toward him, attempting to catch his cock with my darkest, deepest chasm. My hands would grope for him, gripping his ass and pulling it toward me, against me, into me.

I would grind against him: pulling, wanting, closer. He would rise to his knees, poke my swollen, drenched pussy with his fingers, play my ballooning clit with his thumb. He would urge me to touch my breasts as he finally slid the tip of his desire into me, laggardly, delicately. He would wait until I could take a deep thrust, all of him, whispering his desire with every stroke: How tight I was. How he wanted me to hold him there. How he felt when I pulled him in. How I must keep him inside me.

He would reach for my hands, guide them across the sweet flesh of his ass, wanting me to hold on as he started to pump me, tell me to hold him while I started to moan, to tremble, my breasts bobbing with each stroke, each breath ripping through me.

Would I pound him the same way after? Would he let me drape him across the bed, turn him over onto his belly, rise up on my knees, and enter him from behind? He would have to, because that was my exact intention.

I would use my fingers, a dildo, my fist—whatever he wanted. First I would roll onto my back, let him impale me from above, tease his fantasies out of him so that they would oil the space between us, allowing us to slide forward in a way that can only be described as worldly, because it demanded everything—all parts of us, ready.

And I wanted him to straddle me from above, his long, fleshy need hard enough to render it thrilling. I wanted him to dangle it above me, wanted to watch his cock drip with desire as I spread my rosebud for him.

He stepped in front of me now and squeezed my breasts together. I let out a long breath. Was the mammary spanking over? He smiled, holding the weight of my mounds in his palms. He stared into my eyes; I stared back. I slid a hand to his crotch, held his hard package. We stayed like that for minutes on end, each of us pulsing, entering the moment like a marriage of heartbeats. Finally, he released me, and I, him.

"Spread yourself for me," he said.

"I'll do whatever you want," I answered, "on one condition. Do you agree?"

He did not hesitate. "I agree. What is it?"

"That you do the same for me."

His eyes gleamed, gleeful. "My pleasure."

He led me to the bed and lay me down gently at its edge.

"Get naked," I said.

I watched as he removed his pants and briefs. His cock was utterly hard, curved slightly to the right, and even bigger than I had imagined.

I bent my legs, knees up, and spread my legs wide apart.

"For you," I said, but he was already between my thighs, plowing into me with one tremendous stroke. It was just what I wanted, how he held my legs up and open, ramming into me, stuffing me, satisfying every molecule of lust within. I bucked against him, but he suddenly released my legs and held me down by the hips.

"Touch yourself," he demanded. "Keep your legs spread so I can see you."

Still standing, he pulled out his cock to the tip and waited for me to respond. I teased him a bit by reaching for my breasts first, pulling at the nipples so that they rose into the air between my fingers.

He fucked me once.

I licked my fingers and made slow circles around my aureoles.

He fucked me twice.

I spread my legs farther apart and dragged my fingers down my belly to my pubes.

He fucked me three times, still holding me down.

I pulled the lips of my pussy open wide.

He fucked me once again.

"Stay inside," I said, and he did. Mercy, how it throbbed as my fingers fell to my clit. With each stroke, he fucked me; we found a rhythm I could scarcely bear it was so perfectly melodious, charging me to my depths.

And the sounds we made! His throaty groans mingled with the slapping of his balls against my flourishing cunt, my breath hurtling out like an animal giving chase.

He pounded me faster and faster as I ground my fingers against my clit, and my entire body trembled so deeply from the surge, I felt I would explode. When the coming roared through me, sounds I'd never heard rose from the boundary of my soul and sudden tears sprawled from my eyes.

His climax, pounding and pungent, tailed mine as it spiraled to its luscious end.

For the moment, we were sated. We lay entwined, breathing into each other's mouths.

"Suck my dick," I whispered.

"Suck my pussy," he replied.

"Who are you?" I mused aloud.

"Who are *you*?"

I loved his willingness, that look in his eyes. I wanted to suck his cock, needed to. My virile Spaniard. He was stiff again five minutes after his orgasm, after plunging into me again and again. Still breathing hard, I climbed over him, facing him, straddling him. I bent forward and pursed my lips, let a stream of saliva slide down to the deep red tip of his penis, met his wondering eyes. Circling the base above his balls with one hand, I let the other wrap around his suspended scrotum—such heat! And such fragility. I held his testes sweetly, squeezing harder when his sigh told me to.

I leaned down and took him slowly into my mouth, my lips a sudden cock ring. He moaned as I created a rhythm and then changed it each time he got close. I pulled away and took each of his balls into my mouth, letting them rest on my tongue before lifting them to the roof of my mouth, lightly sucking. I moved to one side so that I could watch his face, and I then looked the other way, down his body to his bare feet, which shook back and forth as he came.

Such sway, grace—connected were we. He held me there, pressed against him.

Eventually, I fell into a deep sleep in my lover's arms. Once again, I dreamt of Linda and her Italian duo and the erotic conclusion to their afternoon at the Hotel du Cap.

There in the suite, while Anastagio had watched, Catarina caressed her breasts through the soft fabric of her blouse. Linda swooned with desire and memory, the sweet agony of her love for Olivia resurfacing. Cat again kissed her neck, her fingertips playing Linda's nipples as if they had always done just that. A stirring—heat and longing—basted Linda's nerve endings. At a certain point, while her tongue lingered behind her ear, Cat began to knead Linda's nipples between thumb and forefinger.

Anastagio looked on approvingly as Linda groaned. She met his gaze for a few moments as Catarina's fingertips spread and grasped each handful, slowly undulating them at first, then reaching beneath and lifting them so that their weight would drop into her outspread palms. Linda shut her eyes as Cat held and squeezed each bundle, then released them, grasping the fall with her waiting hands.

Linda shivered from this unexpected intensity, her vulnerability. She had crossed her legs when she sat down, but they fell open now as a moan slid into a long exhalation and the deepening desire coursed through her thighs. She needed Catarina's hands, needed them back on her nipples, but she did not know how to ask for that. She sighed instead, a slipping-away feeling that seemed to go on for ages.

"Ah," Cat responded, "I knew you'd like that."

She came around from the back of the chair now and knelt before Linda, purposely spreading Linda's legs farther apart with her hands, leaning close so that her face was barely inches away. The sharpness of her features had softened, though her gaze remained direct and deliberate, vulpine in its focus.

Would she kiss Linda now? Linda could not move, pulsations beating in the depths of her vulva. But Cat only smiled sweetly and brushed a gentle hand through Linda's dark hair as her other hand began to unbutton her blouse. One button, then a swipe across her nipple. Another button, another swipe.

Finally her blouse hung open; her breasts throbbed. Catarina teased back Linda's bra just enough to make her aureoles visible. She stared into Linda's eyes as she circled them lightly with her fingertips.

Linda trembled again from the masterful touch, the intense stirring between her legs like branches fretted together into budding flame. She felt the heat of her own breath as Cat leaned forward and encircled one nipple with her lips, her smooth tongue just barely grazing the aching nub. Cat began to torment both of her breasts in just this way, barely making contact with her lips while the feather of her tongue lapped first one nipple, then the other.

Linda imagined falling off the chair from the weakness this superlative pleasure caused. Perhaps Anastagio sensed this, for he suddenly pushed himself away from his perch by the window and stepped behind Linda's chair. He ran his hands through her hair as he took in the sight of Cat's expert exploration. He tipped back Linda's head and eased his mouth onto hers. He began to suck her lips and offer his tongue in the same slow, soft way that Cat pored over her inflamed mounds.

Linda groaned into his mouth—she could not hold back. Who was going to slake the oceanic yearning between her legs? Would Catarina take her with her mouth, or would Anastagio plunge his newly erect, naked blade into her? Abandon was where Linda was headed, if the trembling of her torso, if her breathtaking moans, foretold anything. Cat began to stroke Linda's breasts with the tips of her fingers as her tongue slowly stabbed her nipples.

Anastagio dipped his tongue into Linda's mouth, his slow descent letting her know that he wanted her to suck on it—which she did hungrily. Her head still tipped back, she reached up with both arms and pulled him closer by wrapping both hands around his neck. Cat made small sounds now, hot breaths coming from between her lips, which now sucked Linda's aureoles, sending new shivers up and down Linda's frantic flesh.

Anastagio pulled back suddenly, both of his hands lost in her hair.

"Please," Linda whispered. "Please . . ." she begged with a moan.

Catarina responded by softly squeezing her breasts together and, while cupping them in one hand, lashing at each nipple with her dazzling tongue. Then she pulled her mouth completely away, and Linda thought she would faint. Her hands fell from Anastagio's neck as she opened her eyes and saw Cat standing before her, one hand held out in invitation.

Could she even stand up? She was sure the chair she sat on was soaked from the fiery puddle between her legs. Anastagio stepped to her side and helped her up. Cat reached over and removed Linda's open blouse leisurely. She unhooked her bra, sliding it down one arm in a measured tease.

Linda now stood between these two exquisite strangers half-naked—while they were fully clothed.

Did she dare reach out and touch Catarina? Linda was mesmerized by her sultry lips and even more by what she could do with them. How she longed to kiss her!

Cat stepped so closely then, reaching the fingers of each hand to the fleshy lobes of Linda's ears. She gently pulled her nearer this way, caressing her nape, too, but Linda could not still her desire a moment longer and flung herself into Catarina's embrace. Her flesh was trembling, her loins searing, and it was that mouth, those hands that had caused it—"more" was the word she longed to say with her being, every millimeter of skin.

Pressing herself against Cat's unfamiliar body, Linda felt a combination of sensations: She was soft, lithe, supple. Yet overall, she was so luxurious—yes, that was the word—as Linda leaned into the pillows of her breasts. Her sweet, simple breath was the promise of those remarkable lips.

Again she focused on Cat's mouth, the wide, full lower lip, the fleshy shelf at the center of her upper lip that spilled over the one beneath like a diving board over a pool.

Did Linda dare dive? She looked beyond Cat's piercing gaze, hoping to see her deeper being.

Catarina smiled then, a full, open grin, and Linda melted. She leaned into that feeling and felt her lips meet Cat's as if they had landed in a new world. She hung on tight as Cat parted her lips and allowed Linda to kiss her tentatively—slow pecks that soon turned to lingering pronouncements as the soft, moist flesh met this way and that, their wanting mouths intermingling with sighs and wonder. Linda reached around and pulled Cat closer to her, one hand on the back of her neck as she kissed her more deeply, teasing Cat's mouth open with her tongue, near breathless with the thought of sucking the enticing ledge of her upper lip.

Cat's tongue met hers urgently. Linda nearly fell over from the impact of its sudden slippery insistence, from its life. She swooned, barely able to keep her balance as Cat found a rhythm, slowly circling her tongue with her own—just as she had circled her aureoles, just as she had circled her nipples, just as she would . . . might . . .

Linda moaned. Could her body melt away so that she could experience this rapture, this thrill, with replete abandon? Straining, leaning, how close might she get, how much might she flourish?

Anastagio stepped behind her, slowly pressing himself against the soft expanse of her buttocks. She let herself lean into him, buoyed by the memory of the uncut marvel between his legs. His hardness strained against his trousers; she was grateful for the firm support of his chest. He reached a hand to each of her hips and pulled her to him, Cat stepping forward as if in a dance as he did.

Their mouths still mingling, Linda was at Cat's mercy. Her fingers returned to Linda's naked breasts as her tongue darted in, around, out of her mouth. Cat's breath was like a sweet gust as she came closer, her lips curling over Linda's, their titillating center spilling across her mouth like overripe fruit.

Linda wanted to suck that center, but at the moment, she couldn't move. Being sandwiched between this sexy pair was unlike anything she had ever experienced. She panted as Cat's fingers drummed her nipples, as Anastagio's hands roamed over her ass. Cat's kisses were becoming more insistent, her tongue exploring deeper, her touch more adamant.

Linda's hands fell to her sides.

Like a strain of lingering musical chords, the weakness, the surrender that was deepening inside made her sway. When Anastagio gently pulled her from Cat's tongue and led her to the bedroom, Linda's knees literally buckled. Cat accompanied them at every step, of course, pausing momentarily to sail a hand, a caress, her mouth over some part of Linda's exposed torso—the small of her back, a rib, the tender spot where the underside of her arm ended in the soft crease that met her torso.

Linda sank into the carpet with each step. How could even those tiny fingers—those fibers—be so welcoming?

At the side of the bed, Anastagio released her with a squeeze of her buttocks and stepped away. Catarina stood in front of her as before, her hands reaching out, her lips open, wanting. Linda sank into them as she had the carpet; it ached too much to try to hold back.

How she needed the ledge of Cat's mouth now. How she wrapped her lips around it and slowly sucked. Who was she? she wondered then. How could it feel as if she had reached a new horizon, a place she had never known existed? The sensations landed in her like new destinations, dreams she had always longed for, without ever fully realizing before this instant—this lick, this connection—that they were possible.

What did it mean?

Linda sucked the ledge of Cat's upper lip with both of her own, her hands rising to explore Cat's back, the length of her torso, her belly. She could not stop her fingertips from roaming, tentatively drizzling caresses across Cat's sculpted ass, even more shyly approaching the sloping wonder of her bosomy rack.

Again she asked herself: Did she dare dive?

Starting with Cat's supple lip—the pouting shelf that lured her to pounce on it in a way she did not recognize—Linda sensed she was mid-dive. It could only mean that so much had already happened, and there was so much more yet to come, though she could barely imagine what—with Catarina, with Anastagio.

As Linda's hands lingered here and there, Cat eventually lost her balance. She fell against Linda, and they landed on the bed, laughing, bumping against each other amid the soft pillows. Holding onto each other, they rolled around on the bedspread. When Catarina sat up, Linda leapt to her knees and reached for Cat's blouse. She pulled it up and over her head swiftly, mesmerized by the sight of Cat's lacy black brassiere.

From that instant on, Linda surrendered. As the moment sped into fast-forward, they grabbed each other. Cat's bra came off quickly and Linda's breasts crushed against hers. They kissed wildly, swooning from the feeling of their nipples mashed together, their tongues intertwined.

Linda pushed Cat down on her back and eased off her pants—no panties. Linda moaned, spreading Cat's legs as if in a fever, desperate to discover her secrets, her abandon.

Cat was willing; she allowed her.

How could Linda describe what it was like to put her mouth on another woman's pussy for the first time, taste her juices, feel her clitoris swell and harden beneath her lips? At the beginning, she dipped her tongue in the lush red well of Cat's opening, sucking in her scent, the velvety nature of her wetness, her potent femininity. Cat lay back and spread her legs wide, making it easier for Linda to lap and linger.

Between a woman's legs exists an entire world. The vulva is a country boasting so many destinations: the *mons veneris, labia majora, labia minora* and *clitoris,* to say nothing of how those destinations open at the *urethra,* the *vagina.* Open to the depths of her being.

Such intrigue, mystery—a woman.

Linda parted the larger lips of Cat's labia majora, her tongue nestling into the crevices of her slippery, fleshy cave. Her mouth swept up and down the length of her pussy, across its breadth, finally settling on her swelling nub, which flushed a resonant red the more she licked, sucked, and stabbed it.

Cat reached down with both hands, her fingers dancing in Linda's hair. Her small sounds became larger, louder, and Linda sucked slower then, orchestrating Cat's surrender.

Linda felt the trembling overtake Cat as she teased her soaked opening, as she lightly tugged the dark hair covering Cat's mons veneris, as her tongue stayed steady on her clit.

Cat arched with a wailing cry as Linda finally slid a finger inside and pressed her lips against her. Her tongue was the center of the world; it mapped a pathway to ecstasy as everything else fell away and Cat lost herself in the moment. She hollered, bucked, writhed. She twisted, cried, swooned.

When she quieted, Linda lifted herself and lay atop Cat's quaking flesh; she pressed her vulva against Cat's.

It was an astounding moment. She barely moved. She didn't need to, want to. The connection of their clits was galvanizing, paralyzing. But passion never waits: Anastagio was suddenly behind her.

His tongue rolled across her exposed ass, his hardness pushed against her leg. Catarina pulled her closer with both arms as Linda spread her legs, wanting him to lunge as far inside of her as he could go, reach the bottom of her that was burning for more.

Cat sucked her tongue as Anastagio entered her aching center. His solid, sweet mass within her made her clit sear with even more sensation. She writhed against Cat, whose hands had wandered to the cheeks of her ass, petting, kneading.

Sandwiched between these lovers, Linda understood what rapture was. Anastagio thrust into her with a determined delicacy; Cat's fingers caressed her inflamed flesh. With one final plunge, he reached it: her source, the hidden, enigmatic tempest that found its life raining through her. Lightning flashed through every synapse, nerve ending, nerve beginning.

The bliss was consummate, vaulting, oceanic.

Anastagio stiffened behind her, his cock beyond hard inside. She strained to meet him as he fell against her, his cum bathing her to her depths.

They finally lay back, delighted, exhausted. Catarina kissed Linda one last time. "Are you hungry?" she whispered.

"Always," Linda answered.

Cat laughed. "For food, I mean."

Linda laughed, too. "Starving," she answered.

Anastagio smiled. "Bouillabaisse, anyone?"

He called room service, which was soon followed by a knock on the door. Linda leapt from the bed, wrapping a sheet around herself as she headed toward the entrance to the suite.

Opening the door, she was surprised—the bellboy had brought their lunch? The instant he saw her, he blushed.

Though the sheet was wrapped tightly around her, Linda felt suddenly naked. "Well, hello," she managed. "I see you're a man of many hats."

"I . . . just wanted to see you again," spilled out of him.

They stood unmoving until it became too obvious to ignore.

"What's your name?" she whispered.

"Tell me yours," he answered.

"Yours," Linda replied.

They laughed.

"Come on in," she offered.

"I'm Franco," he said.

Looking only at her, he rolled the tray to the dining table at the far end of the living room. Stepping into the bedroom doorway, Catarina and Anastagio had donned the plush white hotel bathrobes. They looked vibrant, fresh, undeniably fucked.

After a glance at them, Franco looked confusedly at Linda—she was part of an intimate trio? He blushed more deeply than he had earlier.

As if sensing their simpatico bond, Cat bounded across the room.

"You again?" she said in a miffed tone. "I'll have to talk to the concierge."

Rather than respond directly, Franco busied himself moving

their meal from the cart to the table. He then laid a pink napkin across his forearm and strode to the suite door. He turned and faced everyone as his heels met, inquiring whether they wished for anything more.

While he said those last words, his gaze searched Linda's eyes.

Anastagio, as ever his style, stepped in. He walked over to Franco and handed him some euros, thanking him once more with a pat on the shoulder.

"Buona sera," he said.

"Arrivederla," Franco replied. He left.

"Che cosa desidera?" Cat asked Anastagio. *"Non voglio essere disturbato."*

What was she saying? Linda had to know.

"I don't want to be disturbed, either," Anastagio replied. "I want to eat. Sit down," he said sternly. "It is rude to speak our language in front of our guest."

Catarina turned to me. *"Non mi creda cosi maleducato. Non volevo offenderla.* Don't think me rude. I did not want to hurt your feelings. Please, sit. Let us eat. We have shared so much together already."

Linda sat down obediently, but she sensed there was a fracas hovering, just below the surface of this moment.

Anastagio served the steaming bouillabaisse. They feasted on it along with a thickly crusted white bread doused with olive oil. They ate in silence, Linda absorbing an increasing tension.

"Linda," Catarina finally began, "Anastagio and I have just discussed it. We want you. To be with us, I mean."

"You are the perfect choice," Anastagio added.

"You complete us. . . ." Cat went on.

"You belong with us."

"We will never fuck you without each other being present. . . ."

"We will never have you to ourselves."

Now they were talking to each other, Linda realized.

"We will share you equally. . . ."

"We will not take advantage of the situation."

The situation? It was one thing to have a spontaneous adventure, Linda thought, quite another to harness life this way. There was a strange energy, how they were ruling each other, reining each other in, deciding what could, and could not, be. And not a word about *her* life or even the idea of love.

Only rules? Never, she thought. The moment was dead. They had killed it with their rules. Being desirable, being desired by others, had brought her this far, to a place she realized was lustfully teeming in the moment, but then, empty of everything beyond it: intention, commitment, loyalty. After lunch, she dressed, thanked them both, and left.

It will come as no surprise, I imagine, that it was Franco who swung the door open as she exited the hotel.

Come dawn, I still lay with my Spanish Stranger in bed.

"I don't even know your name," he said.

"I don't know yours," I responded.

"Do you want to tell me?" he asked.

"For a thousand euros," I teased.

"Touché," he said. "I'm Gaspar. So tell me, what brought you to Paris?"

After room service brought our breakfast, I sipped orange juice and explained that it was Jacques Lacan—or rather, his work as a Parisian psychoanalyst—that had lured me to France. Starting in the 1950s, Lacan had reinterpreted the tenor of Freudian thought by developing his own version of psychoanalysis, based on the ideas articulated in structural linguistics and anthropology. Heady stuff, I know: the penis as signifier, the vagina as signified. Yet while he also influenced literary criticism and feminism during that period, it was he himself who disbanded his seminars at the Ecole Normale Superieure in 1980 and eventually fell out of cultural favor.

I arrived in Paris twenty-five years later, seeking answers to some of my own questions about psychoanalysis. They were in regard to the practice and theory of a handful of concepts that had plagued me throughout my entire professional career. The first question was: Did I believe in Freud's essentially humanist philosophy or in Lacan's poststructural one?

And so, after my arrival, I had taken some newly reprised Lacanian seminars at the Ecole Normale Superieure, I had started my own practice . . . and I was still full of questions.

Actually, I had so many more. And they had nothing to do with psychoanalysis. They had everything to do with my own awareness of what it meant to be alive.

Maybe, in the end, we only get so close to ourselves—by ourselves, I mean. We need other people to remind us of this, as Linda, by sheer example, had done in my life by questioning my boundaries, my beliefs, the reality of my personal sexuality.

If I were to explain that I had grown up in a home where a healthy sexuality was expressed between my parents, would I look there for the burgeoning of my own limitations? No, in this instance I would not. Every person's sexuality—unless its origins are decidedly traumatic—comes into his or her own by a combination of environment, education, and experience—Evelyn's three e's. Rather, I should look at my own sexual history or, more fitting in my case, the lack thereof.

Red Shoes, I promise to try to avoid launching into a shrink-like diatribe. Instead I will simply tell you what my earliest experience was, which centers around a man named Justin.

The instant we met, it was as if I already knew him. We were students then—fresh, flushed, full of possibility.

Fearless.

We met one night at the university library, literally bumping into each other. Our books fell and as we bent to retrieve them, we saw that we were reading the same texts. Which were his and which were mine? From that moment forward neither of us knew—or cared. Because the books were now "ours," shared, the same.

He was blond, like I was, a pile of tousled hair falling in his eyes. His features were more prominent than mine, uneven to my even. He was lanky, which I wasn't, but clumsy, too. We shared that from the instant our books spilled to the ground.

Our conversation flowed as easily as the sex that followed: like a river, a watery dance of shifting currents, tides of feeling, bodies bowed by bliss, interrupted only by rapture.

Three months later, he asked me to marry him. We became engaged, overflowing, teeming, beyond. Along with everything else he taught me, I learned what ecstasy was: It was Justin—*just in*.

One evening, as I waited for him in the car outside a convenience store, he was killed. Murdered in a holdup. An uncomplicated situation, actually.

An accident.

The end of a life.

He had gone into the store to buy aspirin—for me. My headache.

I was numb for at least three years, my heart no more than a buried, petrified stone. I stopped feeling, stopped thinking that it was possible to ever get that close to someone again. The simple terrible fact was that if I did, I might suffer as much or even more than I already had. In that suffering, I had learned that the very act of wanting was the most essential part of what ultimately scourged, felled, paralyzed me.

With Justin there, I had decided that I had everything in my life. Without him, I felt, I had nothing. My life was nothing. He had ignited me, made me constantly yearn, swollen and burning. But that fiery world had died too, the life between my legs.

I struggled to make any sense of it at all. How could I have loved so completely and then lost that love? When death came to claim that life—everything I lived for, everything I had surrendered to: For what? Because why? To lose that depth, definition, such shared tenderness, ripped out every shred of feeling inside. And so love was replaced by irreparable grief. Unutterable loss. Disastrous sorrow.

There was no way to go there again, no reason to risk that much. What had it meant, to be so present that I inevitably gave everything, only to lose so much of myself in that unimaginable embrace when it was taken away? To offer everything, much more than I had ever thought possible: bare being and its beautiful truth, our lovemaking the breadth of all life, our flesh like a landscape of our soul. Only because it was possible to feel all of this with him did it rise in my psyche—to want so deeply, so singularly, so eternally. This was how I loved Justin.

To lose him was to lose a part of myself forever; I lost a grip on life that few of us are lucky enough to ever find. And from the moment he was ripped away from me, I could not move: Act. Be. Open. Experience.

Because a part of me felt dead, too. Killed off. Yet life insisted otherwise, though, and I had fought it for so long.

Lying in Gaspar's arms that morning, what I came to realize was that Justin's vast absence (along with Linda's unwitting nudge) was the very thing that eventually shoved me—an endless breath of wind at my back—over an unexpected cliff, making me want more—naked life and deep experience—and a new wonder thrummed through me.

If wonder had a name, it would be Gaspar. His name, he told me, meant *master of treasure*.

I'll say.

One late winter night, a feathery snow fell as I sat at the Royal Saint-Honoré Hotel bar, silently toasting Justin. Gaspar had left for Hong Kong. We'd been seeing each other for months now. Linda had just ended therapy with me, enthralled and committed in her relationship with Franco. I knew we'd be in touch, especially if she ever needed me professionally again.

And so, Red Shoes, all was well in my little world. From my perch at the end of the bar, I waited for just the perfect eyes, the most inviting mouth, the yearning, the possibility. Ah, there he was: a young man of twenty-five or so, stopping in for a cocktail before a compelling night in Paris, perhaps.

I waited until he sat down and then rose from my seat and walked past, pausing only long enough on the way to my hotel room to slide the plump white envelope in front of him with a smile.

JAKE

"To whom does the psychiatrist go for counsel? In my case I've chosen you, Red Shoes. Please, don't judge me too harshly. Thanks for being there. Thanks for listening."

So that's it, Stella; we are the chosen. What counsel can we offer? All I can say is that I'm left wondering whether there's any other approach beyond the curious ways in which life insists we learn. It's always through the people who barrel into our existence and shake it up, knock it down, ultimately rearrange it to the core, isn't it? The ones that fate introduces, forcing us to lie awake in the long night, blanketing us as the darkness deepens, surrounding us as we lie wondering about the other: Who is this, what is this, and what will be?

As always, I wonder about Alex. What she did, what it meant—what it means. How her actions affect my life today and how I will go forward.

Evelyn freed herself through a process of painful discoveries—not through a decision. Life seems to be decided—or defined—by actions, *not thoughts. Had Evelyn not gone to the Royal that night, she never would have met Gaspar. Had Linda not taken that train to Nice, she never would have encountered Anastagio and Catarina. Had Franco not appeared at the hotel suite offering bouillabaisse, Linda might never have seen him again.*

That leaves us, Stella. What are we going to do with our lives? I honestly do not know.

The first sentence Evelyn wrote to us was: Secrets you can't confess to your mother, shrink, or priest. *She never told us that those secrets were hers; she didn't need to. She told us her secrets, and now she's free.*

And what about you, Stella? There's always you. You tell me all your secrets and I'll tell you all mine. Agreed?

So, where is that bone?

Four on
the Floor

◆

JAKE

I just finished a set of drawings—not my usual skyscraper—but a design for a house that a friend of mine commissioned. The drawings are for a big house for a newly married couple that wants a lot of kids and—you bet—a dog just like you, Stella.

The wife insisted on a large mudroom because when she was a child that was where everyone took off their shoes and hung their coats on wall hooks. They'd watch the mail pile up on the table and inhale the savory kitchen smells that pulled the family together like a comforting embrace.

It was the way she talked about the house that momentarily diverted me from my preoccupation (all right, obsession, really) with Alex, but as I worked on the house plans, they seemed to carve a new pain into my chest. I had hoped—had dreamt—that one day I would share a home like that with Alex. A soft place, a nest that provided safety, love, marriage.

No such luck. The opposite of luck, actually. But I can't focus on that. I need to focus on something else—the soothing balm of the Red Shoe Diaries, *maybe.*

And as I pick up the next envelope, I wonder if the dream for a house with Alex was one I really ever had, or was it merely something expected, a dream I had been conditioned to want? When life slams you, your own life shifts violently. Who you are, who you thought you are, is dismantled, like a building felled, and only rubble remains.

Feels like I've been picking through the remains of my own life for a while now. So far, I haven't found one piece, one shard of myself that makes any sense. Except for you, Stella. Explain the rest of it to me if you can. I mean, what am I to do? Wagging your tail at me that way can't be the answer—or can it?

♦ ♦ ♦

Dear Red Shoes,

Have you ever been affected by something you've seen in a movie? I mean really affected. Haunted might be a better word. It happened to me during my first year of college, when I went to a film one afternoon between finals to rest and just let my mind wander. The story was about two couples on vacation together and how they somehow ended up all going to bed with one another. By now I think you know where this letter's headed.

I've always been accused of having a "vivid" imagination. I consider this a high compliment because, at the tender age of five, I announced boldly to my mother that I was going to write great books and everyone on the planet was going to read them.

Dream on, she had responded, with a wink and a smile and a quick tousle of my hair.

Dream on. Oh, what beautiful words she had spoken. All at once a small fire was ignited inside of me.

Dream on became my own private prayer, enabling me to imagine anything and everything.

Which is why I've never understood why people insist that we get our heads "out of the stars." Really, isn't that a fantastic place for one's mind to dwell? Luckily I did grow up to be a writer of fiction, and I often swirl in a dizzying constellation of words and images in which souls burst forth on the page. It's a kind of dreaming. It's like love—the falling in, the roar of desire, the melting ache of flesh, and the tremulous anticipation of what's next. Writing. Dreaming. Loving. These are all intertwined for me. Each feeds the other; they whisper to me, guide me, teach me.

Remy, my boyfriend, often jokes that one day I will slip away into a dream and find it more alluring than life. He'll then have to visit me at some institution where drool slides down my chin because I'm smiling so open and wide and my eyes are bright and faraway.

I will never leave Remy. Sometimes I believe that the only reason I was born is to love him. At the core, take the rest of the world away and you'll find our love. But—here's the rub—I'm a writer and my imagination has never been contained by limited definitions of love or anything else for that matter. I will never leave Remy, but I'll never stop dreaming, imagining, or being haunted by images from a film I watched a long time ago, either.

Sometimes I wonder if I only dreamt I saw this movie. Or maybe I made it up, told myself I saw a film that haunted me, and then I created a story about two couples, old friends, trusted friends, who went on vacation together. And one night, it just happened . . .

I'll lay it out for you, Red Shoes, the principal actors, the setting, the plot, the drama and pathos, a surprise here and there—all the work of a great storyteller. Keep in mind that this story is true, and even the names have not been changed to protect the innocent. None of us were innocent. None of us were guilty.

PRINCIPAL ACTORS

There's Remy, my boyfriend, a dark-eyed, dark-haired Angel-Beast—my pet name for him. This combination of soft soul and brute man is perfect for me. We met just after college, over seven years ago. He's a journalist, and his passion for the "truth" in his work is matched only by his compassion for the uncertainty and confusion of the human condition. Duality turns me on. One day, his dream is to work at the *Washington Post* as a foreign correspondent. For now he's just landed a job as a stringer with the Associated Press in Madrid.

I fell in love with Remy when he invited me over to watch a soccer match on television. In the course of three hours, I saw him scream, laugh, cry, stomp his feet, pound his fists, and kiss the television screen. He swept me into his arms, twirled me around, and after his team won, we ended up on the floor. He ripped off my clothes ferociously, then his, and it was as if we replayed the whole delirious match with each other. Our bodies were the playing field and from that moment on, I became a HUGE fan of soccer—*and* fucking Remy.

Julia is next, my best friend since freshman year of college. She's a dancer, artist, poet. Anything she expresses, whether through words, images, and especially her body, is absolutely inspired. Do I idealize her? Of course. Does she idealize me? You bet. We try to create a space of adoration for each other because it's so damn difficult to reveal yourself to the world creatively. There's always a critic salivating, poised to humiliate you. Best friends are there through thick and thin, to pull you up, wipe your mouth if you vomit, hold you tight when you're bereft, make you feel as if everything you've ever wanted is right around the next corner . . . and the next . . . and the next. . . .

Did I mention that Julia is exquisite? She's languid and mysterious, delicate and naughty. Here I am again, Red Shoes, telling you that duality turns me on. Julia has always had an ease I've wanted to steal, as if I were standing at the Bloomingdale's cosmetics counter looking at the most radiant, precious bottle of perfume, and I knew I had to have it or my life would not make sense.

Marcus completes the foursome. He's intensely irreverent, with a shaggy head of blond hair and eyes that seem to teeter at the edge of a joke right before the punchline is delivered. He teaches English as a second language to immigrants at a church and developed a program to use rock lyrics in the curriculum. He includes all his favorites: the Doors, Hendrix, Van Halen, Janis Joplin. According to Julia, his classes are the most popular.

I've had a crush on Marcus since the day Julia introduced us over five years ago. They'd only been dating for three weeks, and she wanted to see how Marcus and I would get along. We've always promised that if either one of us had a particularly negative reaction to a new lover, we'd dump the guy—just like that. It's about trust, gut, instinct. We truly believe in women's intuition: Follow it or pay the price.

The three of us met for a drink at Mecca, a trendy gay club in San Francisco, not far from the writers' conference I was attending. My trip coincided with the Napa wine country tour Julia and Marcus were about to embark upon. Poor Remy was alone, back in New York City, where we all lived.

Over shots of Corazón tequila and an array of appetizers each more delicious than the last, we were surrounded by a gaggle of young, outrageously gorgeous gay men. We all danced. Julia and me. Then Marcus and me. All three of us at the same time. Marcus even accepted a few dance invitations from some guys. He had absolutely no problem as a straight man dancing with a gay man.

He had grown up in the East Village, with parents who were left-wing liberals who eschewed tradition; they were not even legally married. Marcus described his upbringing as very "experimental." His dad was a poet and stay-at-home "mom." His mom ran a neighborhood co-op and had many lovers, both men and women.

"What was that like for your father?" I asked.

"A relief," Marcus said. "My dad dug words, hanging out with me, and watching football. He loved my mom, but he knew he could never feed her appetite."

"Appetite?" I queried.

"Oh, yeah, my ma is a singular force of nature. A bit like Julia." He winked at her. "She wants to taste everything before she dies."

I drank in the way Marcus's eyes floated up and down Julia's body and face as she spoke, and whenever she would laugh, his own face would explode with an adorable smile. You know that feeling when you meet someone for the first time and they feel so familiar, like they've always been a part of your life? That's how I felt with Marcus.

After a while, I swear I was about to suggest a three-way between Julia, Marcus, and myself. At one point, Julia pressed me to join her in the restroom. I knew she was dying to find out what I was thinking about Marcus. Once inside the safe confines of our women-only sanctuary, I pushed her up against the wall and said, "I want to fuck him."

Naughty Julia smiled and pulled me against her. "He wants to fuck you, too," she said.

I should explain that Julia and I have always been very physical with each other. There have been moments after long, confessional nights or too much wine or broken-hearted marathons, when we've ended up soothing each other wordlessly with touch, embrace, caress. What we have is inexplicable, yet neither one of us has ever even suggested that we define or box in such deep affection. This is what I've learned, Red Shoes: There is nothing concrete about love. Love is anarchy, irrational chaos, a real fucking mess at times, but oh, the pleasure of its expression—just like dreaming.

"Nina, come with us to Napa," Julia said, her eyes filled with mischief.

"No," I replied, "You'll see . . . someday."

"Someday what?" she asked.

"You have to wait."

"For what?"

It was clear that she had no idea what I was talking about.

I pressed my lips to her ear. In a reverent tone I said, "One day we will have ecstasy beyond our wildest imaginings. You'll see. One day. *Dream on*."

Like I said, it was a foursome that haunted me since I had seen that movie: two men, two women, trusted friends. I was going to wait, wait until destiny served up the perfect moment for my dream. Now that Julia had met Marcus I believed that day was closer to becoming a reality.

In the film, the two couples displayed an ease and intimacy with each other that was immensely seductive. The camera caressed this quartet, bathed them in a soft, shadowy light as they roamed the French countryside, and as I watched, I felt that four people could not have been happier. They swam naked in a pond, then lingered, still naked, on blankets under the shade of trees drinking wine and eating grapes, cheese, olives. Subtle touches were shared, shy, yet searing glances exchanged between them. As the film progressed, the foursome seemed shrouded in a canopy of pure sensuality.

There have been those moments between Remy, Julia, Marcus, and myself, in which I felt the same sense of our being blanketed in a cocoon of desire, lust, and indelible love. We've done the usual "couples" gigs: dinners, vacations, clubbing, movies, and concerts. Beyond this, though, there have been a handful of occurrences that continue to feed my resolve for all of us to wind up in a foursome one day.

Two years ago, Remy rode around for a week or so with a pair of New York cops on their third shift, midnight to eight A.M., for a piece he was writing for the *Village Voice* about late-shift city workers. That was when Julia and Marcus had me over for dinner alone. Marcus prepared pasta fagioli while I took a long, luxurious bath. Remy and I had only a stall shower at our apartment, so I'd take any opportunity to submerge in a liquid cocoon of water.

Julia lit a single candle as she prepared my bath and soft music leaked in from the living room. She brought me a glass of Chianti and went back to the kitchen to prepare the salad. The subdued noises they made were so comforting: the chopping of vegetables, the soft *clink* of metal pans, the uncorking of wine, their hushed giggles. I drifted into the sounds, my eyes closed, when I felt warm hands sliding down my shoulders into the water.

Unmistakably, they were Julia's hands. When I opened my eyes, Marcus stood in the doorway, a glass of red wine lazily swaying in his hand, his eyes drifting between Julia and me.

"I'm the luckiest man in the world," Marcus said.

"Do you mind, Nina?" Julia asked.

Not waiting for my response, she slipped off her dress. She was naked beneath it.

"I correct myself," Marcus said, "not the luckiest man. I'm now the happiest."

I sat up, making room for her, my breasts lifting above the soapy universe, my nipples deep red and swollen. Marcus sighed when he saw them, and I emitted a sudden gasp as Julia slid her foot between my legs. Concealed beneath the lush bubbles, I pulsed against her, her eyes sparking impishly.

"You know," Marcus said, smiling, "in Japanese cultures, whole families, entire neighborhoods bathe together."

Julia reached out her hand for a sip of Marcus's wine, beckoning him nearer. He knelt beside the tub, lifted the glass to her wanting lips. A trickle of ruby liquid slipped down her chin. He licked it away.

"Sorry, baby," she said. "We'd need a bigger tub for all three of us."

"Yes," I concurred, as she wriggled her toes against my pubes. "It's pretty cozy as it is."

"Always a spectator." Marcus sighed. "Never a bather." He kissed Julia again, his tongue slipping slowly across her wet lips.

Without conscious thought, my hand had found my right breast and began circling the hardening nub of my nipple.

Julia saw; her gaze met mine. She let her toes shift slowly against my muff, my pubes like drifting seaweed. I felt she wanted something: I was almost certain it was the three of us together. I was thrilled, terrified, and so not ready.

Riiiiinnngg. The timer device in the kitchen went off. It was like being doused with icy water.

Marcus shook his head. "So close and yet so far away."

As he walked back toward the kitchen, Julia smiled wickedly. "One day," she murmured, "you'll see."

She rose from the tub, toweled off, stepped back into her dress, and left to help with the meal preparations. I was speechless—she had remembered my whispered promise from so long ago. I gulped down the rest of my wine and breathed deeply until my racing heart calmed. If Remy were here would something have happened? Perhaps both he and Marcus would have come into the bathroom while Julia and I bathed. A quiet dinner, flowing wine, two naked women—best friends—bathing. To my mind, a single gesture could have turned a "normal" evening into a sensuous dance between the four of us.

Once again, the film was predominant in my mind: my vague memory of seeing the two women underwater, their arms and legs wound around each other's, pubes swaying like tiny fish. I closed my eyes, wondering what our pubes—Julia's and mine—looked like submerged in the tub.

The next incident—about six months ago—almost led me to initiate a premature foursome. There was a full moon that night *and* I was premenstrual, which translated into my being hell-hot and horny. We went to a new club in the Meatpacking District to dance. None of us knew much about that scene, but Marcus had snagged a flyer from the sidewalk and the words had enticed him: *Searing Movement. Ridiculous Insanity. Sweat and Writhe:* Club Excess! Indeed, we were game.

Upon entering the club, we were corralled, with dozens of others, through a cave-like passage. Water streamed down walls of indigo stone and flickers of light made them sparkle like the blackest sea imaginable. We caught glimpses of distant stars above as thumping rhythms made the floor shiver beneath us.

I wore high heels, my slim black leather skirt, and fishnet stockings with a revealing black lace sleeveless blouse. Julia's ensemble was even more enticing than my own, or so I thought. She'd poured herself into a tight-fitting red dress—a red like no other, not fire or flame, but more like a primal color emancipated from its essence. She looked to me like the sexiest tube of lipstick imaginable, and I could see Marcus and Remy lusting to apply some of her to their lips. I confess: I wanted to as well.

The main room was a flourish of twisting, pulsing flesh. The only light was muted, rising from the floor so that the crowd looked as if it were dancing atop a glowing orb. A hazy smoke poured in that curled and snaked slowly through the crowd. The whole scene was like witnessing a living thing, a throbbing apparition made real by men and women in motion. The air was as ripe as when the earth warmed under a hot sun after a torrential rain. It was sweat-soaked, lush, and profane at the same time.

Remember, I was bursting under a full fierce moon that ignited my every pore, an obsessive desire for sex, touch, tongues reaching down to my very bones. I admit I was already wet, and as I moved through the pumping mass, I began to tremble. Remy grabbed me from behind, forcing his body against mine as a tremor of crazy physical need shook me to the very core.

I imagined bending over, my hands splayed against the illumined floor. Clouds of smoke would camouflage all of me except my ass, which would rise to meet his bulge. The reality was, my swelling puss demanded to be taken right then, over and over—by anyone. Stiff cock after stiff cock. Fingers and fists careening inside my translucent wet cave. Tongues spearing my mysterious dark pearl. I saw it all. Heard the screaming echo of orgasm upon orgasm colliding with the harsh percussive music that filled the air, a music that pounded under my skin and inside my heart. It felt as if each heaving breath I gulped was part of the song, its own instrument of sound.

Loud. Jarring. Rough. Cacophony. That's exactly what I wanted: a cacophonous fuck.

Suddenly Marcus was in front of me. Remy's arms slithered across my breasts as he gyrated against my outrageously wanting ass. Was I even dancing? I had no idea. I had slipped into a dream, completely absorbed by the moment. My nipples were thrilled, giddy, ballooning, as Remy crushed my breasts with his strong, knowing hands. He squeezed my wild nubs, kneading them like precious dough.

Marcus moved his hips and my arms jettisoned around his waist deliriously, pulling him against me.

"Go for it, baby," Remy whispered, as I began to dance with both of them.

Remy was sucking the back of my neck, his lips devouring me as his tongue swam in delicate circles. Were we all under a spell? *Searing Movement. Ridiculous Insanity. Sweat and Writhe.* Absolutely—Club Fucking Excess!

As if stepping out of a dream, Julia appeared behind Remy. Her arms reached past both of us, her hands pulling Marcus harder against me. Our quartet was bound together, our flesh pressed close and pulsing.

It felt as if a torch ignited between my legs. The torch was Marcus—his cock hard, simmering. Remy cupped my cheek, guided my hot mouth to meet Marcus's. My tongue burst forth, lapping his. There were no boundaries. No distinction between my body, these two beautiful men, and Julia's.

Was this the time? Was my dream happening now? My legs felt weak as Julia's eyes met mine, wearing an adoring smile that said, "Take whatever you want, Nina. I'll give you anything."

All at once, loose and unbridled, Remy grasped my waist, turned me away from Marcus, and lifted me from the glowing floor. He began rubbing his face, his hair, his mouth across my swollen tits.

The spell was broken. Had the experience scared Remy? Had we crossed a line he suddenly felt uncomfortable with? There was a fleeting moment, a split-second when I was certain it could happen, that the four of us, after a night of uninhibited expression, might experience my long-held fantasy. But it wasn't meant to be. Not then. Not yet.

THE SETTING

It was the confluence of events: Remy's new job, our moving from New York to Madrid, and our plan for the four of us to take a vacation prior to Remy's start date. I was excited for Remy, but secretly I knew I was going to miss Julia and Marcus; they were so woven into the fabric of our daily lives. Could I handle their physical absence? I knew we'd always remain friends, but the looming distance scared me, and it fueled my resolve that if we were meant to make love together, it had to be now.

Andalusia. Say it slow; whisper it like a prayer: *Andalusia . . . .*

There are certain words that sound like love, words that intoxicate. Our foursome had rented a centuries-old, Moorish-style home there, outside the tiny village of Mojácar, Spain.

We were on our way to the Málaga airport in the plane. Remy, my devourer of facts, read aloud to us about the Andalusia region: its mountains, sea, lush valleys, wineries, beaches, bird sanctuaries.

Images from my beloved film played on the screen in my mind: *A woman with long, curly black tresses, her lips darkly painted, slowly presses her mouth into the dip above the other woman's ass. That one's got sweet, short blond hair, haunted, innocent eyes. Black Tresses' tongue follows a trail up her friend's spine to the nape of her neck, where she lingers, tasting, absorbing the woman's scent.*

The men watch, mesmerized. Their hands reach out, slide across the women's bodies in a lazy, sensual crawl. Close shots of tongues whirling around budding nipples, the long, glistening shaft of a cock piercing a wet slit, a finger teasing a quivering asshole.

The images were in such close-up that I was unable to distinguish exactly who was who.

Remy's voice tugged me away from my reverie. "They call this region the bridge between two continents," he read, "and the meeting point between two seas—the Mediterranean and the Atlantic."

I trembled inside. Two continents. Two oceans. Two couples.

A geography of elements merging and colliding. We were a landscape—the four of us—a region where the possibility existed for us to embrace like two vast bodies of water.

My eyes consumed all three of them greedily. A certainty was lodged within me that this was the time for us.

The plane hummed and vibrated. Soon I excused myself and went into the restroom. The images from the film swirled within and my clit felt like a tiny, demanding fist, just itching to punch, to be beaten. I shoved my fingers inside my jeans while I locked the door behind me with a *click*.

I was raw, swollen, scalded by the Mediterranean-hot liquid that met my palm as I thrust one, two, then three fingers into my pussy. With my wrist and the ball of my hand I ground brutally against my hard, stinging mound. I imagined Julia's tongue against my neck, Marcus's prick inching into my hungry pussy, Remy's mouth sucking Julia's breast. I erupted fast and sent God gratitude for that, because a voice came over the speaker telling passengers to fasten their seatbelts and prepare for landing.

I quickly washed my hands, splashed my flushed cheeks, and headed back to my seat. Remy was still reading aloud to Marcus and Julia about the region's cuisine. I crossed my legs tightly, savoring the thrum of my clit as the plane touched down.

Remy and I had a ritual when we traveled long distances. After we arrived at our temporary quarters, we showered, fucked, slept. It worked for us. Some thought you should stay awake and get into the groove of the new time zone. For us, time zones were irrelevant; we held sacred our pact to christen our arrival with a languorous excursion into flesh.

Red Shoes, I must tell you about Remy's penis. Remember, my

pet name for him was Angel-Beast and that basically describes his cock. Flaccid, it was like an angel in repose—soft as a cloud, endearing in the way it curled up against his thigh as if representing peace and grace at the same time. When he slept, I loved to just gaze at it like a sacred object, a beatific creation of eternity.

When Remy was hard, however, his rod became apocalyptic. Yes, I'm absolutely serious. It was fierce, a force to be reckoned with. Whenever it rose, I imagined that he was capable of parting the Red Sea. I pictured his cock as a superhero, like the Hulk, soft, compassionate and timid until aroused or ignited, and then the Hulk transformed into an unruly, explosive beast capable of monstrous acts!

Lucky fucking me. He could pillage my village for as long as it took to desecrate every inch of me. Plunder my ass. Loot my breasts. Raid my pussy. Ransack my jewels. He was a voracious lover and I was a buffet ready to be devoured. Toss in a really good brawl between us and you get the picture. Usually after a few hard-core bouts, we would settle into a timeless, woozy, hazy state of rocking our hips in a silent rhythm, him inside of me, our tongues twined and tired. We'd be wordless then, thoughtless bodies merged and submerged. Sleep would often blanket us and we'd wake up hours later, Remy's slumbering angel still inside my groggy, grateful pussy.

Upon our arrival at the house we were renting, we discovered that our charming bedroom had huge vaulted ceilings, dark paneled walls, and a luxurious bed swathed in the softest linens. The place was large enough to give our foursome privacy, with the other bedroom located on the opposite side. The kitchen itself seemed to whisper *"home"* with its stone floor and ancient wooden table, marked with stains that suggested many meals shared by families and friends. The walls smelled of lamb stew, rosemary, and baked bread. It was a house that held its inhabitants as a nursing mother would, in a primal embrace.

THE PLOT

There are several definitions that serve my purpose: plot *n.* 1. A plan decided on in secret, especially to bring about an illegal or subversive act; 2. The story or sequence of events in a novel, play, or movie; and, plot *v.* 3. To chart the course of a ship.

In this case, I was orchestrating a sequence of events as if writing a story I was meant to tell. Indeed, I had a plan—a secret plan to bring about a subversive, yet agonizingly enticing, act. And, yes, I really believed I was charting the course of our ship on a journey to absolute ecstasy.

And, as the novelist and dreamer of our foursome, I truly believed that I had been selected to silently and unobtrusively bring about an outcome that all of us desired. The ghostly images from the movie I had seen—or dreamt I saw—had pursued me for years. Why? I could analyze the unconscious psychological underpinnings of such fantasy that a film I saw gave birth to. I could search through my family history for some kind of pathological motivation, but such choices bore me.

Indulge me for a moment, Red Shoes. What if the physicists were correct: What if, as string theory postulates, time and reality are illusions? Imagine that time was not linear at all. What if the film—or my dream of the foursome—was actually Remy,

Marcus, Julia, and myself? What if our encounter happened, is happening, will happen? Where does the distinction between them come from? Am I writing these words *now*? Are they also being written in the past, and simultaneously, filling a page at some unfixed point in the future?

Personally, I found this idea extremely freeing. So perhaps what I felt I was about to orchestrate had already occurred, not as a memory, but as an act in the past, present, and future. I was all for bending time, bending static notions of love, and I was also a huge advocate of bending over—pardon the expression.

A HIKE TO THE CHAPEL

Julia had her own traveling ritual: She liked to spend the first day in a new place on her own. On our trip, her chosen destination was a secluded patch of beach along the warm waters of the Mediterranean. She rose early and disappeared into her rite of passage.

Remy had one work obligation before starting our holiday: a conference call midmorning with his boss and two other reporters assigned to Spain. So, as it turned out, Marcus and I decided to share breakfast—sweet rolls and dark coffee—then take a ten-kilometer hike down to the town of Mojácar, which boasted an ancient chapel.

It turned out we shared a certain fascination with religious relics. Marcus was especially fond of the Virgin Mary, often referred to as the Holy Mother. He confessed to me that as a child at church, he would kneel at her feet and pray fervently while savoring the throbbing woody between his legs.

"She was just so beautiful and sad," Marcus said. "She made

my rocket pop." His irreverence often stirred my own popping rocket.

The village far below the house we were renting shimmered with a cluster of bright houses, their tile roofs glistening under a drowsy morning sun. Splashes of redolent colors—geraniums, bougainvillea, roses—seemed drawn upon the village in crazy splotches by an awkward child with a box of crayons.

Beyond this vista was the water, the convergence of the Mediterranean and the Atlantic. Where did one end and one begin? When they met, was it as if meeting a soul mate? Or did the powerful waters at first collide and resist until finally succumbing to their inevitable liquid embrace? I thought of lovers quarreling through the night and the eventual exhaustive surrender that led to the meeting of tongue and flesh, prick and pussy.

The blue of the sea seemed startled and startling at the same time. I didn't know if it was because of the light, the towering mountains and the giant shadows they cast over the azure vastness, but when I took in that blue, I gasped. Gazing at it, too, Marcus gently squeezed my arm in what I sensed was silent agreement.

We began our descent through the thick primordial green that surrounded our house. The air was a fragrant riot of orange and lemon blossoms, eucalyptuses and spicy herbs. We passed tribes of olive trees with their gnarled trunks and leaves like flapping silver wings that pulsed in the breeze.

We walked in easy silence for several kilometers. Periodically, our shoulders bumped as if to say "hello." Both of us wore silly grins, like babies learning *pat-a-cake, pat-a-cake* for the first time. What was happening? There was a sensation of near hysteria—sweet as it felt—blossoming inside of me. Like a loopy madness, minus the fear. The staggering beauty around us seemed to usher in this feeling. I was sure Marcus felt it, too, because he began to smack his hand against mine—playful and reckless. Then our fingers became excited children playing tag. Soon we were inspired to hum a tune without words.

Reaching a stone terrace overlook, we both sank to the ground to rest. A slight wind caressed our gleaming, sweating faces, the summer sun heating up.

Marcus rested his hand on my leg and asked a question that surprised and thrilled me.

"Nina, do you think that all the kisses we've received—from our mother's lips on our foreheads to all the lovers we've been with—do you think those kisses are stored up like memories in our flesh?"

My eyes must have filled with a subtle shock as I looked at him.

"Didn't think I was such a romantic, eh?" he asked.

I smiled. "You're many things, Marcus. Your question is beautiful."

A shyness crept across his face that I'd never seen before.

I slid my hand on top of his as I said, "I hope all of those kisses are stored and we can trace them back, one after another."

Without a thought or conscious choice, I leaned forward and kissed his full lips, pressing mine against his with a tender ardor. My mouth eventually opened, inviting his wet tongue to meet mine. We were both curious, excited, tentative. Our mouths grew more eager to suck, absorbing our taste, the remnants of the sugary warm powdered bread we had eaten earlier. Then, ever so slowly, almost reverently, our mouths parted and we released each other.

It felt so natural, so instinctual, as if we were always meant to share a kiss. And more?

A sudden stillness wrapped around us and in unison our giddy, silly elation erupted once again. We laughed.

He punched my arm lightly. "That line—about storing up kisses like memories—it always gets me laid."

"Hold your breath," I said, punching him back.

"Don't you mean, *don't* hold your breath?" he questioned.

"No, I mean the opposite." My voice was filled with mischief, as if I were channeling Julia.

"Is this a riddle?"

"More like a puzzle," I countered.

"I like puzzles," he finally replied.

"Me, too."

We stared at each other; his eyes seemed to plumb mine for clarity. The kiss had created a damp pulse between my legs. I swept my gaze away, closed my eyes, and lifted my face to the sun, breathing in the moist, sweet air.

Images played across my mind like those in an unedited film. Yet it was my own film this time, starring my beloved trio and myself: *Remy's hand glides up Julia's impossibly long, amber-colored thigh to her dark, silken pubes. He lazily twirls his fingers through them, as if petting a cat. Aroused, face flushed, breath quickening, Julia's tongue wets her lips. She lifts her hips slightly, shy yet hungry for more.*

Next, my legs open wide as Remy's tongue inches up inside of me like a child exploring a mysterious hiding place. I'm watching Marcus sip cognac then release the warm liquid into Julia's mouth as she strokes his cock, preparing him for me. I'm dizzy, drowning in desire as Remy's mouth sucks my throbbing clit. He expertly beats a rhythm

against it, pulling me to the edge, then slides away, down again into
the wet depths of my blessed cunt.

Abruptly the images ended because Marcus grabbed my hands
and pulled me up to my feet.

"C'mon, little Miss Puzzle Dreamer. We're going to the
chapel."

"Are we going to get married?" I joked.

He smiled. "*Hold* your breath."

The small, white stone chapel stood in the center of town, draped
like a holy garment in purpling bougainvillea. On its right was a
small graveyard with crudely shaped tombstones huddled in hap-
hazard clumps. Mementos were scattered about them: bundles of
herbs, flower arrangements, shells and stones.

As we pushed open the heavy wooden door, a stream of dusty
light filled the entrance to the dark chapel. We stepped in, the
door closing behind us, the only light inside coming from clusters
of red prayer candles.

We walked in silence from one saint to the next: St. Francis
with his wooden staff; Joseph, father of Jesus. The dim light
forced us to approach each figure closely, as near as if they were
intimates. Marcus stroked the serpent crushed underneath the
Virgin Mary's feet. His eyes rose as his hand caressed her robe,
her porcelain hands, her body ascending toward the cloudy heav-
ens as his eyes followed.

"Your first love," I whispered.

He leaned his shoulder against mine. "She broke my heart. It
was all about Jesus with her, twenty-four seven."

I moved toward the glowing votives, each flame representing
a plea or gratitude, a sorrow or a longing. I knelt before them,

running my hand along the worn wooden railing, sensing the tears spilled there like a lover's endless kisses.

Marcus stepped up behind me, leaned close. With his breath warm against my cheek, he whispered, "It's time for your confession."

He grasped my hand and led me to the confessional: two wooden doors like stern parents standing side-by-side, each opening to an alcove the size of a telephone booth.

I stepped into one booth, Marcus into the other. My eyes could barely adjust to the darkness within as I heard a match flicker. From behind the dingy screen between us, Marcus had lit a candle and its faint glow cast a zigzag pattern against my chest as I knelt.

"God bless you, my child," Marcus murmured, low and seductive. "When was your last confession?"

"Well, uh, Father, I'm afraid I've never been to confession," I answered.

"What brings you here now, my child?"

I could see his shadowy presence leaning close to the grill that separated us. His scent reached me—aloe aftershave tinged with a slightly tart sweat—and made me suddenly woozy in this stuffy little room. I wanted to lick him.

The small space hummed with whispered sins that seemed to cling to the walls like layers of soot in a fireplace.

"Father, punish me if you must, but don't hate me for what I am about to say."

"I'm listening."

Our voices were as hushed as those of lovers whispering under a soft comforter.

My clit hummed with its own sweet sin. My fingers inched down my stomach, rested between my legs. My touch was feather-light—the merest suggestion of contact.

"Father, my desire is pure and certain," I went on. "My confession is about a sin that has not occurred. A delicious sin that haunts my dreams, my imaginings, that quakes inside my body endlessly. A sin that renders my flesh, my being into a vessel of horrible, delirious want."

I paused, hearing him breathe.

Marcus, I want you inside of me. Could he hear my thoughts? Could he sense that I was tracing my index finger lightly over my swelling pearl, that I was imagining Julia's tender tongue exploring uncharted territory for the first time?

"Are you talking about . . . sex?" He hissed the word *"sex"* like a randy snake.

"Yes, Father, sex . . . but more than that."

Marcus, cup my ass with your strong hands and thrust your prick inside of me as only you can. Be swept into my roiling sea, rise with me like a rogue wave. Let us churn, Marcus, into the undiscovered worlds of our desire. Do this with me as Remy excavates Julia's fearless ache, her magnificent fount of sensual thrill. Do this with us as we become a quartet of unimaginable love, of such ease and trust, of shared tongues and wet expressions of innocent hunger.

"You must describe your sin in order for me to help you," he pressed.

Oh, God, Marcus, give it to me, give me all of you. Now. Now!

"I cannot," I whispered.

"Why?"

"I must hold the sin inside of me until I know it is time."

A long, pregnant silence filled the air between us. I finally released my finger from my tremulous clit—quivering and nervous at the same time.

"My child, you are a prick tease," he scolded softly.

We both burst into laughter, the sound reverberating against the metal grate.

"What is my punishment, Father?"

"My child . . . you deserve a spanking."

Yes, bend me over, Marcus, splayed across Remy. His beast will scourge my drenched slit as your hands pelt my ass like hail. Let Julia's forgiving tongue offer succor to my mouth, relinquishing her taste, absorbing mine, my cries softened by her hushed sighs. Take me, Marcus, take me with Remy and Julia, and allow me to have my way with you.

Suddenly, we heard the chapel's heavy front door open, and we scurried out of the confessionals. A short, stout scowling woman dressed in black, a rosary dangling from her gnarled hands, wobbled toward the altar.

Marcus grabbed my hand and we rushed outside, the brightness of day shocking. Hand in hand, we fled down the cobbled street like kids who had just stolen candy from the grocery.

By the time we returned to the house it was close to dinnertime. Our hike back was completely uphill and took much longer than we expected. Remy and Julia were in the kitchen making paella. It simmered on the stove in a big pot, and both of them sipped red wine as they prepared a salad. The smells were almost hallucinatory—fresh bread warming in the oven, the Mediterranean spices in the paella mixed with tomatoes and shrimp—and made me swoon.

I moved to Remy, wrapped my arms around him from behind, and kissed his sweet neck. "I went to confession," I whispered.

"Were you forgiven?" he asked.

"I'm not sure. The priest was very stern." I turned to Marcus. "Weren't you?"

Winking at Remy, he sipped from Julia's wineglass before he answered. "Well, what did you expect? She told me she likes to touch herself . . . *down there*."

"Naughty, naughty girl," Julia chimed in.

"And dirty, too," I replied. "I'm off to take a bath."

Remy grabbed me, pulled me close. "Don't touch yourself *down there*. I'll do it for you."

As I luxuriated in my hot, watery universe, I again felt such comfort listening to the sounds of life coming from the kitchen. Actually it was more than comfort—my heart felt fat and giddy. I realized I was in love, absolutely head-over-heels in love, with all three of them.

Remy entered the bathroom with a steaming slice of toast slathered with melting butter. My mouth took it in greedily as he fed me piece by piece.

"Remy, I'm in love," I said.

He smiled. His eyes sparkled as if laughing. "I am, too," he whispered.

His hand dipped into the water and lightly traced a trail from my knee slowly up to my soaked—and soaking—pussy.

A moan dripped like slow honey from between his lips and mine as his fingers delicately caressed my clit just the way I crave.

"Close your eyes," he commanded gently.

I did as he asked, leaning my head back, feeling each infinitesimal molecule that inflamed my nub as his masterful hand radiated hot energy. He slid two fingers inside of me.

"I want you. . . ." I gasped.

Suddenly the languorous kiss with Marcus flashed across my

mind. I clasped my thumb and index finger and squeezed my nipple hard—then soft—over and over. My breath rose out of my mouth, making a harsh sound.

Remy's fingers were silken, wet. They moved slowly in and out of me, returning to my clit, then dipped deeper inside of me. I clung to them, pulsed my muscles, my need growing ferocious.

"Remy, please, fuck me. . . ."

"Oh, baby." He sighed. "My naughty, nasty angel."

My eyes were still closed and his voice filled me, just as his hand did. "You're my Angel-Beast," I whimpered.

"Right, baby," he whispered. His arm splashed into the water around my back, the fingers of his other hand still slip-sliding all over my molten, melting muff. Suddenly, he lifted me out of the tub and spread me on the floor. Even more suddenly, he released his engorged, swollen dick from his jeans, piercing me, stabbing relentlessly. My cunt and every muscle in my body seized his cock, inviting the assault, pulling him in deeper and deeper. My lungs gasped for air, our eyes locked in a force field of human animal lust, unbridled love, and thoughtless, careening desire.

All at once, Remy is fucking Julia, her eyes locked with his, her pussy pleading for more. Her nipples expand against his tongue as Julia's breasts meet his hot mouth, his teeth. Her moans merge with Remy's urgent groans. Julia understands what I do with Remy, my Angel-Beast, a devouring, untamed creature.

A sound shattered the still air, startling me before I realized it was my own voice, releasing a wild scream from the depths of my groin. My flesh trembled, my hips bounced and bucked, my clit exploded. Remy, my fucking beautiful lover, cried out as he came, a brutal, sacred cry.

"ARE YOU OKAY?" It was Marcus at the other side of door. "Anybody hurt?"

Remy collapsed on top of me, and we began to laugh, our bellies bouncing in unison.

Hearing us, Marcus giggled, too. "Guess Nina got her spanking, eh?"

"Oh, he gave it to me, all right," I called.

"What's happening?" It was Julia's voice. The door swung open, thanks to that mischievous, wicked girl.

Marcus and Julia stood grinning, staring down at us.

"Obviously, your first course was pussy," Julia said. "Second course, paella."

"Don't bother to change," Marcus added. "You both look fantastic."

Remy didn't flinch at all at being exposed; in fact, he bounced to his feet with a loopy smile on his face and pulled up his jeans. I caught Julia's quick glimpse at Remy's crotch. Her eyes met mine and she winked, nodding teasingly.

Marcus drank in my nakedness. "You must go back to confession, my child."

"Yes, Father."

Remy offered his hand to help me up, wrapping a thick terrycloth robe around me.

As we all headed for the kitchen, Marcus said, "Can't wait to see what's for dessert. . . ."

Dessert? Julia and I are naked, on our knees, our soft ass cheeks pressed together as we give twin blow jobs to our precious men. I'm doing Marcus, she's having Remy, and as we suck, lick, squeeze, our hot mounds pulse together. Our boys expand and stiffen inside our mouths, against our tongues and teeth, and we begin to shimmy our hips. We grind against each other, our own wet pubes dripping, our simmering teeming wetness mingling and colliding like the Atlantic and Mediterranean. After they come, spurting their silken, salty semen into our mouths, Julia turns to me, grabs my neck, pulls me ferociously to her. She devours my dripping lips and tongue with hers, blending the masculine juices from our beloved fucking men.

There's dessert.

ONE TOKE OVER THE LINE

Julia had purchased a bit of grass from a young waiter at a café she'd stopped at for lunch. She guessed he'd have some because he wore a T-shirt with Bob Marley's photo on it. After dinner we settled into the living room, and sitting on pillows in front of a blazing fire that crackled and sparked, we proceeded to get high. The grass tasted sweet and earthy. The wine from dinner had already made me loose, and the pot transformed my mind into a sensual stew of words and fantasies. My body buzzed, drowsy and stoned, and through my eyes, my friends were the most remarkable creatures God could have imagined.

I leaned back against Remy, and Julia rested her head in my lap, her feet finding a home between Marcus's legs. He massaged her toes, her feet, then her calves, lingering as if to memorize every pore. I stared at his hands, at the little patches of almost imperceptible, innocent blond hairs that decorated his knuckles. His fingers were thick and long; a hand that begged to hammer wood, chop trees, haul in heavy nets of fish. As he massaged her, his veins wiggled and danced beneath his skin, thick with the blood coursing through them.

I wondered what it would feel like to slide my tongue unhurriedly across those veins, feel the pulse and vibration of his swimming life force. How it would be to slowly invite his hand into the deep trench of my vast uterus or to feel his well-muscled arms holding me with their fields of golden fuzz.

Dreamily, my fingers wended through Julia's dark, lustrous hair. The texture was like a revelation, a completely unexpected feast.

Remy inhaled a long toke off the joint, then pressed it once again to my lips. The sodden tip of the joint tasted like moist, fall leaves, and I took it in as if smoking autumn. He passed the joint to Marcus before resting his hand upon mine, caressing Julia's hair with me.

My eyes greeted hers, and we both smiled so widely my lips ached.

"Shall we dance?" she said with a hum.

"I am dancing," I sang back.

All my senses were saturated, and I could feel Remy's growing bulge throbbing against the crack of my ass.

I'm swallowing our world, dazed and consumed, high and soaring.

Marcus's hands roamed deliriously slowly up Julia's legs.

Julia's vulva is a vase planted with blood red geraniums, with succulent, radiant life. Her pussy is a garland of flowers, a feast of blossoming scent, waiting to be plucked, each downy petal thirsting for nurturing water. I am a bee, my tongue, like a stinger. I demand to penetrate her stamen, pierce and stab her very center countless times, drink her in, take what is rightfully, naturally mine.

As if reading my mind, Julia's fingers snaked around my neck, caressing the nape tenderly as she pulled me close, her lips nuzzled against my ear. "Nina, I want to kiss you," she whispered. I hovered above her, time disintegrating.

Lovely pink, hot creature between your lips, open to me. Burn me, sear my wanting tongue with yours. No mercy, no hesitation. Eat me, drink me, devour my teeth, slash at my gums. Obliterate all space between us, our mouths fused into a new being, a suckling, primordial creature causing a roar of unceasing intoxication.

I woke up in bed with the faint morning light sliding across the room. What had happened? My head throbbed, reminding me of last night. Had I kissed Julia? Passed out? Was it all too much for me? Perhaps this constant swirling in a tempest of painful longing and fantasy was just too overwhelming for my psyche and my body to bear. Remy was not in bed, and I could not hear a hint of human activity in the house. I was glad for the silence. The last toke of pot had pushed me over the edge of clarity, of consciousness. I felt badly; I did not want my precious dream to be tainted by a chemical alteration of the purity of my desire.

Maybe I was more afraid of the reality of crossing these forbidden boundaries with them than I realized. Would it change our friendships? Could we find a space to hold the experience without judgment? Suddenly, I worried what consequences the actual foursome would have on Remy. And on our relationship. Would it ignite dark jealousies—suspicions—between us all? My mind raced with the possibilities and now my head pounded. I needed a bath, needed to wrestle with these demons and discover my truth. More than anything, I had to know why, after years of imagining the act, now that it was closer than ever, why did it suddenly thrust me into such doubt?

Two aspirins and a good soak quelled my anxieties and soothed my aching head. Whenever I'm in water I always reconnect with my center, my truth. The demons, I realized, were remnants from an old identity. Yes, I'd always been a dreamer, yet sometimes, after I'd revealed a dream, I'd often felt shame.

For example, when I was fifteen I told my parents I was going to marry Jimmy Mandala, a seventeen-year-old basketball star at my high school. My dad, an avid fan of the team, had rolled his eyes. "That kid is going places, darlin'. Probably he'll become pro," he said. "Don't think you're in his league."

Then my mother chimed in: "Are you dating him?" When I shook my head no, they both burst into laughter. I turned beet red and ran to my room.

Dream on, I told myself then.

It took me a while to realize that others often held dreamers in contempt—even my own mother. I learned not to allow my head-in-the-stars self to be ridiculed or belittled then. I became smarter about to whom I revealed my dreams. In this case, I felt I would dissolve if Remy, Julia, or Marcus belittled me for having this beautiful dream, this fantasy, this vision of the four of us. But I trusted them more than I'd ever trusted anyone before.

I realized that Marcus and Julia, Remy and I were like two compasses drawn to each other through a magnetic force when within a certain radius. There was no denying this force; it was palpable, like the compact energy of an explosive. Instead of giving voice to my demons, I bathed in images and sensations from last night.

I thought of Julia's eyes upon mine, so dark and deep, as if reflecting the evening sky. And her words: "Nina, I want to kiss you." Her voice had been hot, electric, zipping down my spine to my ass, and Remy's prick had thickened, a pure, raw nerve incarnate. Her desired kiss to my lips had traveled through me, down to Remy's resounding shaft as I watched Marcus's powerful hands and arms, his shoulders like the wings of a hawk, sailing up Julia's thigh.

The confluence of events—my time in the confessional with Marcus; the primal, potent sex with Remy in the bathroom; the food and wine; the indulgence of all my senses and emotions with my loves, heightened by the grass—had thrust me into an almost unendurable, convulsive state. No wonder I had passed out.

TENGO HAMBRE
(I Am Hungry)

Although I felt a bit wobbly, the plan was for Julia and me to take a day trip to shop in Córdoba. The guys would have none of it, knowing from past experience that to shop with us was like being stuck in a time warp. We went very slowly, savoring every store, boutique, craft and jewelry stand we encountered, not willing to risk missing out on a potential find. For our men, the experience was like having a vise grip on their balls.

The three had returned that morning with fresh fruit, bread, sliced ham, and cheese. They spread out a feast for me, complete with several espressos that I gulped greedily.

After my second espresso I *had* to know, so I blurted out: "What happened last night?"

Remy took my hand. "You fell asleep."

"When?"

Julia smiled. "Well, right after I whispered to you. You just, well . . ."

"Passed out," Marcus announced.

"Passed out, fell asleep, same difference," Remy joked.

"Did I do anything strange?" I asked, trying to re-create the scene in my mind.

All three giggled.

"Was it horrible?" I pressed, my face reddening.

"Honey," Julia said, her voice soothing, "you just looked at me, said something like, *'Tengo hambre,'* blah, blah something, and then you lay your head down. That's it."

"*Tengo hambre?* But I don't speak Spanish," I protested.

Marcus rose from the table. "Let me be more precise. You said, *'Tengo hambre. Tengo hambre.* What am I going to do?'"

"Marcus!" Julia slapped his ass. "Don't embarrass her."

"What's so embarrassing? 'I'm hungry. I'm hungry. What am I going to do?'" Marcus winked at me.

Remy draped his arm around me. "You were adorable."

"Absolutely," Julia agreed.

"Huge," Marcus said, "hugely adorable."

"Must have been the pot," I said, my face hot. "Grass makes you hungry."

Could they see that I was lying? I knew what I hungered for—did they? Were they putting me on? Had they discussed it when they were buying food for breakfast? Shit, was I that transparent? Not one of them brought up whether or not Julia and I had kissed. Had we? Or had I passed out just as the warm flesh of our lips met? I must have heard those words somewhere, *"Tengo hambre,"* and they'd just popped out.

Okay, I reassured myself, *they said you were adorable. They were very sweet.* And Marcus was just being Marcus—playfully wicked. We had shared our own secret kiss yesterday, and ever since, I'd been feeling even closer to him in an inexplicable way.

Okay, Nina, I said to myself, *this is part of the journey.* Tengo hambre. Tengo hambre. *What am I going to do?*

Soft Spanish guitar notes leaked from the radio as we drove to Córdoba. I was behind the wheel, Julia's feet perched on the dashboard. Her soft-pink painted toes moved with the music. In her blue sandals, they looked like perfect seashells. We were quiet for well over an hour, another quality about our relationship that I cherished. She knew how I loved to wander through my thoughts and fantasies, how I absorbed a landscape into my mind, imagining characters, battles, love affairs gone awry, families facing obstacles.

"Do you remember what I whispered to you last night?" she asked.

Red Shoes, I would have written *she asked out of the blue,* but in that exact moment I was literally replaying her words in my mind.

"Yes," I answered, without looking at her.

She touched my cheek with her palm, resting it there. I leaned against it—so unimaginably endearing. When she pulled it away, I felt a pang of sorrow.

Her voice immediately pacified me. "There are these moments with you, Marcus, and Remy when I feel like we're one being. Is that crazy?"

"Not at all," I replied matter-of-factly, though a part of me wanted to jump and dance.

"I had this dream a while ago," she said. "I haven't told anyone about it."

She paused. I was eager to hear every word, but I wanted to

allow her the space to go at her own pace in revealing her thoughts.

She began to circle the tips of her toenails with her fingers, massaging them distractedly as she continued.

"We were swimming, the four of us, naked. And the water was so blue, a blue I've never seen. And so clear and warm. Our bodies were moving like we were fish, and we could breathe underneath the surface, and slide and slither against each other."

I glanced over; she seemed far away and closer than ever at the same time. In that moment it was as if we inhabited the same soul, yet were separated by the singular, unreachable universes of our dreams.

"I've never felt happier in my life than I did in that dream," she continued.

I reached over, traced my fingers gently across her face. "I love you," I whispered.

"Me, too."

By the time we reached Córdoba, I once again felt that my heart was fat with joy. Arms linked, Julia and I meandered snail-slow down whitewashed lanes, glimpsing dreamily beautiful patios, each one a floral extravaganza. Artisans' craft stands glutted the sidewalks with ceramics, pottery, colorful tiles, inlaid wooden music boxes. There were achingly supple leather goods, delicate embroidered linens, and jewelry that made us salivate. We were not big buyers, just extraordinary shoppers, treating it like an art form.

Julia approached a stand where bright, colorful scarves swayed under a slight breeze. I watched her press a hand against one as if stroking something alive. The delicate silk, undoubtedly warmed by the sun, seemed to answer her touch.

All at once, I felt seized by a feeling of disintegration—of plummeting and soaring at once. Was I falling in love with Julia? I know, Red Shoes, I've told you that I'm in love with all of them, but at the very core, my love for Remy is as essential to me as oxygen. What was happening to me? In that moment, my core seemed to quake like tectonic plates shifting, forever changing the landscape. Could my being hold such immense emotion? Or would I collapse, dissolve under the weight of it? Was I having a nervous breakdown? Many writers were insane. They went crazy, lost their grip, put heavy stones in their pockets, and strolled into rivers.

"Pueda usted ayudarme? Por favor. Socorro!" I heard a voice, obviously in distress.

"What?" Julia asked.

"Socorro! Socorro!"

Julia grabbed my arms, pulling me back into my body, my mind. "Nina, what did you just say?" Her face had filled with concern.

"Nothing," I replied, feeling myself shiver deep inside.

The woman selling the scarves approached. As if she knew me, she wrapped her arm around my shoulder and guided me to sit in the chair behind her stand. She turned to Julia. "Your friend said she needed help. *'Socorro'* means help." Her accent was British.

"But she doesn't speak Spanish," Julia said, her eyes scanning mine, confusion growing between us. Fear snaked up my spine.

The woman poured Spanish sherry into a small cup and handed it to me. "Drink all of it. Don't sip, take it all at once."

I did as she said. The sherry was sweet, with a hint of cinnamon. It warmed my mouth, my throat, even my stomach. I was immediately calmed. In fact, I felt wonderful. Julia, however, was clearly upset.

Sensing her distress, the woman poured another cup of sherry and handed it to Julia. "You, too, drink up," she directed.

I focused on the woman, finally able to see her. In her fifties, she had black hair with flecks of gray swept back into a bun. Her face revealed a life of fullness; each wrinkle seemed to disclose pleasure. And her eyes, a shimmering green, murmured wisdom.

"Let me explain what happened to you. I've lived here, in Spain, for over thirty years." Her loving gaze rested on me. "I watched you and could see you were overtaken—captured by the old souls of Spain. They can be very tricky, especially when one is too open, too expansive, as you are."

"Is she possessed?" Julia asked in reference to me, her eyes wide and scared as a child.

The woman laughed, a throaty, joyful sound. "Yes, she was. Possessed by unsettled spirits that roam this landscape searching for young, open hearts. They long to feel, if only for a moment, what it is like to inhabit flesh once again, to be inside a beautiful body. To feel desire, passion, *amor*."

She grasped my hand. "You swim in these places, drunk on love, yes?"

"But what about the Spanish?" Julia insisted, before I could respond.

"That's their language, dear," the woman replied. "If you were in Italy, it'd be Italian."

We bought four silk scarves from her. Afterwards, she directed us to an out-of-the-way restaurant for tapas—encouraging us to partake in a bit more sherry.

We sat in the farthest corner of the small room, a simple, family-run place. It was no-frills, just good food, drink, and far away from the bustle of shoppers. Julia had bought a pack of cigarettes on the way, and she lit one for each of us as our first glasses of sherry were delivered.

"Well," I said, lifting my glass. "That was interesting."

"Tell me something, Nina," Julia said, her voice somber. "When you were a child, were you picked up in a long school bus or a short one?" That wicked smile of hers flashed wide, and we both laughed.

"To insanity," I toasted.

"Drunk on love," she replied.

"*Tengo hambre.*"

"*Socorro,*" she breathed.

"*Socorro,*" I repeated.

Help, indeed. Was my vivid imagination now posing a threat? Was I slip-sliding into my dream world, the foggy fantasy that haunted me? If time was irrelevant, even bendable, didn't that render reality anybody's guess, just a collective impression we all agreed to?

All I knew was that on top of all my questions, I had Spanish souls to contend with at this moment—souls that could scent my redolent desire. In previous times, people suffered from "spells." They were attributed to women mostly, who would go out to the countryside to recover from their "nerves" or from "the vapors." Perhaps it was just part of being a woman, especially an expansive, open woman, willing to dive into that delirious, indescribable universe of love—anarchy, chaos, mayhem, turmoil—but, oh, what a ride it was.

Julia and I agreed to keep this experience to ourselves.

———

On the drive back, I remembered the time shortly after we met, Remy and I had gone to see an Eric Clapton concert at Madison Square Garden. The seats were third row center, given to Remy by a reporter friend who worked for the music industry's hottest magazine, *Spin*. I was absolutely mesmerized watching Clapton play the guitar that was nestled between his legs. He created sounds of melancholy, expressed turbulent longing and bottomless desire. Sitting there next to Remy, I closed my eyes, trying to imagine what it would be like to be Eric Clapton. Then I had the strangest sensation. In my fantasy, the guitar I held became a penis—and then I was Nina with a penis. A woman with a dick that played guitar like Eric Clapton!

Women were hollowed out, mysterious vessels to be penetrated and filled. Men had a solid, fixed, exposed penis that ruled, dragging them like dogs on leashes, with boners threatening to constantly erupt. They had to get inside of women, had to plumb our mysteries over and over, though they could never unlock our secrets. As a woman, I would have given anything to have a penis for a day, just to feel that maddening mass between my legs.

What would it be like to fuck Julia, as a man? How would it feel to thrust inside of her, to have her wet walls clenched and trembling, pulling me in deeper and deeper? In many of my fantasies it was my tongue (a petite penis?) that wriggled, inch by inch, inside of her wanting puss. Her hands would force my head to go further, to fill her more singularly as my wet muscle twisted and curled, lapped and licked, drenching my face in her juices. What would she taste like? How would I taste to her? I wanted to feel her bud swell between my lips, the heat of her blood engorging her molten slit. And as I feasted, Remy and Marcus, fueled and charged by seeing the women they loved fucking, would have no choice but to fuck us both, fuck us in every imaginable way.

Dive! Dive! I wanted to scream as the car brought us closer to our men. Just like in Julia's dream, I could see us all, naked, swimming, our bodies as one being, fluid, liquid, teeming with life.

Tengo fucking *hambre!*

TELL ME A STORY

Remy's angel nestled inside me as I lay on top of him, our skin linked by sweat, my raw, stinging nipples pressed against the damp fur of his chest. We breathed slowly, steadily, in sync, and the pungent scent of our lovemaking filled the air.

"Tell me a story," Remy whispered, his voice low, saturated by pleasure.

We would often tell each other stories before we fell into dreams. Tonight, however, after my intense experience in Córdoba with Julia, I didn't feel I had one coherent synapse left in my brain.

"Baby," I replied, "too tired. Your turn."

"On one condition," he said.

Still straddling him, I sat up and gazed into his deep, love-drunk eyes.

"Touch yourself. I want to watch . . ." he hummed.

"Better make it a good story," I replied, lifting my hands to my breasts. I cupped, then lifted them as if presenting a gift to a king. My nipples, still erect, were like ruby red jewels.

He began: *A woman's husband fell into a coma after a horrible car accident.*

I interrupted: "Remy, a coma?"

"Hold up, hold up," he said. "I'm giving you background."

I nodded.

He continued: *They were deeply in love, newly married, and the world spread out before them, filled with possibilities. Her best friend . . . I'll call her Red, because she had long, deep copper hair that glowed and shimmered . . .*

"Nice," I said, cutting him off again. "What's the wife's name? The husband?"

He frowned. I was pressing for details, interfering.

"Sorry," I apologized, squeezing the sore nub of my right nipple in supplication. A soft grunt escaped from my lips.

He smiled.

Sad Eyes would sit vigil with her husband in the hospital every day, all day and night, sleeping by his side. She talked to him endlessly, touched his body, kissed him from his toes to his mouth, to the top of his seemingly dead brain. Eventually, she took him home, providing around-the-clock care.

Red, her best friend, would visit daily, bringing food, offering unconditional love to Sad Eyes. But she was worried. The flush in her friend's cheeks was gone, her voice, once exuberant, had become flat. Her body, once brimming with curves that echoed with womanliness, was now silent under the weight of her sorrow.

"Remy," I said, "this is a sad story. Is it sexy?"

He lifted his eyebrows, chastising me.

I pinched my left nipple.

"Harder," he demanded.

I squeezed, wincing, but felt a heated quiver shoot down to my groin.

He went on: *One night, Red took Sad Eyes by the hand and guided her downstairs, into the living room where a blazing fire roared. She poured them both a glass of absinthe and made her friend sit with her on a pile of large, soft pillows as they drank.*

No words were spoken between them. Red slowly unbuttoned her blouse, allowing her breasts, full mounds of life, to spill forth. She wasn't wearing a bra. She lay back, lifted her ass, and slipped off her skirt—no panties. Her trimmed bush was like a tiny fire.

"Wow, Remy, that's gorgeous," I whispered. My hand slipped down my stomach and found the moistening pearl between my legs, just as Remy's angel expanded slightly inside of me.

Sad Eyes lifted her glass of absinthe to her eyes and gazed through the diaphanous light green liquid at the undulating image of her naked friend spread out before her. After so many months attending to the seeming emptiness of her husband's body, this vision was a welcome, unexpected gift. She lowered the glass, her eyes floating over Red. Her breasts rose and fell with each breath. The dappled light from the fire made her body seem like a constellation of stars, an undiscovered universe all its own.

My finger, like a child zipping down a waterslide, slid up alongside Remy's thickening cock, still a guest in my cunt. I twirled my finger, drenching it, then glided it back to my blossoming clit. I rapidly flicked my finger against it, then stopped, pressing hard as if ringing my own doorbell.

"Great, Nina," Remy said in a hushed voice, "do it. Feel it."

"Keep going." I moaned. "Tell me more."

Time hung in balance for a moment, then Sad Eyes, famished and desperate, pressed her mouth forward, bringing her tongue out to meet Red's. Without hesitation, Red stripped Sad Eyes of all her clothes so no barriers existed between them. She brought Sad Eyes down upon her, pressed her flaming pelvis forward, and they ground hard against each other, hot pussy to hot pussy. Red grasped her friend's ass, stroked it for a while, then held it firmly. With hard jerking pelvic thrusts, she offered her friend everything inside of her, focusing all of her life force into their movements.

For Sad Eyes, it was as if a thick layer of skin all at once dissolved, and as it did, a new layer of flesh infused with hope emerged.

I moaned, rocked my hips up and down. I could feel Remy's balls against my ass cheeks. I didn't want to come, not now. I rested my finger against my growing clit.

Finally, Sad Eyes' legs went high, her knees to her chest as Red's mouth dove in, her tongue licking the thin slit between her outer lips. . . .

I was breathing fast, and with each exhalation, a mini groan came out of my mouth. "Oh, Remy, fuck, keep going. Keep going," I pleaded, images of Julia flitting behind my eyes.

Remy held my hips between his strong hands, stopping me from bouncing. "Almost there, baby, almost."

Red used her hands to slowly peel the lips back, revealing her best friend's radiant snatch. How it begged to be sucked, slashed, consumed.

His eyes on fire like Red's cunt, Remy licked his thumb, and he began to work at my clit, slapping then stroking. Yes, the story was sexy.

Something overcame Sad Eyes, as if her cunt demanded to be fucked hard, harder than she could ever imagine. The empty space between her drenched walls had to be filled, had to feel excruciating pain.

My hips longed to bound up and down Remy's ram-hard rod but he held me steady, prolonging each moment. I flung my head back, my mouth open. I suddenly wanted Marcus's cock to fill the space all the way to the back of my throat.

She grabbed Red's hand, curled her fingers around it, forcing it into a fist. Understanding, Red stroked her friend's gushing hole, slipped two, three, four fingers inside, then her thumb.

"Fuck me," I yelled. I grabbed his wrists and freed myself from his grip. "Deeper, Remy, deeper." I was gasping now, as if I couldn't catch my breath. I slammed my body against him, my mawing cave sucking him in as his knowing thumb plied my throbbing clit.

"Open it up, baby," Remy whispered. "Give me all of it!"

I didn't know I had more to give, but his words, his cock, became like a fist inside me. The pain was searing, exquisite, and awful at the same time. All my thoughts were devoured. I wailed as my entire body shuddered when Remy slipped a finger into my tender asshole. I grabbed my nipples as hard as I could, yanked at them as if pulling stubborn weeds from clay soil. All at once, I flung my arms into the air, cried and groaned, just as Remy showered my cunt with his sticky hot stream. The bone-deep trembling of our flesh felt timeless as wave after wave rippled through us, our tongues suckling softly.

Eventually our breathing slowed, and I pressed my lips against his neck, feeling the rush of blood beneath his flesh.

"Did you like the story?" Remy finally asked.

"Oh, yeah," I said. "But what happens in the end? Does the husband come out of his coma? Do the women fuck again? Do they all fuck?"

Remy slapped my ass. "You're gonna have to wait to find out."

"I have a story, too," I cooed, the sweet sting pulsing under his resting hand.

"Oh, yeah? Tell me."

"No," I growled.

Slap! Slap! The sting deepened, delicious and hot.

"Tell me," he commanded.

"No," I whispered gently.

Slap! Slap! Slap! My clit beat like a cheering spectator—a witness to sublime torture.

We both giggled, sighed, and just like that, sleep quickly enveloped us. Our bodies as one entity, exhausted and transcendent, sailed off into dreams.

WHEN IT RAINS, IT POURS

The rain came down in sweeping torrents, so hard it seemed to bruise the earth. Our foursome was undeterred by this sudden change in weather, however: We were going dancing. As Marcus drove, I was mesmerized by the grand curtains of water that slashed the dark night. The pine and eucalyptus trees leaned over, pushed by the harsh hand of the wind. Such drama nature offered, stirring emotions inside of us, reminding us of how fragile we were, how small compared to a simple storm that wielded such power. It humbled us—or at least it should. We were flesh, bones, spirit, soul; each a unique creation, and our existence on earth was so decidedly tenuous. We often had a hard time holding that truth, it seemed, and instead lived lazily, as if we'd go on and on. Although moved by this kind of sentiment in instances like these, we could still put off seizing the moment. Myself, I refused to live my life passively. It was way too precious for that.

Enclosed in the car with my loves, I felt safe and excited. A thrill hummed in every pore, and my heart was already dancing.

I rested my hand on Julia's shoulder. "Remy told me the most amazing story last night."

"A true story?" Julia asked.

"No, he made it up," I said. "About a woman whose husband is in a coma and her best friend—"

Marcus began to laugh, cutting me off. "Her best friend with a red bush?"

"How did you know?" I glanced at Remy, who shrugged.

"*Coma Party Girls,* best porn movie of 1999," Marcus continued. "A real classic."

Remy cupped my crotch. "My version was hotter."

"Do share," Julia hummed.

"It was a *porn* story?" I said, still disbelieving.

"The end is fantastic," Marcus said. "The husband's in a coma and the two girls have been going at it like wild things."

Remy interrupted. "Hold on—I'm telling the story. Red and the wife end up fucking on top of him, hoping to revive the guy."

"Wait, wait, wait!" Julia bounced in her seat excitedly. "Going at it like wild things? Fucking on top of him? I need details!"

Marcus and Remy laughed, as if sharing a private guy joke.

"Babe," Remy said, "we're guys. Give us two girls doing it and we're happy."

"Two girls, great. Five, even better," Marcus added.

"We want details!" I commanded.

Marcus savored every second of the story. "Okay, the guy's got this dick, and it's lying there like a dead gopher. And the chick with the flaming bush is on all fours, straddling him, while the wife is lapping at the shore of the Red Sea."

Remy slapped Marcus on the shoulder. "And the machines attached to him are buzzing quietly, remember, beeping real slow. But suddenly, as the brain-dead dude's tool starts to rise, the machines go berserk."

Marcus continued: "Guy's lying there all comatose but then he's got this ten-inch boner, like the fucking space shuttle, ready to blast off."

"So they both start blowing him, purely medicinal," Remy added.

"Enough!" Julia yelled. "I know what comes next, pardon the pun. Coma Boy squirts them all over their titties, and they giggle like little girls."

Remy sighed. "Got to love a happy ending."

"Amen, brother," Marcus said.

We arrived at the small club where the strains of flamenco music erased the incessant pounding of the rain outside. The room was small, dark, lit only by candles on the tables and along the windowsills. Blue-gray cigarette smoke curled in waves from tables where couples sat close.

The music had just started. The chords were haunting, melancholy. They sounded like a lament, a pitiful cry of despair. We ordered a bottle of local sherry and sat silently, inhaling the mood: erotic and tense, lust and longing leaking from us—as well as from the other couples at the club. Our chairs were huddled close, Remy seated on one side of me, Julia, on the other. Her leg was pressed against mine, carrying on our secret language.

Julia's eyes lit up. "This style of song is the *jondo*. It is profound and serious, the sorrow of people oppressed for many centuries. They begin with this song to prepare the listener emotionally. Next will come songs of exuberance and love."

She lifted her glass to us. "To exuberance and love."

We toasted. I felt in that moment that the four of us were an inseparable, sacred being.

A female dancer dressed in a flamboyant, frilly red dress moved to the center of the floor. Accompanied only by guitar, she began to perform. Her eyes were dark like hot asphalt, her lips a splash of dazzling red. There was intensity in her movements, which were graceful and explosive at the same time. The percussive sound of her high-heeled shoes against the floor was hypnotic, her hands like poetry. Each movement was a stanza telling a story without words, one blood-deep and mysterious, containing the whole world.

"I can do this," Julia stated. She leapt up and joined the woman confidently, executing the form and style with perfection, yet also expressing her own essential nature. She was fiery and playful, bursting with innocence one moment, then sultry, dark, and enticing the next.

As the night went on, we all danced, switching partners, fluidly offering our bodies to each other. We pressed limb to limb, cheek to cheek. Our hands slid down hips, across backs, caressing shoulders. Our searing glances created a combustible heat; fire passed between us.

Remy pulled me hard against him. "Are you attracted to Julia?" he whispered.

"Yes," I responded.

Then, "Are you attracted to Marcus?"

"Absolutely," I replied.

"Good," he said softly, accepting.

"And you?"

He nodded.

I didn't ask him directly if he was attracted to Marcus because I realized I hadn't ever thought of the two of them touching each other sexually. Was that odd? I knew that they'd taken showers together in the gym's locker room. And we'd all skinny-dipped at night—and in broad daylight. Neither of them had ever seemed the least bit uncomfortable being naked, though I knew straight men had a more difficult time admitting attraction to other men. It was so much easier for women.

In my fantasy of the foursome, however, I hadn't imagined Marcus and Remy together, and yet I'd been extremely aroused in the past watching two men fucking. Well, it was in a movie once, but I found the muscled physicality, the almost competitive and brutal sensuality extremely hot, and so had Fitz, my boyfriend at the time. He had been my everything then: broad-shouldered, coffee-brown eyes, bald, and tattooed.

It had been a French film, shot in black and white, about men in prison. We were bombarded with an endless wrestling match of soulless cocksucking. Raging dicks pounding anonymous assholes. A collision course of tongues and teeth drawing blood. Tenderness emerged after the brutality, when the men showered and washed each other in a ritual that was so loving it was almost motherly.

As Fitz and I watched, a surprising ache erupted between my legs. I dropped my hand onto Fitz's lap. He was hard, his jeans tight and hot over his throbbing tool. I unzipped him quickly, grabbed his hand, linked our fingers, and stroked his shaft. I let him guide our touch, our eyes fixed on the screen. He spasmed and jerked in his seat, his warm, gooey cum showering our fingers.

After the film, we returned to Fitz's dorm room, lit a few candles, collapsed on the futon and smoked some grass. We were silent for a while, both still caught up in the power of the film.

"That was fucking hot," Fitz finally said.

I turned over on my stomach, then up on all fours, and stared down at him.

"You gonna be my bitch?" I barked.

"Bring it on," he growled.

We began to wrestle and quickly he had me naked and pinned. I was facedown, one of his hands holding my head against the pillow, the other easily gripping both my wrists.

"Fuck me, asshole," I grunted, raising my ass, inviting something I hadn't yet experienced: backdoor action.

He pressed his hand roughly against my gushing cunt, slathering his fingers. I writhed underneath him, felt as if I was going to spasm uncontrollably. He deftly rubbed his fingers on the slick bridge between my clit and anus, that delicate, sensitive in-between place that was neither here nor there. He teased and tortured me, my clit begging for touch, my unexplored hole dying to be penetrated.

Finally he gave me everything. He lubricated my virginal hole, first sliding one, then two fingers into the tight pulsing chamber. Using my hands, I spread my ass cheeks, feeling the insistent tip as his snail-slow, hard cock began to penetrate. My teeth clenched down on my hand, curled into a fist. The pain was searing, delicious, consuming. It was a pain of elimination, a frenzied obliteration, and in my mind, the only words were *fuck me, fuck me, fuck me.*

At the very moment I felt I couldn't go on, I was about to scream for him to stop, his fingers gently stroked my swollen, ignored clit. That tenderness, combined with the rhythmic, painful pounding of his cock in my ass, overwhelmed my senses. Suddenly my body convulsed, a quaking shudder ripping through my flesh. Both of us cried out as he shot me full of hot sperm.

I don't remember how much time passed before we regained full consciousness. Fitz lit up another joint and offered it to me. "That was fucking hot," he repeated, smiling. I took in a deep drag, my ass throbbing, and I felt strangely proud of us.

In the film about the foursome, there was no brutality. The two couples' lovemaking was like a flowing, fluid river: limbs lifting, diffuse mouths sucking, fingers and hands dipping into shadows, exploring every inch of flesh. There was no distinction, no separation between male and female. Many of the images were undefined; who was touching whom, who was fucking whom, was left ambiguous. Watching that experience was so freeing, so radical to me. I witnessed how we could be released from gravity, from logic, from restriction—which suddenly made anything possible.

On the dance floor, I felt released from my obsession, freed from the persistent fantasy that had haunted me for so long. Dancing with the three of them in that moment, I felt as if we had already made love—bending time, yes. Yet, truthfully, I was so in love and felt so loved that if I could, I would have chosen to replay this memory on my deathbed. Such was pure bliss. Whatever unfolded beyond this moment didn't matter anymore, no longer seemed to possess me. The flamenco music swelled, engorged with exuberance and love—as were the four of us.

When we left the club, we had to race to the car because the rain was pounding, the wind a ceaseless howl, with lightning and thunder having joined the drama. After hours of dancing we were in a dreamy, drowsy state, enclosed in our secret circle. Nothing could touch us—or so I thought.

Out of nowhere, a speeding car careened toward us from the opposite direction, forcing Marcus to swerve out of its way. I heard Julia scream. The tires screeched. Metal crunched. Tree branches slapped loudly against the car as we spun then jolted forward, creating a path where none existed. Finally, we slammed against a tree and lurched to a violent stop.

"Anyone hurt? Anyone hurt?" Remy's arm was pinned against my chest, holding me in place.

"I'm okay," Julia said, her voice shaken.

"No," Marcus mumbled as he opened the driver's side door. Both he and Remy climbed out to inspect the damage.

I leaned forward, wrapped my arms around Julia from behind. Her hands grasped mine, stroking them, seeking comfort at the same time that she offered it.

The curtains of rain were still relentless. Completely drenched, Marcus opened the passenger door and reached inside the glove box for a flashlight.

"Time for an adventure, ladies," he said, "we're stuck here. Remy saw a building about a half mile down the road, so we're going to have to make a run for it."

And run we did. Great booms of thunder accompanied by flashes of lightning fueled our legs with marathon power.

The building turned out to be a dilapidated barn in which someone had obviously set up makeshift living quarters. There was a box of candles. Matches. A few blankets. A pit for a fire and a pile of wood. And, lucky for us, a case of dust-laden red wine.

Remy and Marcus immediately kicked into caveman macho mode, providing for their women. They built a fire while Julia and I stripped off our sopping clothes and wrapped ourselves in blankets, sitting close, letting our body heat warm each other.

"It was a dark and stormy night," Remy said, as he pried the cork off of the first bottle of wine with the car keys.

"It was a dark and stormy night," I repeated, leaning against Julia. "Two couples were stranded in a barn."

CRASH! A part of the ceiling gave way and fell just beyond our fire.

We were all stunned for a beat, watching the rain pour down.

"It was a dark and stormy night," Marcus added. "Two couples were stranded in a barn with a hole in the ceiling."

Remy handed the wine to Marcus, who took a long swig.

"A hole in the ceiling where rain showered in," Julia offered.

"But just out of reach of the fire that heated their bodies," I continued.

"A case of forgotten wine was all the sustenance they had," Marcus said, offering the bottle to me.

I took a sip—it was delicious, dry, slightly fruity. It soothed me as I drank more. I then held the bottle to Julia's lips, lifted it gently, and she took it in slowly, purring with pleasure.

Marcus stripped off his clothes and wrapped a blanket around his waist; Remy did the same. They draped all of our wet garments over a low wooden bench, away from the rain but close to the blaze.

My body was already dry and cozy from the fire and the nearness of Julia. I rose, slipped off the blanket, and naked, gathered the candles, pushing them into the dry areas of earthen floor, while Remy lit them with the matches. We created an altar for ourselves before the primal inferno of the fire, the sacred tongues of candle flame painting our bodies, as we shared the wine.

I went back to sit next to Julia. She opened her blanket, her legs wide, inviting me to sit between them. As I did, she wrapped her woolen cocoon around us. Her breasts pressed against my spine, and I felt her nipples begin to bulge from our nearness. She squeezed her legs tight, pressing them against my thighs as her arms wound around my stomach.

Seated side by side, Marcus and Remy both stared, their eyes flickering with absolute adoration.

"Y'know," Julia began, "in those porn movies, the chicks lick each other's pussies like birds picking at seeds. It's just not real. If you ask me, there's nothing worse than bad head."

Marcus and Remy nodded in unison, passing the bottle to each other.

"Reminds me of Jay, this guy I dated once," I said. "When he'd go down on me, he'd put his hands on my stomach like he was getting a manicure. It took everything I had not to yell: *Grab my ass!*"

"Absolutely!" Julia responded.

"He had this really long tongue, but he'd only use the very tip of it," I went on. "He'd go up and down and up and down, like he was some kind of paint roller."

"Harsh," Marcus stated, nudging Remy with his elbow.

"Yeah, well, I felt like I was on a painfully slow roller coaster," I continued.

"Did you tell him?" Remy asked.

"A thousand times." I sighed.

"Geez, Nina, I know. I had a guy who would only go down on me using this cinnamon-flavored lube. He'd squeeze it all over me like syrup on pancakes." Underneath the blanket, Julia's hands inched down between my legs.

"Tasty." Marcus hummed. "So was he any good?"

Her fingers waved softly through my pubic hair.

Julia laughed, remembering. "'Cin-o-min, let me in,' he'd sing, and I'll tell you, he dug right in. Got his nose wet, his cheeks all sticky, his face lost in my luscious space."

"Right on," Remy cheered. "To the cinnamon girl!"

I dropped my hand to meet Julia's, still caressing me, and I led her to go further. Her index finger slid into the liquid heat of my pussy. A sigh escaped from her lips. Ever so slowly she started to rub her breasts against my back. Hidden under the blanket, our secret dance flooded me with desire. She teased my burgeoning clit with her finger languidly—so knowingly, so naturally, it could have been me touching myself.

Remy reached out to hand me the bottle of wine. "You do it," I whispered, not wanting to free my arms from beneath the blanket.

He offered the bottle to my lips, tipped it back, and I swallowed a mouthful. Next he offered some to Julia.

I looked over at Marcus, saw the twinkle in his eyes. Did he suspect what we were doing? Were we leaking pheromones that his body was reacting to? They both knew we were naked underneath the blanket and that alone had to be a turn-on.

"I would give anything," Marcus said, winking at both of us, "to see two women eating each other out in a way that you feel is a true representation of the act."

"Not like birds pecking at seeds," Remy continued, "but realistic, y'know. It would help men around the world to, uh, improve their . . ." He fumbled for the right words.

"Yes," Marcus assisted. "To see the real thing, men would finally be able to offer the pleasure all women—as the greater sex—deserve."

"I don't know about Remy," Julia cooed. "But Marcus, you're fantastic in the going-down department."

She quickly slipped two fingers into my wet cave.

I grunted, then cleared my throat as a ruse. "Remy is also *very* skilled." I hummed.

Julia pressed her lips against my ear, whispering, "Let's give it to them."

I was ready, the enticing ache between my legs already so intense. I slipped off the blanket, exposing Julia and myself to Marcus and Remy, as Julia's fingers continued their knowing journey.

Their eyes widened and both of them gasped.

Julia curled her entire body around to face me. I lay back on the warm blanket, my legs wide and happy, and watched—with my men—while Julia slipped her hands under my ass, lifted me slightly, and lowered her head.

At the very first sensation of her tongue flicking against my hard nub, I felt as if my groin emitted a sound all its own. Julia moaned, her voice vibrating against my ache, filling me. Her tongue snaked deeply into my cunt, tasting me, circling the wet walls. My eyes were pulled by a magnetic force toward Remy and Marcus. No longer wrapped in their blankets, they both sat, legs wide. Their gorgeous cocks thickened and engorged, rising slowly as their eyes danced with flames from the fire.

I reached down to hold Julia's head, my fingers gliding through her hair as she sucked my clit. Then her tongue beat against it fast. I was drowning in love, the vibrant pulsing energy of passion surrounding us.

A tremor exploded into a full-blown quake as my clit thrummed wildly. Julia squeezed my ass cheeks, keeping her face buried against my trembling cunt.

"Oh, God," she groaned, the sound of her voice trailing a path deep inside of me, through my groin, my belly, up into my breasts. It made me dizzy, hungering for more touch, from Marcus, from Remy, from Julia.

Soft grunts—emanating from the guys—caught our attention. We gazed at them, both stroking their glistening, solid cocks in unison. What a duet of pure, masculine power. Without a

word, we crawled to them; I went to Marcus, Julia to my beautiful Remy. As I had imagined, Julia and I were positioned so that
our ass cheeks, flushed with heat, were pressed together as we
both knelt to take in these throbbing creatures for the first time.

Marcus tasted like rain, his blond pubes smelling of damp hay,
earthy and natural. As he continued to move his hand up and
down his quivering shaft, I pressed my lips against his head, my
tongue drawing lazy circles around the very tip. He moaned from
his belly, deep and satisfied. The soft, fleshy mass of Julia's ass
pulsing against mine made me swoon.

I heard the familiar, harsh sighs coming from Remy. Although
I could not see Julia's mouth upon him, I knew by the timbre of
his voice that he was swimming in pleasure. My heart swelled.

My mouth began to inch slowly down Marcus's enlarging penis. What a profoundly sacred and profane experience to feel
such enormous life inside one's mouth. I wanted all of him, to the
very depths of my throat, as deep as possible. I wanted to swallow
his essence so a part of him would always be inside me.

Marcus, my confessor, my irreverent friend, the lover of the
most precious woman I knew. What a gift it was, this act, this
time together. His hands held my head, showing me the singular
rhythm of his need: a slow sliding up and down the length of him.
I licked the long, throbbing vein that ran down the back of his
cock as my hand found his balls. I began to caress them, squeezing slightly. I longed to taste the furry loads, and pressing my lips
together, they crawled down his cock. I replaced my hand with
my mouth as my tongue and lips tortured his sack. A long, luxurious groan filled the air.

I could hear Marcus's harsh, fast, breathing mingling with
Remy's hot, quick grunts; Julia and I released twin moans. My
mouth returned to Marcus's cock, and I devoured it, feeling the

raw tip pressed deeply against the back of my throat. On fire, my tongue slashed at him as my mouth moved rapidly up and down, almost releasing him, then devouring him once again.

He thrust, then jerked, finally losing his load into my mouth, some of it dripping down my chin as his pelvis shuddered over and over, and he released a cry of supreme ecstasy. The echo of his cry reverberated as Remy's familiar guttural groan punched the air and my damp ass ground against Julia's.

There was no room for words now, only sounds—touching, sucking, fucking, loving sounds.

I turned as Julia's hot mouth met Remy's lips, their kiss deepening hungrily. My hand had to feel her liquid mystery. I reached out—her ass so inspiring—and I caressed the length of her crack. My fingers glided farther down between her legs, greeting her simmering wet slit. Startled, I gasped. On his knees now, Marcus came up behind me. He grasped my cheek, turned my face to kiss him. Our second kiss. Here we were again, eager to play with each other.

My delirious fingers continued to fondle the folds of Julia's dripping labias, darting to her delicate, hard clit, then entering the depths of her. As I felt her muscles pulling my hand in, I suddenly had to taste her.

I pulled away from Marcus and lowered myself onto my back, positioning my face beneath Julia's wanting gash. On all fours, she lowered herself against my hot breath, my tongue careening out of my mouth into her sweet, pink wetness.

My legs wide, I invited Marcus or Remy to do whatever they wanted. In this position, either of them could have stood above us and penetrated Julia from behind, while the other entered my insanely hot cunt from the side. *More, more, more,* the only possible words.

Julia rocked her pelvis back and forth, as if dancing with my mouth and tongue, slippery with her distinctive flavors. A sudden moan escaped from my lips as a warm, slick finger circled my asshole then began sliding up and down the path between the two luscious holes. A mouth landed on my right nipple, and I knew it was Remy, his familiar tongue grazing lazily across my thickening orb.

I reached out my arms and found Julia's breasts, hovering above me, bobbing slightly from the rhythmic movement of her hips. I teased her nipples, offering them slight twists between my thumb and index finger. She swooned, releasing an "ahhhh" of absolute elation.

Remy's mouth was on fire, nibbling then sucking my nipples just as I felt the tip of Marcus's firm cock rubbing against my cunt.

I clenched the muscles of my ass, lifted my pussy slightly. It was a silent invitation to be penetrated, but Marcus took his time, wetting his prick with his own juices as he moved his shaft against my aching mound, making me dizzy with excitement.

I focused on Julia's clit, solid as a miniature fist, flicking my tongue hard against it. Her breath quickened, her pelvic thrusts faster and faster against my mouth. I felt as if I were melting under the power of her growing orgasm as it neared, and all at once, writhing and groaning, she came, my grateful lips surrounding her beating clit.

I cried out as Marcus, on his knees, entered me fully, and Julia sat up, crawled to Remy, pushed him down on his back and leapt upon his eager and erect cock.

I fixed my gaze on Marcus as he lifted my legs and feet over his shoulders. He slid in and out of me maddeningly, deliciously slowly, my ache intensifying with each deliberate thrust.

The air was charged with our heat. A palpable energy seemed

to erase time and place. We were four creatures: two men, two women, sharing our most precious primal selves. I felt no separation, only a marrow-deep connectedness that was beyond definition.

Our bodies, our sweat, our fluids, tongues, lips—all parts of us were a piece of a deeper erotic mystery. Because such a door had finally been flung open, there were no constraints, no limits to where we would travel, no maps that dictated direction.

Marcus had asked if all lovers' kisses were held on the lips like a memory, an imprint eternally held. My answer was *yes.* Now we were all etched indelibly upon each other, layer upon layer of flesh memories simmering in our bodies.

Which meant that all of these images had also become a part of me:

Julia's glistening breasts are two radiant planets. I watch as she dips one nipple, then the other, between Remy's full lips. Those lips have been bitten, sucked, licked, thrashed at with my mouth—and now, Julia's.

Remy's Angel-Beast extends, rising, blood-engorged, his balls swinging, as he stabs Julia's slippery dark cavern. I'm kneeling above her, our eyes locked, and my tongue matches Remy's cock as we stab and stab her glorious openings.

Marcus's hungry tongue pulses against Julia's tender, innocent, pink asshole. It's wrinkled and puckered like a newborn, and he laps away as she holds Remy's rock-solid cock captive inside of her. My tongue and hers are knitted and dazed from endless suckling.

Julia's hand curls into a fist inside of me, a globe of such soft power, and Marcus laps at my succulent clit. Remy, my Remy, murmurs into my open mouth, whispering words that release me, free us, a wet fusion of undying love.

I dip my tit between Julia's legs, her pubes molten, slick, and I press my aching nipple against her clit, my ass rising to meet Remy's bursting beast. My hands spread my cheeks wide, wanting him to take me, fuck me, overwhelm me with his love. I cry out as he enters me, my ass quivering, and Julia grasps my tit and bucks against my breast. Marcus's fingers find my slit, and he massages me with a comforting tenderness, helping me take in the excruciating ecstasy of Remy fucking my ass.

My hand holds Julia's, clasped like we are schoolgirls skipping in unison, as Remy fucks her and Marcus fucks me. All of us are sated, exhausted, our breath heaving in great gulps, our men spilling the last of themselves into our cunts. As they come, we clench our fingers together, binding us in a secret pact for life. Silence descends, save for the last trickles of rain still falling through the ceiling. Remy and Marcus collapse on top of us and we stay silent. We listen to our breathing, the gentle thrum of rain, and the periodic snap from the dying fire. A sigh emerges from one of us, then another, and soon, depleted, drowsy, we fall asleep and slip into a quartet of dreams. . . .

HAPPY ENDINGS

That night was extraordinary. Partially as a result of how we arrived there—that harrowing accident. And because of the circumstances, we found ourselves in a separate world, able to drift far, far away. The rain, the silence, the strangeness of the place. We were all somewhere we had never been before. We were simply being free.

When the sun rose, we dressed silently, shared shy smiles, and walked back to where we'd left our car. A tow truck was parked in front of it, and a burly, older man with a thick moustache leaned against it, smoking a cigarette while he hummed a tune.

When we approached, his eyes lit up. "Ah," he said in a thick Spanish accent, "I sensed you would show up and need my assistance."

After he secured the car to his truck, we all climbed into his cab. I sat on Marcus's lap, Julia on Remy's.

"Poor kids," the man said, "stranded on a night like that. Must have been awful!"

"Harsh," Marcus said, his eyes all twinkly.

"Brutal," Remy concurred.

"You have no idea," Julia cooed.

"Unbelievable," I murmured.

And then we all laughed—along with the truck driver—caught up in a pure moment of infectious joy.

In case you're wondering, Red Shoes, we never talked about it afterwards, and we never judged each other. We were all guilty, all innocent. In the end, our secret actually brought us closer than ever.

Dream on, my mother had said so long ago. I knew I would never stop following her advice. As for my writing, I had started thinking about a story that involved two couples, trusted friends, and they go on vacation together, and, well . . . you get the picture.

JAKE

As I slip the thick stack of papers back into the envelope, Stella, I'll confess that I feel a knot of shame lodged in my chest. The truth is, Alex was so much freer than I am. Hey, my life is all about convention: Become an architect, find a woman, ask her to marry you, buy a house, raise some kids, take vacations, build up a respectable retirement account. Shit, it makes me sick; how predictable, unoriginal, deadening.

I see now that my plan was a cage in which Alex would have suffocated. Her spirit was so adventurous, so wild and bold. Is that why I wanted her so—because she was everything I wasn't? No wonder she sought out another man, took a risk, choosing chaos rather than my stifling sense of order.

What I'm realizing, Stella, is that I thought love was concrete—like a building! How wrong could I be? Perhaps it's Nina who's right: Love is anarchy, irrational chaos, a real fucking mess at times, but oh, the pleasure of its expression—just like dreaming.

Yet how can I ever love again? Aside from loving you, I mean. You who love and obey me, depend on me. In a way, that's what I'd come to expect from Alex—love, obedience, dependence.

Fuck, I realize I don't understand the first thing about love. Not one damn thing. How many diary entries and letters will it take before I change? How many? How long?

Whatever it takes. I promise, Alex, whatever it takes.

Emily's Dance

◆

THE INNER DANCE

How do I know the other is even there, much less believe that I am loved, completely? How do I know that it is me you see and not merely some making of your imagination? How am I to trust the sweet murmurs that trickle over your tongue, the meeting of your lips on mine that equally take and give, ask and answer, forego as they claim?

I have envisioned you forever, it seems, somewhere in the shadows of myself, the hidden corners of my being that surface in slumber's dreams in which I often turn, or fly, and finally dance into your arms. Or sometimes, when my eyes open slowly from sleep, I sense you behind the frail lids as they flutter against the light and vision floods in. I know then that once again I am miraculously alive, teeming with every possibility, the insistence of being.

My limbs sway from the tremendous urge to spin, to move, to leap with life. I want so much to express the wonder it fills me with, the inextinguishable light of each dawn, the dazzling drumming of unexpected rain, the way its sudden existence freshens the air, the atmosphere, every breath.

That is how I feel each time you appear, when opportunity arises and grace invites me to remember you exist evermore.

I would dig myself into the ground if you asked me to, grasp each strand of grass with precise abandon, cling with hungry palms to the sky, kneel haphazardly before the horizon, keen ever after under the stars.

All this I would do for you. Give you everything and all of my heart, even always knowing that they could never be enough.

JAKE

The diaries and letters, they roll in as steadily as each day. Stella, tell me you figured otherwise. I confess: It never occurred to me how many of us were so sore in the heart, distraught to the very heels on which we stumble forward. I guess that's what happens when we launch into relationships. We find ourselves so often catapulting through them that sometimes we land where we do—not in but out of love.

If we're lucky, we made it to abandon, encountered ecstasy, embraced the bliss of meeting another, momentarily merged into one. When that blurry moment fades away—as it must—we eventually return to ourselves. Sometimes that's perfect; we've expanded, our hearts have grown. But sometimes, if our hearts have been broken, the longing to be one with another shifts. We long to cut away, flee the pain—given how deeply we hurt.

We might search to be heard then, to make sense of our wounds as we wonder just how our rapture finds itself flat on its back, and other truths—however *poisonous they seem to be*—*sprout up like plants:* Betrayal. Deception. Misunderstanding.

Yet, *sometimes, those nasty truths can be in relation to our own selves. I wonder if that's because we've more often been so disappointed by how our dreams turned out*—*or we're even more disappointed in ourselves because we were just too afraid to dream them.*

Emily's got a lot to say about that. Stella, here's the diary entry:

♦ ♦ ♦

Dear Red Shoes,

I feel your pain. And I know that sometimes the pain can be so great that fantasy takes the place of reality, especially when you're alone. I know because for a long time I thought I was living my life truthfully. I thought I was pushing myself as hard as I could. . . .

Oh, Stella, how I know that lie.

THE OUTER DANCE

September 8 . . . my time in L.A. is almost up. Either I get this Freedom video or it's back home for me. See, I promised my momma when I left if things didn't start to move in six months, I'd come home and get a real job.

I've gotten close a few times, but for some reason, something inside always stops me from letting go. Maybe it's because there are just so many good dancers out here. I mean, really good dancers. Or maybe it's because deep down I just don't believe I'm good enough. I don't know. And to make things even worse, the moment I laid eyes on Freedom, I knew I was in trouble. He's just so focused, so disciplined. Every time he looks at me it's like he's looking right through me.

At today's casting call, the director showed up at the studio dressed all in black, a sweater draped across his shoulders. He was very cool, together, total business.

"How you doin'?" he said to everyone. "Here's what's happening. Everybody knows A.C.? A.C., where are you?"

"Right here," a voice called. And then A.C. stepped up. He was sweet-faced and fresh, with a light brown brush cut that stood straight up, a simple white T-shirt over jeans.

I took that moment to cut my eyes at the other dancers. Lots of spandex, boots, and buff bare midriffs.

I felt a little out of place. Yeah, I wore my beat-up motorcycle jacket, but underneath, I had chosen to wear my favorite black-and-white print dress. Fit me like butter, felt like butter. Truth, it was my lucky charm, sewn for me before I left home by my very own momma. So what if everybody else looked more hip, more downtown.

"A.C. is a choreographer," the director explained. "He's in from New York."

A.C. smiled, nodding. "We'll take it from the top," he said to everyone. "Really strong, right here." He pointed toward the stage.

A red-haired woman in shades strode into the room. No nonsense there, I could tell right away from the chill that surrounded her.

"This is Tampa. She's the casting director," the director said.

"Hi," she said to all of us, but she didn't look at anybody. She walked over to a long table and sat behind it.

"What we're going to be doing is we're going to interview most of you," he explained, "and then we'll cut those interviews against the footer that we're doing for the video. We're also gonna film the whole thing."

There it was—the pressure, cutting through my belly like a phat, wicked knife. I felt it so often these days it didn't slice me so deep anymore, but it didn't help make it any easier for me to bust out, either. I lined up with the other dancers as Tampa started firing questions at all of us. She hadn't even looked at me yet.

"How long have you been dancing?" she asked the first chick.

"All my life," the skinny thing answered.

"All my life," said tiny chick number two.

Such attitude they both had. Yo, girlfriends, I nearly came out of the womb moving, and I had more meat on me then than either of you could get your swirl on today! Let her ask *me* that question.

"All right," Tampa went on. "Name? Place of birth?"

"Paula Venice," said the first one. It was "Ven-eece," not "Venice," like in Italy. She wore hoop earrings and a nose ring, straight black hair falling sharply to her chin, making her look more severe than skinny.

"Alison Cramer," said the second one. A mane of long, mussed dark hair surrounded her pale face. She was vamped out, totally goth, toothpick thin.

Tampa finally looked at me.

"Emily Johnston," I blurted. "Columbus, Ohio."

"To-ooo-ny Ree-ee-ed," said the chick standing next to me, as slowly as she could.

"Faster," barked Tampa.

I saw Tony's shoulders stiffen into belligerence. She had fight in her and at least one extra handful of flesh.

"Loss An-gee-less, Cal-eeee-for-n-ia," she dragged out.

What was up with that? Like myself, Tony was African American, a sistah. The other two were white chicks. In fact, most

everyone else there was white—not Freedom, of course. He was
a force of serious brown muscle, damn straight.

And. He. Had. Just. Walked. In.

Hair pulled back in a ponytail. Jeans so tight like they'd been
painted on. Bare arms pumped big enough that they seemed they
could hold the world. Yet it was the way he moved that transfixed
me, every single muscle in agreement with the countless, connec-
tive others at each step.

"Faster!" Tampa ordered. "We're talking energy here. How
old are you, Alison Cramer?"

"I'm twenty-two," Alison answered.

"Twenty-somethin'," Paula said with a coy smile.

Tampa stared at her blankly. "Twenty-somethin', huh?" She
looked at me. "How long do you give yourself to make it, Emily?"

I swallowed hard. "Six months . . . a year," I said slowly.

"What if it takes you longer?" Tampa pressed.

"Well, if it's meant to be, it'll happen," I managed. Did I believe that? I didn't really know anymore.

"What if it doesn't?" Tampa asked the other chicks.

"I wouldn't have any peace," Paula answered.

"Then I'll do something else," I added.

I glanced across the room. Freedom's gaze was fixed on me. I
flinched a bit—the knife inside twisting.

Alison said, "I . . . I don't even want to think about it."

Tampa smiled for the first time. Thin, but a smile. "Okay.
That's a good attitude. Now I'm gonna ask you all to go over there
by that wall." She pointed. "I'm gonna say a word to you, and I
want you to say the first thing that comes to your mind. Got it?"

Damn, we moved our butts over to the wall. About a dozen
crew guys watched us. Freedom stood there, too, hanging quietly
away from the lights. I could see he still looked right at me.

"Ready?" Tampa called. "Emily—freedom!"

"Um . . . equality," I answered.

Alison said, "Moving."

Paula hesitated, her mouth open, but then she said nothing.

Tampa stared. "Step forward, honey. It's okay." To all of us, she said, "C'mon, I wanna see in your body that you're a dancer. Move!"

I started slow, my special shimmy. "Freedom," I called out to Tampa.

"How does it make you feel?" she asked me.

"Alive. Free . . ." I said easily. That was true, as long as my hips were rocking.

"Good, good," she answered. "Move! Good—freedom—say it."

Oh I moved all right, that I could do. I was free when I shook it. "Freedom!" I called.

"Scream it!" she ordered.

"FREEDOM!" I hollered even louder.

Tony was beside me, dancing, too, but so tight-ass.

"Dancing," she muttered.

Tampa was on her in an instant. "Do not give me an attitude. Tell me the first thing that comes into your mind."

Tony's hands flew to her hips. "Honey, that *is* the first thing that comes to my mind!"

Tampa scoffed, then turned to Paula. "Freedom?"

Paula sighed. "I don't know."

Tampa looked us over. "Freedom!" she called. "Let's move!"

After we changed into our dance gear, A.C. showed us the routine on the dance floor. The music was already pumping, a low bass pulsing through the beat. It sent me right into the middle of it, carrying me to its core. I did my best to let my body go with it, turned out in a skintight, backless black bodysuit, spaghetti straps just barely climbing over my shoulders. I'd tied my favorite flannel shirt around my hips.

Red Shoes, I'm only telling you what I did with the shirt because I can be a little shy. I admit, I'm a healthy squeeze, not one of those tiny things that turns sideways so you can't even see her past a memory. You know, what can I say? This baby got back—and it's fine to cover my booty from time to time. Especially when I'm auditioning. See, that's because I am not the type of female who gives it all away at once. That is definitely not my style.

Besides it was Daddy's old shirt. I still wore my special necklace from him as well, the one with the hanging pendants. It made me look like an exotic goddess, like I was from Egypt or beyond, or so Daddy would maybe say . . . before he left us for good.

Like that necklace could take his place. But, yeah, I wore it anyway.

There was A.C. talking: "One . . . two . . . three . . . down on four. You're looking at the floor. Right hand goes on the back. Bring the butt up."

The director called: "We're changing the lights, get some atmosphere, put some smoke in. Let's get down now, girls. . . ."

I *was* down, already juiced. Everybody—the director, Tampa, A.C.—they were conferring together. Freedom was watching, too. When I saw his eyes on me again, just like that I grooved down deep to my knees. My head back, neck exposed, I pumped my booty up from the floor, as if it was just for him.

But you know what? I did it to get away from him—lose the knife inside by dissolving into the beat.

Red Shoes, like I said, I feel your pain. That's because I feel my own, this sudden place where I petrify. When someone's looking at me, expecting me, wanting me to be something . . . I'm not sure I am. I mean, I'm just me—little Emily from Columbus, Ohio.

I don't mean to slam Columbus, but, really, what's it got to say for itself? What special thing did I get from living there that's going to fuel me up for the rest of my days? That it was founded in 1812, the year the United States declared war on Great Britain? That Columbus is the capital of Ohio? Really, I'm just a girl like so many others, got to play on the swing set at the school yard, got to get loved by my momma and daddy in the regular type ways in the early days of my childhood, got to have the mainstream American experiences that I eventually found left me feeling pretty empty. Alone with my dreams . . .

Once I made it to L.A., I got to see that so many of us have dreams. I mean, what's America without them? Dreams are what the U.S.A. is made of! So there I was, one of how many million who had come before me, walking the streets of West Hollywood, taking in the faces, the expressions. After just a few days, I decided that there were two types of people here: the hopeful, fresh-faced, yearning, dreamers and then the hopeless, dead-faced, disappointed, dreamless.

Dance! I told myself. Let it rip and dance! My feet, my rhythm, my talent, they were my only hope. And yet I had come to know something about my inner workings. Even though I could see beyond myself—into the world and what it could mean—as I did the instant I got to Hollywood and felt the magic vibe, I wasn't sure that meant I could catapult beyond what I had come to realize about those two L.A. types. Could I carry the possibility of such disappointment—or success—and still step far? How could I bear the weight and still soar?

But more importantly, how could I not?

All this rolled through my mind like a thunderstorm as I wriggled and twisted on the floor in front of everyone, a part of me just daring them to take me in: Do you see me? Do you feel it? Do you know where we can go?

My booty banged the floor, my legs climbed toward the ceiling, my arms bit into the air here and there. After a few minutes, the director nodded to the others before he walked toward us—toward me, specifically.

"Emily," he began, "so you're gonna dance opposite Freedom, I believe. . . ." He reached for my hand, helped me up, and led me toward the group.

"I'm gonna give you to A.C.," he explained. But then he paused, so subtly I almost missed it before he offered, "You know Freedom?"

Freedom seemed to glide closer to me, his eyes beating down on my being. His breath landed on me along with the words, "How you doin'? You did great, sistah."

What sweet breath and even more sugary words. Freedom complimenting *me*. Wait until Momma heard! I soaked him in as best I could, given the reality that I had never been that close to someone so famous. I mean Freedom had one of the top-selling rap CDs of the decade playing all over the radio these days. He had also starred in a bunch of other videos before the one we were about to make.

His skin was as clear as the sacred brown earth, his jaw jutting and direct. Pinky finger-sized silver hoop earrings hung from each earlobe, a silver necklace around his neck. Not bling at all, but real taste. Yet it was the gentle seat of his eyes, how I felt I could be myself—even rest—in them. That unusual sensation made me want to drink him in like I would fresh morning juice.

"Thanks," I whispered.

When he touched my hand, I went into a kind of trance. Without my really knowing how, my mind stepped back from the moment. It was as if I entered some kind of inner world on rewind, and there was a sudden swirl of images filling my eyes, images I realized were snapshots from early on in my life.

There's me and Momma. There's Daddy at the piano. There's Daddy and Momma at the parade, my grandma in her big round glasses and sun hat as my baton soars high up into the air. There's my daddy's back as he walks down the alley from the apartment to the street where his car is parked. Daddy's a fine salesman. I see his face in the audience when I dance at my first performance in my white tutu, my tiny pink top, my sweet little ballet shoes, but that's only because I wish it so . . . Daddy's not there. Not then or ever again.

According to Momma, he left the necklace I'm wearing today with her, to give to me when I turned twelve.

After he left, my momma's sad eyes took his place. I would dance for her—pirouetting, leaping, jumping about, hoping to find her smile, but it was never enough. Her smile had gone sad and never changed back. After my grandma died, we were all alone for good.

Like I was dreaming, I heard the director yelling to everyone, "Dance!"

The same team that had chosen me just chose the back-up dancers, too. Those of us who had been selected followed A.C.'s lead as we did a run-through of the routine before the actual video shoot.

After we finished, everybody applauded. Damn, it's sweet when the very same people who not twenty minutes earlier have been your competitors are now your appreciative audience.

A.C. beamed. "Okay, Steve's gonna work with the girls; Paige is gonna work with the guys," he called.

The director took center stage as the part of the video he had already shot appeared on an overhead screen above us.

"Yeah, and there's a story that goes with it, too," he explained. "Emily's gonna be dancing lead. She's gonna be playing Freedom's girlfriend. The back story is that she was brought up in the projects. She was a really talented dancer, but she's gotten really frustrated lately and she's fallen onto bad times. She's got a gangster boyfriend now.

"But Freedom, who also grew up in the projects and really, really loved this girl—and this girl loved him—has just cut a new song, you know, 'cause he's left the projects and he's worked really hard. He's come back because he knows how great a dancer this girl is and he begs her to dance in the video with him. When the gangster finds out about it, he goes ballistic because he's frightened of losing the girl. He doesn't want to hear about Freedom, so you know bad things are gonna happen."

Gangsters, guns, chase scenes, filled the screen. A rush of energy swept through the studio like a train charging by. Damn if the story wasn't full of danger, romance, surprise!

"So what've you got?" the director went on. "You've got your bad guys, you've got your gangster. . . ."

Everybody laughed.

"You've got Freedom," he said as he gestured toward him. "He's the hero. And you've got the girl in between. . . ."

Meaning me. He started to clap his hands, and everyone did the same.

"Freedom!" the director shouted.

"Freedom!" the dancers shouted.

The director shouted it once more—and so did we.

"Okay," he said, "cut the house lights. I wanna bring the gang-sters in. C'mon, guys," he called. "I'm gonna show you exactly what we're gonna do. We'll walk through it first, okay?"

A half-dozen guys shuffled forward, gangster attitudes all! What a bunch of homies, decked out in skullcaps, bandannas, shades, and threads. Yeah, the threads: hoodies, baggy jeans, puffy jackets. These dudes were ghetto fabulous.

"What's crackin', man?" said one.

"How you livin'?" said another.

"What's tha dily yo?" put up another.

The director just smiled. "Okay, you guys are over here. You're here. . . ." He showed each one where to stand, what to do.

"Freedom's over there," he went on. "Okay, here's what hap-pens. You ready? I'm gonna be you." He pointed to the gangster boyfriend and explained where he wanted everyone to be when the boyfriend shows up with a piece, the other gangsters stepping in my—the girlfriend's—way, physically preventing her from hooking up with Freedom so that she didn't even get the oppor-tunity to leave the gangster if she wanted to.

We ran through the rest of choreography, Freedom's part, my part. How the gangster would threaten to kill Freedom, but we get that he really didn't want to.

Then the director said, "Freedom, at a certain time, man, it's the attitude. Just get . . . you know, this guy's got a fuckin' gun on you. Now keep on movin', keep on movin' . . . Get an attitude. Break away, everyone. Break away. Music!"

We all got the scene, the energy. We all started moving. The music shifted into high gear, and we focused, feeling the charge. I felt myself swoon when Freedom danced close and held me in his arms, his hands roaming up and down my exposed back, teasing my bodysuit's spaghetti straps. He pressed tight against me, and I shimmied in his arms.

We revved into a rhythm of grinding close, then pulling away. I found myself swaying to one side, then the other. He met the movement like the pro that he was, dipping to the opposite side each time. It looked like our desire pushed us together, yet tore us apart an instant later.

Was that really happening? I had no idea if it was happening for him, but it suddenly felt real to me—too real.

He kissed me on the cheek, the edge of his tongue teasing my earlobe. His hands lingered on the small of my spine. Yeah, I got that, grooved on that. *Baby got back*, like I said to you before, Red Shoes. We ground against each other as the music climbed to a climactic pitch. Just as the moment should have exploded into pure ecstatic movement—sheer physical abandon—I leapt away.

And off the dance floor.

I could barely see, a blur of stars filling my eyes. But I could sense the immediate shift—everything and everyone stopped.

"I'm sorry," I sputtered, my breath in gulps. "Just give me a minute. I'll get it. I feel it, it's just not coming out."

As my vision began to clear, I realized the director was next to me. "It's okay," he said. "It's okay. A.C., just go over the routine with her."

I heard A.C.'s voice. "Hey Emily, just go with the music. I know you got the routine. Just let yourself feel it."

There was a slow-motion quality in the atmosphere. I shook my head to clear it. When I could really focus, it was Freedom's gaze I met.

"That's not her problem, man," he said, staring at me. "She knows the moves. Right?" he asked me.

"Yeah," I whispered.

"Yeah, I know," he said real quiet, "'cause I had the same problem, too, when I was starting out. You see, I felt all this emotion inside. . . ." He gestured to his chest. "Then one day I was at this club, right? And this guy, you know, he was so sly, smooth, you know, crazy moves. So I stepped to him, and I said, *Yo, man, what's your secret?* And he said, *Simple* . . . If he ever got blocked up in his mind, right? He'd pick out somebody who he knew he could fuck with and fuck with him straight on!"

Crazy all right. Freedom grabbed one of the guy dancers and shoved him against the wall, screaming at the guy to hit him.

"He kinda flies up against the wall like this and . . ." Freedom went on.

The dancer's hands rose, palms up in surrender, confusion.

"Do it, man, do it!" Freedom spat. He batted the guy against the chest, baiting him.

"Cody, c'mon, you a daddy's boy?" Freedom taunted. "What up? What up?"

Cody finally pushed him back.

"Yeah," Freedom said, "just like that . . . You understand. It's real simple. That guy in the club, he said that that expression of emotion would start to center him, and his juices would start to flow. Sort of like a jump-start, like a boost. You know I'm sayin'? You know I mean?"

He was looking at me now as he explained, but I could only shake my head.

"You don't know what I'm tryin' to say?" He went on. "You can—you can push me."

Freedom left Cody standing against the wall and sauntered over to me.

That walk. Those muscles. That grace.

"You can push me," he repeated.

I laughed from nerves, my feelings frayed by his insistence. "No, I don't think so," I breathed.

And then he pushed me, against my collarbone.

"C'mon, just push me." he said. "Push me, it's simple. Just— just let it go. Don't be scared. C'mon, baby. I'm all yours. What up? Push me. Come for me, come for me . . ."

I was paralyzed. Couldn't move. He started circling me, pushing me, tapping my collarbone, my chest, with his fingers.

"Come on, come on," he challenged me. "You gotta release yourself. You gotta stop thinkin' so uptight. Release it. Let it go. Let it go. Let go. . . ."

I was mute. It was impossible to move. I wanted to slam him, and yet I found I couldn't respond at all. When a timid little laugh came out of me, I wanted to slam *myself*.

Maybe the director saw my feelings. I don't know. But I guess he got that I couldn't respond, because he broke in then with, "Okay, okay. Here's what we're gonna do. We're gonna break for today, and—A.C., make it work. Come back tomorrow. Eight o'clock."

Everybody split except for me and A.C., Freedom leaving behind a big smile for yours truly.

"Do you wanna talk about it?" A.C. asked.

I shook my head. "It's not about words."

"I know what you mean," he said.

He stepped closer to me. I backed away.

"We can run through the routine together," he offered. "If you want."

"I got the routine. That's not it."

"Then tell me what it is," he said all soft. "You're special— anyone can see that."

He stepped toward me again. I didn't move. He reached out and touched my face, simple, tender. I didn't stop him.

I looked into his eyes, but I felt nothing for him. Couldn't he see that my feelings were all wrapped around Freedom?

"You're a beautiful creature," he whispered. "Let me show you what it feels like to look at you."

He tried to wrap me in his arms, but I pulled away. There are certain things I can't pretend about, and hitting it with someone is one of them. No sexy feelings means no sexy action.

Was I making a mistake? Did I have to sleep with some-one to get the part? The classic girl-from-small-town-heads-to-Hollywood to make it big? Or in this case, to make it just a little?

I would take my chances.

"I . . . don't even know you," I said. "I don't work that way."

He reached for me again. "I got that, gorgeous. But it might help loosen you up."

He pulled me close. I looked deep into his eyes.

"It's not gonna help," I said simply. "It's not what I need."

He let me go. "Okay. Tell me what you need. Whatever it is, you got it. That's my job."

"To be alone," I replied.

His eyes showed surprise, but what he said was, "No problem. I respect that. See you in the morning."

And he left.

I stayed for a while, wanting to rehearse alone, to do the moves in front of the big mirror on one wall of the studio. I sat staring at my reflection. There was too much going on, too much feeling I couldn't explain. *You gotta release yourself. You gotta stop thinkin' so uptight. Release it. Let it go. Let it go. Let go. . . .*

Freedom's words.

I didn't know what they really meant, but I so totally wanted more of them, wanted to drink them in like a cocktail, a mixed drink, something sophisticated.

Sophisticated? I guess I wanted that because I was so not sophisticated. In L.A., everyone's sophisticated. Glossy. Shining. Well, I mean the first type—the dreaming, hopeful ones. Not the others, the downtrodden, disappointed ones. They drooped like dead flowers.

Would I droop, too? My dreams unwatered, left to wilt?

No! I had not come all the way from Columbus to fail! I made myself work the routine twice, and then I took a short break. I mopped away my sweat with my red kerchief as I faced the mirror.

There I was, deep brown, burnished, ready to blossom.

Would I droop? I asked myself. I was so nervous about tomorrow I could barely breathe. No more excuses. Freedom was right—I had to rise above my technique and let my emotions flow. *Gotta stop thinkin' so uptight. Release it,* was what he said.

I stared at myself in the mirror again. Was I special? Was I beautiful, like A.C. had said? How come I couldn't see that?

I just wished I could see what other people saw in me. I curled up in the corner, suddenly so tired my eyes closed, my mind drifting, my lids like a curtain going down.

Freedom approached me from behind, the silk of his touch matched only by the soft blanket of his smooth, bare chest as he pushed himself against my back. How could something as strong and solid feel so lush, plush, so deceiving? He inched closer as I lay on my side, and I softened into him while he sank his knees into the tender scoop behind my own, our bodies spooning. His fingertips grazed over my hand, my elbow, along my arm, meandering here and there as he touched parts of me for the very first time.

I was naked.

I leaned back into him, marveling at how his pumped muscle yielded, the supple rise and ebb of the musculature below the skin each time he moved. He edged closer still, my delicious booty the perfect resting place for his pile of manhood.

We both went *ah* at the same time.

He breathed against the nape of my neck, that sweet reality the only part of him I had known before now. It landed on the sensitive flesh there like an invitation, sent me tingling all the way down my spine to where my nerves nestled around my snatch, and I had no choice but to arch back.

He answered with a sudden sigh, grinding against me gently. One hand stroked my head, the other roaming across my torso. He did not let an ounce of me escape his wandering. No, he seemed to want to memorize every inch of me with that spectacular hand. I began to squirm, from the pleasure and strain both, not wanting him to stop but also needing to see his eyes, meet his gaze, kiss those sumptuous lips.

His mouth met my nape then, nibbling slightly as his open palm pored over me. He kissed me lightly as his hand climbed to my breasts, shivery handfuls just waiting for him, my chocolate pearls standing tall, looking for attention. Between my legs I felt the wetness seeping, my hidden lips billowing, my secret spot swelling.

As he leaned over me, I swooned from his intoxicating smell. It was pungent and sharp—like fresh soil cut with fertilizer. His face was above mine now, and I lifted my lips to his.

Damn, that lavish mouth!

The moist, sexy pillows of our lips had finally found each other. My hands rose to encircle him in my arms as his tongue parted my lips gently and met mine. He dipped it in slowly, my lips closing over it. I pulled him into my mouth and began to suck, simply, unhurriedly.

He nestled in deeper as our tongues danced together, circling, slippery. I let him take mine into his mouth, felt those heavenly lips close around it, begin to suck.

Soon a sound rose from us, like a solid humming, but with a long "mmmm" attached to it. We might as well have been musical forks, for we kissed at a pitch that seemed orchestrated, it was so perfect. We turned onto our sides, facing each other fully, our knees touching front to front now.

How could it feel as ideal as this, though we had never before been together? How did he know to circle his tongue around mine just so, creating an indescribable clamoring inside me? One hypnotic revolution, then another—my budding clit leaping.

Our breath turned fast, hot. Our voices hummed, hands caressed. I kept mine on the slope of his chest, tantalizing his nipples with my fingertips. He sucked in a mouthful of air the first time I touched them, letting me know how sensitive, how desirous they were. I rolled them between my fingers, teased the supple nubs to hardness, squeezed them until he groaned.

He kissed me deeper then, one hand pulling me closer still, the other lingering at my cleavage, my breastesses waiting for more. He reached for one, gently held its weight, then released it as he reached for the other. Each time he held one, he stabbed my tongue with his, then started to squeeze each of my fine mounds. I mirrored his ministering, squeezing his breasts, his nipples, with every caress.

I kissed him back, letting him explore the inside of my lips, the ridges of my teeth, the lapping wonder of our tongues. I pushed my knees against his, kept our private parts from touching on purpose, wanting to watch his nature harden, rise into its glory. Wanting to savor the wet fire flaming through the center of myself.

"Couldn't wait to hit it wit' you, baby," he crooned. "Been temptin' me from the instant I set my sorry eyes on you."

"Yeah, brotha," I whispered. "You so yoked, I knew I had to tear it up wit' you before the end of this day."

We giggled, innocent, revealing. We inched closer, our mouths ever against each other's, our words moaning out, senses way stimulated. As we kissed harder and faster, I kept a steady attention on his nipples—and he did the same for me. We both began to squirm, our knees no longer keeping us separate. Our limbs lengthened and our torsos slowly met as we pressed together.

The hum of our *mmmm* intensified as we found each other, melded into each other. Our hands still played our nipples, our mouths still featured our tongues. With each breath, I drew him closer to me, inside of me. I lifted the leg on top over his hip, the sudden gaping aspect of that shift making us both gasp. One of his hands finally left my breasts and grabbed the hip that rode the air.

Would I allow him to enter me just like that, simply because he was perfectly poised to?

Maybe if this Columbus, Ohio, chick had not had to wait this long for her dreams to come true . . . I leapt up, straddling him, my knees pressing into the floor on either side, looking for some control.

How could I control Freedom?

Freedom!

His touch was everywhere now, trailing over my shoulders, my back, my belly . . . my being. I kissed him hard, stilling his hands. I ground my baby against his hard thang, letting him know I was right there. *I feel you,* the words ready to soar out of me, my everything for him inescapably there.

Pretending I didn't want his soul.

How did I know he was even really there, much less believe that it was me he wanted? I could feel my precious face twist with pain, my heart start to ache with the thought. Had I lost too much with Daddy leaving us the way he did to believe that someone could be there a different way? That someone could love me and want to stay?

Yeah, I was lost in my own rap now.

Freedom, let me love you this way, this mesmerized way from the moment I met you. I looked into your eyes and wanted only to live in their gaze, launch a thousand feelings, lap you up with my own sight. Believe me, it's what I've longed for, what I truly need, what my spirit seeks completely.

How can any of us be whole without the love of another to soften our edges, argue us to reason, enrapture us with another way of being, seduce us with a separate self? If I tell you my secrets, will you tell me yours? If I reveal my vulnerability, will you embrace it? I want so much to linger in your arms, find ways to love you that nobody ever has, make you cry from the enthralling connection, the jarring thrill of climax, the momentary marriage of our bodies.

Don't answer my questions with words, please. Words so often get in the way of meaning. That's why dancing is the answer.

Come, will you? Dance with me. . . .

Freedom responded by grabbing my hips and pulling me even closer. Still straddling him, I spread my legs farther apart so I could swoon harder against him, my tingling mounds pressed against his chest, my tongue playing his. I rose to my knees again, let his hands catch my breastesses as I pulled away from his mouth long enough to suck his earlobe, lick the side of his jaw, feel his breath like a small wind on my face.

He started to say something, but I covered his mouth with a

curl of my palm. I leaned back and lifted the other hand to part the lips of my tempting possum, wanting him to see the dark wet gleam of my deep juices for him. I dipped a finger into my special sauce and slid it up alongside the sleek folds of my baby, finally finding the blossoming nub with a slow, slippery *mmmmmmmm*.

Freedom's lips lay open, his panting like a song. I wanted him to show me what an animal he was, prove what a brute of discipline and creature of wildness he was, too. He answered by shifting his hips, his boy finding my slit with no hesitation. With a lift of his pelvis, he grabbed my booty with both hands as he slammed his passion inside me.

Oh, it is beyond immense when dreams do come true! I had been waiting for this moment—for so long. And with him particularly, once my eyes set on him, every breathing nanosecond of this day.

"Baby, gimme that grill," he growled.

"Straight up, lover," I whispered, leaning down once more to find his luscious lips with my own, my tits mashed against his solid shelf of muscle. I arched up slightly, dipping this way then that, dragging my nipples across his.

"Sprinkle me, girl," he whispered.

His style was his own. He made me sit still on his baby, then ground against me just like he had on the dance floor, when he had been a world away from being inside me! He gripped my booty and lunged deeper. I lowered myself just enough to tongue his mouth, took him deeper into my feeling.

I slid a finger from his lips to his nipples, played them before I dipped the fingertip back into his mouth and then hightailed that hot, dripping digit back to my enormous nub. I spanked it, waiting for Freedom's attention to take that in, how I punished myself, waiting for his desire to dig deeper inside me.

He pulled out to his tip, watching me slap my pootay at least half a dozen times before he slid himself back in. This time he moved slowly, watching my eyes, fingering my nipples, pulling them slightly downward so that I had to bend toward him as he thrust into me.

Damn, he dug into me like we were sugar footing on the dance floor. I started thinking of stepping into a heel fan and then turning out one hip when he met me there—open, gaping, waiting.

But we were horizontal, not vertical. No reason that need stop us from dancing though, especially because his touch was like a blanket of water, inviting me to immerse myself in it with each stroke. I sank against him, my nipples shimmying to and fro across his. Our mouths kept hovering, tongues meeting at the tips, lips sliding across the other's, breath ragged.

I stiffened my whole body, especially the inside of my baby, and held him there. I pulsed, squeezed, released, commanded. I poised my being for each response—would it be frustration? Or demand? Satisfaction? Submission?

I wanted all of these—and more that I had no names for.

I gripped him, held him far inside. He arched, all of him insisting. I tried to meet him, curling forward to offer more depth. A long breath slid out of him as my mouth met his once more, always again, wanting that fresh surprise. My fingertips squeezed his nipples before burrowing down his side to the sleekness of his hips, spreading them wide to take a handful of ass cheek into my hands.

What a superb event. There is nothing in the world like a black man's booty. Especially a black man who danced with it every day, expecting it to be the primary companion to his frontal vine.

When dancing, a vine is a continuous step pattern with feet crossing behind or in front. Freedom seemed to move this way below my touch. Can you feel me? Do you understand?

Can you feel us?

We're dancing now. Daddy's big black shiny shoes what I'm stand-ing on as we bound about. Momma is at the piano, banging out a tune that makes my daddy sway. He holds my little wrists in the air above me, barely reaching his hips. I am that small. As we spring from side to side, I see my parents meet each other's eyes and watch them with my unbound curiosity, hunger, longing to be part of what love is.

What is love? Something that washes in like a giant wave, and just as unexpectedly, ebbs away? Because it seems so fleeting, does that mean there is ever more than those moments—a flicker of wings, the closing of an eyelid, meeting the endless gaze of your lover's eyes?

That would mean there's no great love, only tenderness.

But what of rapture and of ecstasy? Isn't love essential to those ex-periences?

And maybe even more beguiling: What is <u>falling</u> in love all about?

Freedom thrust inside me as I held his booty tightly, pulling him in even deeper as he held onto mine. Each time he pumped, I clenched the hidden walls of my snatch, holding him there as long as I could, slowly releasing as he pulled out.

I leaned ever closer, and we rocked against each other then, rapping to each other without the need of words as soft sounds arose from our lungs. When he withdrew one last time, I teetered on his tip's dark bark before I twisted slightly to the left and slipped away completely.

His frustrated groan accompanied me, but that was because he didn't know where I was going next.

Can you guess? *Come on now, use a little imagination. You gotta stop thinkin' so uptight.* Was I moving into a loop turn—twirling underarm to the left as he twirled to the right? Didn't think so. Would I pivot—a turn done with thighs locked and feet apart in ex-tended fifth position (heel to toe, often used in a rock step)? Hardly.

Yet how could I do either with both of us horizontal like that? Neither was in my vision, but vaulting up was, before slamming into a one-eighty turn. Crouching to my knees was not out of the question as I set myself to work on this deep brown miracle beneath my touch. I needed him to fuck me with both hands, my baby in his full gaze, but his mouth, his tongue, beyond that reach. I wanted him inside me puss *and* booty, feel him everywhere at once, while I took the purplish hues of his shadowy pole between my fingers and pulled it firm, circled it with my touch, adored it with my gaze.

Freedom found me. Two fingers trailed up my sleek beast, teasing me with yet another presence at the entrance to my desiring back alley. I dipped down, lowered myself still more to his touch. I felt the sudden absence of any pressure whatever at my phat cavern, but then I heard the luscious sound of his finger slipping into his own mouth, juicing it up before he returned to that precious place, now poised for more.

He slid the solid wetness in, waiting for the tight walls to absorb him, accept him. A beat went by when neither of us moved, then another, one moment more.

"I gotcha, girl. Give it to me," he whispered.

Damn, I did. My booty proud in the air, I opened my knees wider, spreading my cheeks farther apart, and shook it hard!

The thumb of his other hand, two fingers already plying the need inside my baby, found my teeming ache.

My clit. My swell. My bliss. My stairway.

The music of my *mmmmmmmm* met the slit at the tip of his thang. I wrapped my lips around the head, still moaning so that his sensitive flesh would soak up the sound's vibration. Freedom bucked from the sensation, and his moan rose, mingling with mine. We moved this way for a while, so slight, almost swaying.

He poked me here and there while I allowed his boy to just barely poke past my lips. Our moans deepened, as did his fingers inside me. My booty thrummed as his finger fucked it, the pair from his other hand rubbing against my pootay wall with purpose. His fingers like amative vines climbing inside, I had no choice but to feel all three straining to meet, that length of slippery, delicately tortured tissue all that separated them from finding each other.

And then his thumb, resting there until now, started to spank my clit.

I sucked in his dark rod all the way at that moment, opening my throat to make room for him, desperate not to come right away. My head bobbed as I slathered him with my wet lips, savoring his salty cum, my fingers playing his tender balls like a musical instrument.

Both of us shimmied as we moaned, our limbs all shivery, starting to tremble as the moment deepened. I clung to him as he started to buck, as the pistons of his fingers slammed my sweetest spots, his thumb on my clit bringing heaven to earth.

Was I dreaming? Pillowy clouds filled my veins, the sky soared through my belly, the horizon embraced each nerve ending that trailed the most miniscule parts of me, every molecule I was made of. Nature itself seemed to roar from our throats as Freedom bucked wildly one last time, his manhood seeping hot into my waiting mouth as his climax tore through. My clit somersaulted then, releasing one shudder before another surged ever deeper inside.

Our cries catapulted into the air. When they eventually subsided, I fell against him, then tumbled gently to my side. He rolled just far enough away to swivel around before finding my mouth with his.

We lay in the other's arms, slowly sucking tongues, waiting for our hearts to wade beyond desire, toward love.

When I woke up, I reached down between my legs. The crotch of my last pair of clean panties was now entirely soaked.

Red Shoes, are you telling me that I merely *dreamed* this stunning experience with Freedom? That in my waking life, I still had not even kissed him, much less loved him the way my unconscious had just had me beyond belief imagining?

Damn, I am nothing if not a dreamer.

How much can I hope? Wanting makes me so weary sometimes, and yet I can't help but feel it fly deep. It's awful strange to be in a city like this, bursting with big dreams, and far away from my momma, too. But Columbus was so meager a place. What surrounded that little metropolis could not even approach how lush these valleys and phenomenal hills are, the entire Pacific Ocean rolling out into infinity at the edge of the land.

In Columbus, there was a stretch of space here and there in the city, but such barren, unplanted land, never dreamed on. Yeah, I know, L.A. is no natural wonder in the real sense, either. Yet I knew the instant I arrived here that it was planted with dreams.

Was my daddy full of dreams? Was that why he left?

All it took was a look deep into Daddy's eyes to see the weight he carried in them. After he left, Momma's eyes went in the opposite direction. When she would look past me, I could see how her loneliness emptied her gaze so. I know it was loneliness, because I watched it grow in my own eyes, too.

But then my dreams began.

Once I arrived in L.A. and discovered the two types of Hollywood dreamers, I started to wonder: Where did my daddy go to find his dreams? Which ones did he let go of by letting go of us? And, how much did his absence lead to the presence of my own dreams, so insistent?

It's too blurry to know. Daddy would sometimes sit at the piano, tapping out one note over and over. It drove Momma crazy, that I remember clearly. But me, I would sit with my back against the piano and let the sound enter me through the vibrating wood. I waited for the sound to touch me each time it came out. Such a deep sound—low and sorry, yet so captivating, alluring—the one note he would tap out with his left hand.

So plaintive. Wanting. Pleading. Needing.

Maybe it's enough to remember just that, how Daddy must've felt that low, deep note inside. That's what made him leave, I know it. Maybe I knew that then, too, because when the sound leaked out of the piano, I'd soak it up into myself.

It was a piece of Daddy.

Once he was gone, I'd close my eyes and feel the sound inside me, over and over. It was poignant, enveloping. When it started to move around in there, that was when I started to dance.

It hurt to remember this, but that was better than forgetting. It hurt, but I was willing. To learn to dance, to become a dancer, your body has to hurt so much, and you have to dance through it. How else can you push yourself beyond your limits to a new place?

Momma said if you want to get anywhere in life, you have to be willing to deal with the pain that comes with it: failure, rejection, mistakes. They're all part of dreams, part of what it is to be alive. If there's pleasure, you can be certain that at some point there will be pain. It's just in the nature of things.

The reason we had the piano at all was because Momma's a piano teacher. Her own career had only taken her that far. In other words, as Momma would say, she was not very gifted. She said that there were very few really gifted students, but some of the "ungifted" worked so *hard, they got almost as good as, sometimes as good, as some of the gifted. She explained that it was because they had one thing in common: They were willing.*

"Whatever you want, sweetheart," Daddy said to me once, "go out and get it. Ain't nobody gonna give it to you." His gravelly voice still rumbles inside of me when I think of it.

And you know what, Red Shoes? I do want and I'm willing, too. I have got to remember this even though I'm so scared, truly terrified of that shoot tomorrow. Will I fail? Will I soar? What will become of me?

I admit: part of it's about Freedom. How do I know he's even there? How close can I ever really get to him?

What a question: How close can I ever really get to Freedom?

I could not get that question out of my mind.

When all else fails, washing dirty laundry is great therapy. That was my thought as I entered the Laundromat on Fountain, near La Brea in West Hollywood, a few blocks from my apartment. I had changed into a soft blue blouse with little white leaves scattered all over it and my jeans. When I glanced in, the place looked pretty empty. But when I got inside, I could hear someone on the pay phone.

I found an empty washer and started sorting the colored clothes from the whites. I could hear the voice of whoever it was talking on the phone: "Joe, man. Let me call you back. . . ."

It was such a familiar voice—it sounded so much like Freedom! I shook my head to clear it. *Get a grip, Emily,* I told myself. *You're awake now and what you got is a case of Freedom on the brain.* But then, that voice again: "In five minutes, Joe. Trust me. I'll call you back in five minutes. . . ."

I turned around just as he hung up the phone.

Freedom! It really *was* him.

"What are you doing here?" I blurted. I could feel a big sloppy smile slap across my face.

He sidled over like he'd been expecting me, a black button-down shirt hanging completely open, exposing a nest of muscles across my torso and chest. His chest was like a sculpture carved from mahogany.

Damn! I had to force myself to look away. He was even *more* amazing than in my dream.

"I'm outta clean underwear," he said with an easy smile. "Just like you."

I laughed, both nerves and pleasure strutting through me. My dream flashed behind my eyes—and between my legs, too. My panties were still moist. I felt my baby go tight, its juices trickling.

"I . . . I guess I never imagined someone like you doing his own underwear," I finally managed, telling myself there was no way he knew how I felt about him.

"Well, you guessed wrong, sweetheart. Somebody's gotta do it. I mean, I'm not that famous yet, and even if I was, I wouldn't be handing out my underwear to someone to clean."

We both laughed.

"Yeah." I said. "Look, thanks for being so understanding today."

"No problem. Don't mention it. You're gonna be great. You just gotta . . ." He hesitated.

"I gotta what?"

"You gotta release. . . . You gotta rise to the occasion,"

You gotta stop thinkin' so uptight. Release it. Let it go. . . . There were those words again—Freedom's words.

Like I let it go in my dream, you mean?

"Yeah, I know," I blurted aloud. "I mean, I don't understand it. Nothing like this has ever happened before," I lied. "It's like I felt all this emotion, I felt all the energy, you know. And then, *boom,* something happened and I just, I mean, you saw it . . ."

I tried to act like the way he looked at me didn't cut right through me. I pretended that my heart wasn't thumping against my ribcage though I could barely remain standing.

Freedom just smiled. "Yeah, that's probably 'cause you've never been pushed before."

"Hey, I've been pushed!" I argued, though my own smile pressed through. "I'm used to being pushed."

"I don't know, sistah." He shook his head. "Not the way it looked today. Not under this much pressure. I don't think so."

"Ah, you are one pompous son of a bitch, ain't you, brotha!" I blurted out.

Laughter burst out of him. "Ah . . . you should try what I suggested. Go ahead. Push. Push me."

He tapped his naked chest with his fingers. "C'mon, I'm tellin' you. You'd be surprised at the things you find when everythin' just comes out. Pow! Push!"

He reached out as he had earlier at the studio and gently pushed me. It was so *not* what I wanted from him right now. I longed for his arms to wrap around me and for him to pull me close, like in my dream. Let me lose my fear thanks to tenderness, not violence. I didn't get it. I was so confused, staring into his eyes, unable to move.

"Freedom," I eventually said, "I'm not gonna push you."

"C'mon, push," he pressed. "Push!"

He pushed me again.

"That's ridiculous," I hissed, my voice turning shrill. "I'm not gonna push you!"

He put up his hands in mock surrender. "All right, I under-stand. You'll be doin' this for the next ten years. So what you gotta do is rise above your inhibitions *now*. Come from *out* of order."

"Fuck you!" I exploded.

"Ohh! Seriously, look around. There's no one here but the sound of you and me. Oh, baby, just listen to the groove."

He started rapping and stepping with the words: "You know how to do your thing. You know how to make your moves. . . ." He began to dance, slowly moving toward me as I backed away.

"Let me move you up and down, turn you left and right. . . ." He heaved himself into the air, his beautiful butt landing on top of a washing machine. Just as quickly, he bounded back down.

"Let yourself go to the beat and the sound. Get down with me tonight."

He jumped right in front of me and pushed me again.

"So, c'mon," he whispered, "push, push, push. You can do it, c'mon. You can do it, do it, do it."

He reached for my hand. I let him press it against his shoul-der. Was this the only way I would ever get to touch him? I battled back the hot tears bubbling up behind my eyes—from frustration, fear, how much I wanted him.

"C'mon," he went on, "I wouldn't push you if I didn't believe you can do it. C'mon, release it. Let me have it. If I didn't want you to I wouldn't ask you to. We wouldn't be here. . . ."

What were we doing here? How did we both end up in the same Laundromat in all of Hollywood anyway? He wanted me to push him? What was that going to do? I wanted him to get close to me—I did not want to push him away!

"C'mon," he pressed, "I won't stop until you commit. You've got to get this part in the video, so come on, push me."

He was right. I had to get that part. I was losing it, couldn't stop the tears. There they were, seeping out like hot disappointments—my disappointment in myself. Enough of my limitations! Enough of my fear! I was the one holding myself back.

"You want me to push you, I'll push you!" I shouted. I pushed against his chest with both hands, as hard as I could. Once, twice . . . without even realizing it I shoved him against the wall, and I could not stop crying. My fists pounded against his chest, broken sounds busting out of my throat.

"That's it," he whispered. "That's it . . ."

He wrapped me in his arms and caressed me slowly, talking to me the whole time.

"There you go, baby, I knew you could do it. That's what you gotta do. You gotta commit. All that anger and tension you got bottled up inside you, it's gotta come out. You gotta reach. You gotta dig deep. You can be whatever you wanna be, but you gotta believe. You know how beautiful you look tonight, gettin' mad? Lettin' it out?"

"Beautiful?"

"Bee-yoo-tee-full," he dragged out.

I laughed, in spite of my tears. With his arms around me, I finally felt safe enough to let it out. I held on to him tight as I could and inhaled his scent. He smelled just as intoxicating as he had in my dream! Such a pungent mix of manhood and his own earthiness. I breathed him in, not wanting to let go, wanting only to rest my weariness on his strong self.

Maybe some of it could rub off on me.

He lifted my face all tender, brushed the tears from my cheeks with his fingertips. I looked into his eyes and drank in his gaze, so thirsty for it I could have stayed there all night, just like that.

To look at him. To bring him closer. To believe he existed.

Freedom gazed back at me, his hands climbing up and down my sides, his mouth slowly approaching mine. The heat of his flesh near mine made me tremble, but I tried not to show too much. Tried not to let that one note fill me so entirely that I lost myself completely.

Could I kiss him? Should I? Did I even think these thoughts or did I imagine this reality? Was this reality? I was losing it, had lost it, was not in control of myself. All day long, I had experienced *Freedom*.

Earlier, my eyes found him for the first time ever, and I do mean that. Then he watched me so. He chose me to dance with him. We danced. He touched me all over. And after all that, he talked to me. About my wound, my paralysis, my curse.

Damn, how I had wanted to open up to him immediately, when he had actually said, "I was just like you when I started out."

But what is it about someone that makes you really believe them? I wanted to, I mean, I think I did. But could I truly believe myself believing him?

It was hard for me to give myself away like that, to open up to someone I did not know at all and believe my feelings were telling the truth. Why should I believe this stunning black man? Why should I believe that he thought I was something at all, even beautiful?

The way he spoke to me made it seem as if his heart was really open. Was it?

Which begs the question: What about my own?

You tell me, Red Shoes. Is your heart open? Can you even pretend that it is? What I sensed from your ad in the paper was that you were as searching, as desperate, as me. Trying to understand, man. What goes on between two people, what goes on just inside yourself, how much you want, and how little you know what to do with that wanting. Especially when you're alone, seemingly bereft. Searching.

And. You. Are. So. Alone.

I can feel it from here. It's damn clear you got special hurt by someone, but I don't possess the details. All I know is, you put your ad in, you ask for deep, personal details from whoever might be reading it. Yet you make no mention of when I might hear back from *you*. You ask me to tell who I am, expose my struggle to you, but just who the fuck are you?

Not my style. I like a little back and forth in a relationship, an attempt at understanding. When will *you* come forward? When will *you* spill yourself in my direction?

There I was in Freedom's arms, reeling from the sensation. His hands were everywhere around my waist, the dip of my lower back, the tiny shelf above my booty. They teased, pleaded, wanted.

Would he kiss me now? How much did I want him to?

"Whatever you need, baby," he whispered into my ear.

I made myself pull away. "I need to rehearse."

"You got it, sistah," he responded with a smile. "Let's go get yo' swirl on."

"No," I said, leaving his embrace completely. "I need to do it alone."

Freedom understood. At least he said he did. And you know what? I believed him, considered that look true in his eyes when he wished me good night with a chaste kiss on the cheek.

I left my laundry and walked around the mostly empty streets for a while wondering if I had just made a big phat mistake by leaving him. It didn't matter if I did—I had to rehearse! Still, I doubted myself all the way back to the studio. A.C. had handed me the key earlier, told me to lock up later when I was through for the day.

But he hadn't said anything about the night.

After I unlocked the studio door and stepped inside, I saw that I must have left a light on in a far corner. As I walked in that direction, I heard a sound somewhere in the studio, muffled as it was. Instinctively, I stopped.

The stage.

As my eyes adjusted to the shadows, my gaze focused on a pair of people. Both were standing on the dance floor, but one was doubled forward, the other ramrod straight behind. The groaning sound I had heard—and still heard now—came from the one who was bent over. Who, I instantly realized, was getting it good from the standing one.

And. He. Was. A. Man.

I was mesmerized, watching the guy behind plunge into his lover with determined, relentless strokes. The guy in front could barely remain standing from the rapid pumping. I watched him spread his legs a bit wider so that his hands could reach the floor and help him find his balance.

"That's it, bitch," growled his lover. "Gimme all of you, now!"

What? Was that a male voice? It was so high-pitched. Yet the other's, decidedly deep, was unquestionably male. I froze, both from the surprise of coming upon a pair of lovers in this private, amatory act, but also because my sense was that whatever was happening here was something that I did not understand.

"Tell me you want it, cunt," the lover commanded. "Tell me you want me to fuck you harder. Beg me."

Cunt?

"Please, please," panted the one bent over, "fuck me harder. Please!"

How can I describe how amazing it was to be privy to someone else's deepest intimacy, to hear how much a man wanted to be fucked by—whoever that was.

Even from my dim view in the shadows, I could see that the lover was deep inside, grinding against him, reaching around his hips to grab his cock.

"You hard, bitch? You better be. . . . Ah, there you are. Tell me you want it now!"

That voice was just too high-pitched—and how the lover was ordering him that way. Strange, but again I thought I recognized the voice, just as I thought I had heard Freedom's in the Laundromat. Who was this? What was going on?

"Now," the man panted, "fuck me!"

Without a word, the lover worked the man's cock with one hand, using the other to grab a handful of hair on his head and pull it toward him as the ride intensified.

The man's head now forcibly tilted back, his legs spread, I saw his shaky arms struggling to hold himself up. I witnessed the moment his climax consumed him, not only because it made him tremble from head to toe, but because it rendered him otherwise completely still. His breath came haltingly then, sounds ripping from him like bedding suddenly tearing.

"That's it, bitch. Give it up," growled the lover.

A pungent, bleachy scent cut through the air as he came. Damn, the olfactory proof of testosterone! I inhaled it reflexively, a significant sniff.

Whoever it was pulled out from the man slowly. In what seemed like an unusual moment of tenderness, the lover draped across him as they slowly crouched down to the floor.

And. Then. The. Lover. Whirled. Around.

"Who's there?" the voice called.

Apparently my inhalation had been loud enough to demand attention.

I froze, holding my next breath.

"Who is it? Speak up!" the lover ordered.

I knew that voice, I was certain. Before I could associate the name of the person to connect it to, whoever it was strode across the stage and flipped on a light switch.

So it was me who would be identified first.

The sudden light above the stage had us all blinking fiercely. When I was able to focus, my gaze had fallen on the man who had just been fucked. He was now clearly naked, reclining on the floor.

It was A.C.

A.C.?

So the choreographer was AC/DC?

And who . . . ? I wondered, as my eyes swept up and stumbled on the unexpected sight of Tampa, the casting director.

Tampa?

She stared intently at me, and I at her. Neither my gaze nor my being could have left this vision if life had insisted otherwise, I believe. I was completely entranced by her. Bound in a skintight black blouse, a pair of black leather chaps barely covered her otherwise naked legs. But it was the enormous black dildo that dangled from its smoky midnight-hued harness strapped around her hips that held me so transfixed.

Tampa smiled a slow, tight one. "Well," she said, "look what the night dragged in. A.C., I didn't know we were expecting company."

A.C.'s expression showed only wonder. "Me neither, but life is full of nice surprises sometimes. Hi, Emily," he called to me, making no attempt to cover his nakedness.

"Uh, hey," halted out of me.

"To what do we owe this pleasure?" Tampa called.

This I had no answer for, especially because as she asked the question, she strode off the stage into the diffuse studio light where I stood. The closer she stepped, the bigger that black dildo became, the more I could not move.

With each footfall, the dildo bobbed. Damn, aside from its cloudy dreamlike color, it looked real—and enormous. It was at least the length of two fists, one atop the other encircling it. Those hands would have to be oversized themselves to be able to wrap around the cock's thick diameter.

I was gripped by a stony paralysis as she neared me, my mind a blur of images. Why was I thinking about how huge the dildo was, how it would take such large hands to hold it? Did *I* want to hold it? The idea that A.C. could take in something so massive amazed me. Was he gay? But he was hitting it with a *woman*. Yet, the woman had a *boy* to fuck with, even if it wasn't real. And what about hitting on me earlier?

My thoughts skittered about, trying to make sense. I glanced in A.C.'s direction then—a flash of red filling my eyes.

Then Tampa stood directly in front of me, daring me with her unswerving stare. But daring me to what? Did she want me to touch her *thang*? I was captivated as I watched her slowly unroll the condom surrounding its girth. She watched me as she teased the moist translucence from her boy's tip and let it fall to the floor.

Then she grabbed her dream with both hands, shimmied her hips so that it swayed.

I was speechless. What was she doing? What did she want?

And me? I swallowed hard, a sudden leap of my clit allowing the dream to be real.

"Do you want to suck me?" Tampa asked.

My flesh had turned to stone. I was unable to move or speak. I willed my mouth to open—but to say what? I had no words.

"Come on, girl," Tampa whispered. "I can see from the look on your face that you're dying to suck me."

My nerves flushed through the deepest parts of me as she said those words, but I still couldn't move.

You gotta stop thinkin' so uptight. Release it. Let it go. . . . Freedom's words, one more time, echoing through my mind.

I saw the flash of red—what was that?—I had seen a minute earlier, and then I realized: It was A.C., a red robe draped over his shoulders. He sidled up behind me, slid his arms around me.

"What do you want, Emily? Tell us what we can do for you," he whispered.

I broke out of his embrace immediately. "No!" I said.

Tampa started laughing.

Was she laughing at me? I felt another flush run through me. What was that? It's true—I had been intimidated by her chill, her authority, the instant I saw her this morning. But this was different. She was challenging me in a way I did not understand.

You gotta stop thinkin' so uptight. . . .

"What's so funny?" I spat out.

Her eyes met mine straight on, blazing.

"Nothing's funny," she answered. "I'm just enjoying your attitude."

"And what *attitude* is that?" I demanded.

She smiled full out. "The one that wants to watch but doesn't want to participate. The one that wants to dance, but then flees from the dance floor." She stepped closer, a touch away from my face. "What's stopping you, Emily?"

My face burned from her nearness, her questions. She was so close I could feel her breath on my cheeks.

What seemed only an instant ago, I had felt Freedom's breath there. Was that for real or in my dream? What was happening? I was so confused.

"I'm thinkin' maybe Freedom had it backward before," she went on. "Like maybe what you really need is to be pushed rather than be the one who does the pushing. What do you think of that?" she pressed.

With those words, she reached out and pushed me against my collarbone. Just where Freedom had made me push him. Of course I ended up pounding his chest, backing him up against the wall in the Laundromat—and what was all that? Tampa, of course, knew nothing about what had happened.

As she challenged me with her gaze, I realized what I needed: *all* of it. To push *and* to be pushed. But how? Tears burst out of me.

"Ah, I see I hit a soft spot," she said quietly. "You want more?"

In spite of my chaos, my unknowing, I nodded. What did that mean? What was I after?

"A.C.," she directed, "her hands . . ."

What?

From behind me, A.C. immediately reached for my wrists. He pulled back my hands gently until they touched each other atop the pillow of my booty.

Baby's got back.

I twisted as Tampa stepped closer, willing my tears to stop. She wiped them gently from my cheeks. With her face so close to mine, I could forget for a moment that she boasted that big boy between her legs. But then she inched even closer, and as her lips approached mine, so did her toy—pressing against my hidden lips.

I could not keep still, squirming from both of these unfamiliar sensations.

"Okay?" she whispered to my mouth.

Incredibly, I uttered, "Yes."

And so she kissed me. Her mouth landed on mine like the patter of warm, soft rain on my naked flesh, and as A.C. held my arms behind me, the rest of me lunged forward without a thought. My lips parted and I let her in, seeking her tongue with my own, wanting this dance that I had not even known was inside me.

It was Tampa who finally pulled away. "Damn, girl, you're hot. I knew that this morning. Besides that, there's the fact that you need to give it up, that you *really* need to give it up. And I mean now . . . before the scene tomorrow. Can you trust me at all?"

"Yes," slid from my mouth, no hesitation.

"Good," she said, breathing heavily into my mouth. "I want you to pick a word right now, so when you really don't want it, we stop. Pick any word . . . just don't pick *no,* 'cause you might be saying that a hundred times before you get what you need. Understand me?"

You feel me?

I thought I did, even though I didn't really know what she was saying. She was kissing me again, her lips like soft breaths, her mouth never completely leaving mine as she spoke.

The word "baton" fell from my lips. What did that mean, and what did *when you don't want it* mean, too?

When I didn't want *what*?

I wanted always to be willing to welcome whatever the *what* might be.

But I'm telling you now, Tampa scared me.

Maybe as much as she thrilled me, too. The *what* of Tampa was everything she might actually do, in relation to what she might just say. It felt like she was really willing to go—to leap off a cliff.

Was I?

But more than that, she'd know what to do with that leap—at least inside herself—once she did.

What about me?

And where was A.C. in all of this?

To say nothing of Freedom.

Let it go. His words, so inside me now. *You gotta stop thinkin' so uptight.*

Can you feel me?

What I understood was A.C. gripping each of my wrists, restraining me. It steeped into my senses that Tampa relied on this aspect, demanded my willingness to submit. After she started kissing me, her boy pressed insistently between my baby's lips, she wrapped herself around me. I mean she deepened the moment by touching me with her hands, too. At my waist, my sides, all the time that she prodded my mouth and my baby.

And I let her . . . let him.

Her palms climbed, pressed against my breasts, her fingertips exploring their sensitivity. She circled my aureoles slowly, lingered at my nipples way beyond their shivering from it. This was new territory for me, a woman's touch. Where on earth were we going tonight? I didn't know, but I was willing. Maybe even ready. Which meant I had left Columbus, Ohio, I thought, for good.

Tampa slowly unbuttoned my blouse as A.C. pressed himself against me from behind, hard already. He let go of my hands long enough to remove my blouse as Tampa took control.

"Keep your hands at your sides," she directed.

I did.

"Good girl," she said. "Emily, I want you to take off your bra now."

After I unfastened it, I found myself instinctively trying to keep my breastesses covered as long as I could.

Tampa smiled, reaching for the scant swatch of fabric. She pulled it away with a single yank. There I was, my brown handfuls shivering and exposed.

"Beautiful," she whispered. Her hands rose to circle my sensitive saucers, me trembling from the splendor of her touch. She went round and round with her fingers, crushing my nipples into the cup of her palms. I reached up and grabbed her by the wrists, pulling her harder to me.

"Drop your hands, Emily," she said. "A.C. . . . ."

With a groan, I did. I felt something being wound around my wrists and tried to glance back over my shoulder.

"Look at me," Tampa said, turning my face with the tips of two fingers beneath my chin. "He's tying your hands with the belt of the robe. It won't hurt, okay?"

As I nodded, she kissed me, then pulled away with a laugh.

"Unless you want it to," she went on.

"Do you want it to?" I said breathily.

She kissed me again, hard this time, her tongue meeting mine like a tiny whip. Her fingertips suddenly mashed my nipples, a moan slipping out of me.

"Good question," she finally answered. "A.C., she's a fresh one." To me, she said, "I'll ask the questions. Now, I asked you this before. . . . Do you want to suck me?"

My mouth opened to answer, but no sound came out. I could nod.

"That's good, Emily. Start with my tongue."

When she kissed me again I surrounded her tongue with my lips and sucked slowly, intensifying the pressure as her breath quickened.

A.C. responded by grinding against me from behind. I felt Tampa reach around me, pulling him closer. His hands grabbed my hips, his hard boy pressing into me.

"Off!" she directed.

I didn't know what that meant, but A.C. did. His hands soon found and unbuttoned, unzipped my jeans. In an instant, he'd tugged them to my ankles.

"Panties," she ordered.

With a finger on either hip, he slid them down.

I was naked. Trapped, too, by the confines of my clothes at my ankles. Her intention, of course.

"How do you want it, baby?" A.C. whispered from behind. "You want to bend over for me right now, or do you want Tampa?"

Bend over, just like that? Or Tampa's big black boy, slamming into me?

He slid between my cheeks and tap, tap, tapped my back alley. One hand softly kneaded the newly naked flesh of my booty, while his other rose to my breasts and played them between his fingertips. He twisted and pulled my chocolate nubs until they stung. I leaned back against him, nowhere else to go.

Tampa dipped her head then, started to suck the nipple of each mound as he held it out to her.

I was dizzy, ready to lose my balance as Tampa reached down and parted the lips of my baby with an expert hand. One finger on each side spread them, a third dipping into my dark, juicy pond.

"There you are," she whispered. "She needs some of this first."

She scalded my stinging pearls with her tongue, my baby already overflowing as she poked at me slowly. A.C. tapped at me, stroking my ass until I tingled to my core. It was hard to stay standing.

My hands were still tied behind my back, my jeans and panties crumpled in a heap around my ankles, so I couldn't even spread my legs. Sandwiched between these two this way, I was really at their mercy. A.C. slid the hand in front from my breasts to my ribcage, holding me up with his forearm. The hand in back suddenly slapped across one cheek with a crisp sting, and I flinched.

"That's right," Tampa breathed. "Spank her good and slow."

With one last flourish of her tongue, she stabbed my nipples and then stood straight again. She held the back of my head with one hand as she watched me take each slap from A.C. I'd flinch, a little yelp I could not contain escaping me.

Macho as she was, she spread her legs, claiming her ground. But she was such a contradiction, too, cooing as she finger-fucked me. After each slap from A.C., she'd poke me deeper, then pull out and slide that syrupy glory all over my blooming clit. I was hypnotized by her sacred touch.

Whimpering now, I could barely stand. A.C. switched cheeks then, starting his slapping pattern all over again. Tampa slipped two fingers inside me, pumping me faster as I struggled to escape the stinging. The more I squirmed, the heavier his hand. When he spanked me across my crack, Tampa pulled out of my baby and started to thrum my clit relentlessly.

It was too much. I tried to yank my hands apart as I scrambled to flee, forgetting about my twisted heap of clothes below. I stumbled as I tried to get away, caught by their embrace. They saved me from tumbling to the floor, and as I struggled to resist, the more insistent their hands became.

What was the word? What was the word for *stop*?

But I didn't want to stop. Some long, low sound that I had never known let loose from me as his blows intensified, as my clit burst beneath her touch. His hand wailed against my searing flesh, the sensation a sudden leap from pain to rapture, into the sprawling depths of my being.

I fell against Tampa, whose boy was ready, slamming into my ecstasy with one tremendous stroke. From behind, A.C. spread me, finding his way easily after my complete surrender.

I was free.

Surrender had made me free.

"Emily, is that you?" I heard. As my eyes opened, I saw that A.C. had slipped into the studio while I dreamt.

What? I had fallen asleep *again*? But I had danced the routine once—twice—at least three times. And then, I remembered, I had lay down on the stage, just to catch my breath. . . .

"Enough is enough," he went on. "It's after midnight—I knew you'd still be here. You need to go home and get some real sleep before the shoot tomorrow. I bet you've rehearsed the video so many times you could do it in your sleep. Am I wrong?"

Wrong? Right? Do it in my sleep? A.C. had no idea—this little Columbus, Ohio, babe doing a three-way? Not in my wildest dreams! But there it was, literally in my wildest dreams. And what an experience, overflowing with domination and submission—such imagination. Had I gone there because my dream lovers were a choreographer and a casting director, yielding so much power over my waking life at this moment? Was I willing to submit to whatever they wanted so that I could be part of the project?

Truthfully, I had no idea. My mind reeled from where it had just taken me. A.C. and I shared a cab home in silence mostly. The wheels dropped me at my apartment first. There was my laundry bag on the steps, my clothes obviously neatly folded inside, with a note on top.

Damn, Freedom could be so sweet.

When I awoke the next morning, a blur of images battled for my attention. There was Freedom and me, dancing as we did on the stage yesterday, our fever and yearning. There was us in the Laundromat, me pounding against him, his mouth so close to mine. Flashes of dancing with him horizontally—but that happened in my *dream* between those two realities, remember?

Then it was just me, surrounded by shadows as I bore witness to the intimacy of a pair of lovers my mind gave imagination to, as a result of which my being soared. Because of that, I broke out from the shadows of myself.

And now, here it was: *D day*. The day of the shoot. I had barely slept, couldn't think of eating. Even with my tight black possum so satisfied in ways I'd never imagined before, that same old feeling started to knife through my belly. Could that be possible? But it was.

As I made my way to the studio, I heard my daddy's voice: *Whatever you want, sweetheart, go out and get it*. I listened real hard, finally hearing Freedom's words, too: *You gotta release*.

Damn straight.

When I walked in, the crew was prepping for the shoot, the

dancers stretching. A.C. and Tampa were locked in discussion to-gether in the corner. When they saw me, they both waved and smiled, and I shined one back.

Tell you the truth, Red Shoes, it shined between my legs, too. I welcomed that feeling and rued it, too. I did not want my shy-ness to overtake me, especially now.

The director strode in then, all styled out in a long coat and cowboy hat. "What's happening, A.C.?" he called. "Talk to me. You ready? The girls ready?"

"Yesssir," A.C. punched out.

"Let's do it then!" called the director with a smile. "Everybody up here, let's see what it looks like. . . ."

The crew began filming the instant the music started slam-ming. The backdrop was a chain-link fence behind which three gleaming eighteen-wheelers shone their headlights onto the dance floor. Way sleek, sexy. The concept was that the part of the video that took place outside was shot in black and white. It trailed the gangsters as they approached the inside scene, which was us making the music video—a video within a video. The bal-ance of the video was shot—in color—inside the studio. Smoke and sound wafted around us as we commenced dancing.

The chorus boomed: "Freedom . . . Freedom . . . Free . . . Free . . . Free . . ."

And Freedom started doing his thing, dancing and rapping. "I got the beat, I got the rhyme. This here the place, right now the time. . . ."

The chorus sang: "Freedom . . . Freedom . . . Free . . . Free . . . Free . . . "

Freedom belted it out: "Gonna prove to you, baby, just what I stand for. Gonna show you, sistah, what you need this man for. . . ."

Damn, it was revving beyond. The chorus pumped: "Free-dom . . . Freedom . . . Free . . . Free . . . Free . . . "

"I'll make it all good. I'll do it all right. You're gonna feel me, night after night. . . ." Freedom went on.

We were exploding on the dance floor. Freedom was all over me, our bodies thrashing together, grinding, pawing each other, churning, then purposefully pulling back. Magnets meshing together one instant, flinging away from the other the next.

I literally reeled from his touch, that sweet breath of his coating me like honey . . . nectar . . . dew. One moment more of being that close, drenched, enveloped, and then some other part of me rebelled, somersaulted, and I broke away from the moment.

And. Careened. Off. The. Stage.

"What's happening?" the director shouted. "Cut! Cut it! Cut!"

As I flung around to face him, he leapt onto the dance floor.

"I thought you had this worked out!" he shouted.

Stunned myself, I was speechless. Not a word in my mind.

Freedom's hands danced into the air. "Just give us ten minutes, man."

"I don't have ten minutes," the director said flat out. "Let's do the European version," he called to the others. "The European version, let's do it now!"

"Hold on, she can do it," Freedom protested.

I was . . . Words still eluded me. After such abandon last night, now this?

A.C. chimed in. No choice, I guess. "Okay, we're doing the European version!"

He turned to me, bullets seeming to spray from his lips. "Emily, clothes off. You're gonna need body makeup."

"W-what?" I finally managed.

A.C., avoiding my eyes, said, "All you girls signed a nudity rider."

"I am *not* taking off my clothes," I announced. Could I hear anything beyond my own hysteria? What the hell was wrong with me?

Freedom tried again, his hand held out like a stop sign. "Just give us ten more minutes, man. I'm telling you. . . ."

But the director cut him off. "We don't have ten more minutes. We've got so much time and so much money."

He moved toward me then, touching my arm. "I don't want you to do anything you're not comfortable with. . . ."

I had no time to react—not that I could—before Freedom rejoined, "What? Listen, if that's your attitude," he spat, "then do it without me. Great."

The director ignored us. "Hey, wait a minute. I got another girl here. . . ." He snapped his fingers at the crowd of dancers. "C'mon . . ." he beckoned.

"No, no, no . . ." Freedom complained.

The director turned to Freedom. "I got another girl ready to go."

"I'm out!" Freedom said. "That's it. That's it, man. Without clothes, you don't get *me*."

He started walking away.

The director freaked. "Jesus Christ, man, get a grip!"

I couldn't take it, the chaos, the tension. Freedom would lose the video for me?

"Why don't you stop it!" I shouted. "Both of you! Stop it! I don't care! I really don't care!"

But they continued to scream at each other. It reminded me too much of my parents, at the end, before Daddy stormed out. I took off, a creature sprinting away from danger.

Where was I? My head was spinning, the lights of the eighteen-wheelers blinding me.

Behind me, I heard steps and Freedom's voice approaching. "Sweetheart, come here!" he called.

And farther away, I heard the director's voice, "Unrated version! Now! Put the music on! Put the music on! European version. Let's go!"

The music jacked, filling my ears, at that moment, with nothing else but my own limitations. I fled.

Freedom reached me and flung me around.

"You don't give a shit? Bullshit!" he spouted. "You're full of shit, I'm tellin' you!"

It sounded just like my momma talking to my daddy. I couldn't take it. I whirled around. "Just leave me alone, okay? I had my chance and I blew it!"

"Hunh?" he responded. "You ain't blown nothin' so far. But you know what you're doin'? You're blowin' it right now! What, after last night, it's all of a sudden not comfortable so you just go bail out on me?"

Behind us I heard Freedom's rap going on: "This ain't just jive talkin', so hear me when I say, I'm gonna make it better, day after day. . . ."

Day after day? Like you'll even be around? I felt my heels dig into the ground under me, my fingers curled protectively, poised to cut through the air if they had to.

Ain't nobody gonna give it to you, Daddy said. *You gotta dig deep!* Freedom's words.

I was digging deep, deep enough to lose that phat knife that had been cutting at my dreams since I started dreaming them.

You know what "phat" means, Red Shoes?

It means: *P*retty *h*ot *a*nd *t*empting.

Do you get it now? Do you understand how I've needed that knife, needed it to stab me so deep, make me stop, still my dreams, like my daddy's leaving was my fault?

No more!

I stared at Freedom, crazy for him, but scared beyond belief.

"What was that last night?" I demanded. "You knew I was down and you took advantage of me!"

What was I saying? That was not what I felt at all! What was I doing? Then I got it—feeling so close to him in the Laundromat, wanting him so much, needing to pull away.

How do I know the other is even there, much less believe that I am loved completely?

No—it was not my fault that Daddy left!

Freedom recoiled as if I had hit him. "What? Ohhh, if that was me taking advantage of you last night, then I need to check myself into a loony bin for an overhaul."

"Right," I answered, willing my heart to close like a fist. "You do that and send the bill to me!"

The expression in his eyes clouded. "O-kay," he said. "I understand now. This is over. Thank you."

In a second, he was gone.

I stood there, a stone where my heart should have been. Closing my heart would not protect me, I realized. It would only hurt me—and anyone I loved.

Then I heard him, back on the stage, calling to the director, "You want to do the European version, let's do it! We can do it right now; it's not a problem."

Not a problem? I lost it, spun around, crouched down, like I was pressed against Momma's old piano. But in an instant, I felt everything, understood everything. That moment was long gone,

my daddy a mere memory, not something to hold on to. I catapulted up, into action. Leaping forward, I found myself in front
of Freedom.

"What do you want?" I shrieked. "What, you want me to hit
you? Want me to hit you? I'll hit you . . . I'll hit you," I yelled,
and I meant it, already slamming his chest with my fists.

I could not stop it. I stepped back, seeking enough momentum
before I slammed my whole body into him, the way that one low
note would slam inside me when Daddy would play it.

"Great!" I heard.

What?

"Great!" the director repeated. "That's exactly it! Take all
that emotion you're feeling and just start to dance. . . . Start to
dance."

And I did dance then, everything inside me sending me this
way, then that. I was going to lose that knife twisting deep within
once and for all.

"That's it," the director crooned, "just reach down. You got it.
You got it. Now what I want to do is pick up the video exactly
where we left off."

Where we left off was with me and Freedom whipping our
arms into the air simultaneously, whipping ourselves into the kind
of frenzy that I could barely even imagine with him last night.
And that I could not keep myself from bounding into right now.

Because nothing existed but us.

"Everybody get into position," the director went on. "That's it,
honey, just reach down. . . ."

Damn, I am reaching down.

"You got it. Just reach down. I'm gonna pick it up on three.
One . . . two . . . three."

The music blasted. I echoed the routine as before, but this

time, I flung into abandon, never leaving Freedom's arms. I hurled myself against him as if he were my entire life—that piano I used to lean against, my daddy's back as he walked away, my momma's eyes.

You are everything and I am nothing without you. We are grass, air, being, and I cling to you as I cling to life itself.

That is how I feel each time you appear, when opportunity arises and grace invites me to remember you exist evermore.

I would dig myself into the ground if you asked me to, grasp each strand of grass with precise abandon, cling with hungry palms to the sky, kneel haphazardly before the horizon, keen ever after under the stars.

All this I would do for you. Give you everything and all of my heart, even always knowing that they could never be enough.

The music finally ended. Beyond tender, Freedom kissed my cheek. I wrapped my arms around him tight as I could. Different from what I'd done in the Laundromat last night, this morning I did not let go.

When he kissed me full on the lips, the rest of the world fell away. It was just us, in each other's arms, mouths, in our real live dreams.

A sound surged into the air like a crescendo then, deafening, deliberate. Like our two hearts meeting.

The sound of applause.

"'Take advantage' of you, I'll remember that," he whispered when everyone's clapping finally faded. "You little sneak, you finally got what you wanted, huh?"

"You bet your ass," I replied with a booty-full smile.

Red Shoes, I did. I got what I wanted. Now what to do? Not with my career, I mean, but with the way I feel about Freedom. The last thing my momma said before I left Columbus was, *Rule number one: Never fall in love with a rock star. If you do, go immediately to rule number two: If you got to love him, make sure you love yourself first.*

JAKE

Somehow what I learned from Freedom was to push past what I thought my limits were . . . and most importantly, to trust myself. That was the moment, I realized, when I could finally stop asking whether I was good enough.

Because I did love myself.

So tell me, what about you?

Stella, I'd love to learn to trust myself, too. But trust myself to what? Push past my own limits? Dream a new dream?

Love my . . .

Find a way out of this loft for change?

Tell you what—you'll go out first, do your business. Then it'll be my turn—my first time out alone since Alex. . . .

Sex in the Hamptons

◆

The Writers' Confessions

STACEY

Me, in love?

Like I even knew what love was. Clue. Idea. Notion. Whiskers on kittens and warm woolen mittens, wasn't that it? No, that was favorite things. Love was much bigger than that sweet crap anyway, more like a force of nature: mudslide, hurricane, earthquake, tornado. Sounded significantly closer to a natural disaster than the big, bellowing, busted open heart that it was, didn't it?

Apparently, I thought so. In my experience, to be blunt, love was the thing that grabbed you by the throat and led you away, off to Fatesville. What happened there was anybody's guess. Kind of like the old vaudeville days when a disembodied cane would suddenly appear from behind the curtain and yank someone off the stage.

Yet life is but a stage, no?

Which made Jocko and I mere players. Hmmm, interesting.

In that case, the question begged to be asked: What roles would we play?

During our debut in the sculpture studio, I'd become deeply enamored of marble. I'd even go so far as to admit to being utterly smitten with the smooth white clouds of a woman's enormous buttocks. Quite simply because those buttocks had been Jocko's consummate creation, formed by his very experienced, erogenous hands. Could hands be erogenous? His were, especially as he bent me over one of the cool, curved globes of that ass before he took my own in his masterful, vitally sexy way.

And, to be clear, he took me only *after* he had made me come, and I do mean multiple orgasm careening into abandon. Only *after* I had lost myself completely in his hands, under his fingers, puddled by his touch. And there I was: howling, offering, relinquishing, possessed by bliss.

That was when I knew that I was—quite literally—in the hands of a maestro.

It only added to the already shimmering magic of the moment that his cock was just my style—a big fat stick of stiff passion. And how he wielded it, like he was pulling into a parking space singularly designed for his exact make and model. For me, it was as if his arrival was somehow part of my own destination. As if he had finally arrived at a place I had long sought, yet had not even been aware of.

Vroom, vroom.

For Fate's sake, was that how love got you?

And by the way, couldn't I conceive of something even slightly more romantic than these tortured metaphors to express feelings? Cripes: parking space? What was I, a garage? And where was my heart in all this? Bleating beneath a trash can in some hidden corner of said garage, perhaps?

Ah, with love so many questions came.

Pathetic, really. Me, I meant.

But I did like the part about the arrival, the destination; that had depth. Maybe I could find a meaningful way to add those concepts to the special sauce that fed my spirit. Besides cars, then, what else arrived and departed?

(Elise, suggestions please. I've been injured. Romantically, that is, in case you did not know. *Vroom vroom,* yes. Followed by long stints of *vroom*lessness, when my heart left the scene. Can you understand at all, Ms. Twelve-year-relationship Thang, or should I start a blog? Just being realistic, writing partner . . .)

What I realized the instant those car-bent words raced out of me (see, there it was again: *raced*) was that my initial attempt to discuss "it" (meaning: love) the way I did was so far away from approaching (again: *approaching!*) the real feelings that roiled deep within. To be clear, those were like a thunderstorm (wet, passionate, evocative, remarkable)—but with the lightning and thunder landing in all the right places.

It might be best to stick with the allusions to nature because they all seemed so entwined together: the way Jocko had tossed the oysters (back) into the sea when we met that August night, how the trees had swayed when we arrived at his place, the screech of the barn owl above us as we stepped from the Lincoln to his driveway.

(Elise, I know. I didn't mention the swaying trees before, but I can't be expected to recount every single moment, count every blade of grass, can I? Girl, my tresses will go gray long before I'm forty, in that case. What is that Whitman poem about the blade of grass, by the way? So much depends on a blade of grass? No, according to Williams a lot depends on a red wheelbarrow, apparently. But that's poetry for you.)

As a fiction writer, I'd learned to change gears (amazing! That theme again: *change gears*) when in search of the perfect word, phrase, metaphor. Better change than go mad, that was my motto.

So let me try to express myself from another angle, employ a more realistic perspective. Here goes: It might be hard to believe, but I've been accused of being a tough, hard-ass type chick. True or false? Both, actually. For what I believed was that inherent in anything was its opposite. What that meant was that if I were tough, I was also the opposite of tough: mush, to be exact. Not everyone knew that, but not everyone knew me, either.

Or me, in love.

Ah, so we were back to that again. (Note to fellow scribe: Did we depart from elsewhere to arrive there? Did you think of any other themes to apply this notion to?) Obviously, I couldn't stay away from Jocko for that long. Or his stiff cock, actually. Because there it was, insisting, inside my back door.

And there I was, wanting it to never leave, as the subtleties of dominance, submission, and surrender insinuated themselves in my mind. How much of each would completely captivate me in Jocko's eventual absence? How much could I savor, luxuriate in, long for, even as he filled me?

Barely consciously thought, these questions appeared more like shadows in my mind, undoubtedly deepening the experience. They also deepened the pleasure that saturated my senses as he pumped me, slowly at first, my pussy pressed against the buttock of smooth marble I was draped over, delectably heated up now by my own orgasmic juices.

As I ground myself against the sleek heat, my clit somersaulted, delirious for more. I reached back and spread my cheeks for this dark, sultry, bullet of a man, inviting him in deeper. He responded with a throaty, satisfied grunt, plugging me with tender aplomb.

Who would have guessed that Fate had arrived with such singularity? It was no secret: I was a sucker for sodomy.

Jocko's superlative hands had grabbed my hips and pulled me closer now, each inch of him pulsing against the tight walls of my throbbing velvet tunnel. My gash was suddenly bereft of its hot wet berth, catching but a waft of mere air. Almost instantly Jocko's fingers crept between my legs, parting the swollen lips of my vulva before beginning to spank my clit with a slight rhythmic slap.

I shuddered from the thrill, the thrall, what rapture. Somehow, Jocko knew exactly how to stretch the senses beyond their customary limits. Such Italianitude! I needed to show him (Double Pisces, did you hear me? I *needed*. This was way serious.) just how passionately I dug his moves.

My feet were on the floor, my heels pressed hard against it to anchor me as my love poked ever deeper, filling me with spiraling feeling as the sensations pounced upon one synapse after another. The delicious sting of my clit was interrupted only by each riveting plunge of his artistry, one luscious fingertip alternately stroking my explosive clit before spanking it once more. I held onto the gorgeous marble buttock before me as another, even more fervent, climax ignited within. My legs began to tremble as Jocko rocked me back against him, his balls now softly caressing my sweetly sensitive perineum.

At once, the orgasm ripped through me, roaring like a hundred-mile-per-hour wind.

Was that my voice howling into every corner of Jocko's studio, barreling out into the dark night beyond?

Were those my hands, gripping that marble expanse so hard their whiteness seemed to meld into it?

My ass, quivering as something solid would melt into liquid, as if an invisible torch had found there its hottest flame? Combine that with the bliss of my flourishing clit and the way Jocko held me still as his passion suddenly spurted deep inside me. His throaty groans cut through the late summer air, and ours was a wedlock of ecstatic surrender.

Ah, so that was one role we would play. In my humble experience, to put it very simply, there was nothing like getting fucked in the ass.

(Elise, my ears are burning—in addition to other parts of me, natch—which means I know you have questions. Because you're such a curiously swimming-against-the-current type of sea creature, I will bust open the answers. Hop out of the water, follow a trail of imaginary crumbs leading into the forest of sexuality, and you will have arrived. Hey, why not bring a few fishy schools with you, too, so that we might spread the word to the masses as best we can.)

Drum roll, please, as we reveal the most frequently asked questions:

Does it hurt?

Perfect question. What hurts most is an insensitive lover. Someone who is not paying extreme attention or doesn't take the time to *read* your body's responses to this superbly primal act. For there does indeed exist the delectable pain of initial penetration, the *ohhh* of insertion. Time dissolves as the body opens and accepts the offering, and then, in turn, demands more. What transpires during the act is a dance of dominance and submission. Sodomy can hurt, but the pain can be so unbearably sweet that you can't help but beg for more of it. Does it hurt? Bring it on, baby!

In some instances, I can take it in one fell swoop (as with Jocko, my newly, unexpectedly, premium squeeze). In others, I might like you to tease me slowly, spill some saliva or sex grease (lubrication *is* essential in this area) upon the sensitive lips of that tender well, lick or finger me into relaxation, rev me up into rhapsody. Then, and only then, do I want you to fill me with your desirous, upright soul.

For *soul* is the operative word. You need to be that deep, that tender and commanding. Aware of the precise instant when the plunge into the virgin, unplumbed passage needs to be coupled with a finger's sating touch on my perhaps forlorn, momentarily forgotten clit. It calms the searing throb, assuages all fear as you enter me, soothing me as you simultaneously force my entire being to submit.

Is it dirty?

Is sex dirty? Only as dirty as your own little mind. Myself, I like to be clean before I meet and greet. I bathe, soap lathered and lingering inside my private chambers, both front and back. To my mind, cleanliness is next to sexiness. Which is not to say that a sweaty, pungent, nasty fuck is completely out of the question, either. I can be convinced to go anywhere, as least once. (Notice: *Go.* Again we return to theme of arrival and the departure. . . .)

Is anal sex better than regular sex?

That's a very personal question—and I think you mean "vaginal" rather than "regular" sex. You really must investigate for yourself to determine exactly how you might respond. Not in the mood? Sometimes it helps to share, shall we say, some smut with your partner to get you there.

Welcome to Smutsville!

(Writing bud, my shiny, silvery minnow, your turn. Working on that section made me very hungry—and I do *not* mean for food!)

ELISE

We had an agreement, C and I, to not ask each other about outside sexual experiences. That was one of the reasons I liked to talk shop with my arguably oversexed writing partner. With C, there were no questions, no confessions. As long as we continued to support and love each other, we did not impede exploration. There was always the risk that either one of us could fall in love with another and want to rearrange our arrangement, but life was flux and change. It was unpredictable, not linear at all; spirals we traveled within. We were both open to the ever-shifting world inside and outside, because that was what worked for us. Our creative lives were paramount. Our love swam bone-deep. Our tenderness extended to the tiniest hair follicle. We were many things—family, friends, lovers, and confidantes. And we both knew that no one person could be everything, fill every need, fulfill every desire. Perhaps, in exceptional circumstances, that was true within the rare couple, but it was indeed rare, despite the rhetoric and fairy-tale promises made the world over.

In my own world, I'd recently taken two erotic hits. Hungry for my usual half-pound of turkey bologna after the Labor Day crowds had finally left our little hamlet, I discovered Marisa wasn't at the deli. I wondered if she was out sick, but I was too shy to ask the owner about her. I went in the next day and the next—still no Marisa. Finally I inquired and found out that she had gone back to Colombia with her entire family. I was going to miss sucking her cilantro tongue, tasting her spicy sex. And I was really sad that we didn't even get a chance to say good-bye.

The next hit was Joe. In order to make more money to support his family, he had taken a construction job up-island with his wife's brother. He'd be gone at least six months to return only on weekends to be with his family. I didn't take the news well. I begged him to let me drive to Ronkonkoma—a town name I'd always loved to say aloud, but he said "no," he was staying at his brother-in-law's house and couldn't risk seeing me. I cried. He held me, whispered tender words, but I was inconsolable.

I couldn't tell him that another lover, Marisa, had just disappeared without a trace. He knew I was with C, but he didn't understand how central he had become every week. Max. Buddy. Joe. Me. Skipping stones. Soaring seagulls. His clumsy yet knowing hand pawing my pussy. My lips and tongue submerged on his working-class, solid cock. I got attached to sexual ritual—as if my body depended on it as it did on eating, peeing, and (excuse me) shitting.

No more Montauk sunsets with my Spanish deli-girl. No more dog barking, stone-skipping fucks with Joe. Frankly, I was bereft.

As if that was not enough, C was leaving soon for a three-month trip to Europe where a traveling exhibition of her photographs would take place. Without her, and now, without Marisa and Joe, I would turn into a phantom, a ghost, a girl with no groin. Autumn looked mighty lonesome. How would I write? Plus with Stacey head over heels with Jocko, I wouldn't have her attention and time to belabor my misfortune. Every party had a pooper (in this case, me), and I doubted she was about to join mine.

Yet lo and behold. How biblical! Lo and behold, I got a phone call, a call that at another moment might have derailed me. Yet because of when it came, the charge was erotic enough for this fish to bite.

Which meant that I was going into New York City to meet

Rachel, my first love, and now complicated friend from Los Angeles. She was a bigwig at Paramount, overseeing all the advertising campaigns for their films.

We'd gone round and round the sexual maypole since we'd first met too many years ago in the dankest, worst possible dyke bar on Santa Monica Boulevard.

She was in the bathroom, holding a beer, stroking it like a cock. She asked me where I'd bought my watch as the smell of urine, patchouli oil, and beer soaked our nostrils. In the line of bladder-bursting dykes, she was behind me.

"Fred Segal," I answered.

"How much?" she asked.

"Too much."

"Yeah." She smiled. "I love to buy stuff that's too much."

When the available stall door swung open, I gestured for her to go ahead. Rachel gestured for me to join her. I did.

It was one-thirty in the morning. We were both wet from the lusty stench of desire that wafted from the candy-box mix of dykes in the bar. Her blue doe eyes made me wetter. So did her brassy head of hair, thin lips, firm breasts, long legs, and especially her withdrawn intensity. It was like watching a brush fire from miles away and wondering how dangerous it was. Were homes perishing, filled with memories? Was there a trapped dog, cat, child, turtle, or goldfish in the heart of the flame? Should I run in, despite the danger, to rescue life? That seemed to be Rachel's invitation.

I closed the stall door and she pushed me up against it, her greedy hand immediately unbuttoning my 501 jeans, her fingers rocketing between my legs as if stranded in the desert and racing toward a mirage of water. I spread my legs and thrust my own hand down her jeans—she had unzipped them already. We rocked and bucked in unison, intensely staring at each other, feeling the pressure of the line of waiting women in the bathroom.

She still held her beer and she raised it to my opened mouth, slid the bottle between my lips. I gave it a blow job, slashing my tongue across the cool glass. Our breathing was ragged as she released the beer from my lips, crushed and ground her breasts against mine. Our hands dug faster and faster, hot palms against sodden pubes, and just as I came her wet mouth met mine and our sounds were swallowed whole, hers into my belly, mine into hers.

The stall door rattled and shook and a burst of applause filled the space around us. Just like that, Rachel zipped up and turned toward the toilet. With her booted foot, she flushed it. Together we emerged from the stall to the randy smiles of a half-dozen women.

We washed our hands, our eyes meeting in the mirror.

"Rachel," she said.

"Elise," I replied.

She grabbed my hand. "Let's dance."

She was the needle. I was the vein. She was the full bottle of Jack Daniel's. I was the hopeless drunk. It was love. A match made in heaven and hell. My desire was a train wreck. It was the *Titanic*. And I'd crashed and sunk over and over so many times I'd lost count. Hundreds of torn out and ripped up pages from my journals had been trashed recounting each and every collision.

The problem was that when I was with Rachel it often took months for me to recover. I was the proverbial moth drawn into her flames. I would begin to fantasize about being with her and only her for the rest of my life. I would shut down sexually, wanting only Rachel. It made me sick on every level of my being. I was in physical and emotional agony and had come to learn that time away from her was the only way I could heal. Once the agony passed, I would vow never to see her again. Never.

Over a year ago, after one of our visits, we made THE agreement, the contract, once again. I called and told her that although I loved her, I could no longer afford to see her. It was just too hard. After three hours of wrestling on the phone, we agreed that we would still see each other, but we would no longer be sexual.

Our friendship, our we've-known-each-other-in-past-lives bullshit history was too precious, too important; we couldn't put that in jeopardy. We couldn't endanger our bond with sexual confusion even though it was combustive, chemical, and beyond reason. That was the bottom line. We did not want to fuck it up. "Okay," I said. "Okay," she said.

Relationships, especially when they enter the sexual realm, reveal us at our most fragile. How endearingly transparent we are, telling ourselves and each other lies—well-meaning, heartfelt lies, but lies nonetheless. God, how hard we try to do the right thing, whatever that is, and how often we fail abysmally. Yet there we are, continuing to put up the good fight until the day we die; our confused, murky little hearts, minds, and groins absolutely spent.

So, for me, Rachel was the one—we all had one. The one who permanently set up a kind of living quarters somewhere inside of us. Because there was no surgical procedure, we would have to kill ourselves to get whoever it was fully out of our systems. Barring suicide, we had no choice but to survive. Sometimes I wondered if the reason I had taken so many lovers was that I was still searching for someone who would erase Rachel from my flesh memory, my mind. Or maybe I was like the addict hoping to experience that one moment—the transcendent high—that was ever elusive and, thus, always sought.

Now that I lived on the East Coast, Rachel and I only saw each other once or twice a year. As I'd gotten older, had many lovers, and lived with someone for the past twelve years, her hold on me had diminished somewhat. However, just when I thought the brush fire had been put out, all flames doused, only a few simmering embers smoking, all it took was one strong, swift wind to ignite the madness all over again.

Rachel lived alone, as she always had, with her secrets, with nameless, faceless lovers, men and women. There were no strings, just her muddy promises to each, I imagined. This time around, I *absolutely had to* go into the city to see her, because if I didn't she'd *be beyond hurt,* she'd *be devastated.*

When she came to New York for business, she always stayed at the Four Seasons, insisting that I stay there with her. In the past, if I tried to maintain distance by crashing somewhere else, she'd reel me in with whispered words over the phone: *We mean so much to each other. You were my first real love. We're best friends. No one understands me like you do. Maybe, someday, we'll be together, as we should, as it's meant to be.*

These bizarre, seductive, ridiculous words always soaked under my skin—like heroin.

And this time, in the middle of my lonely September, I was in the mood. When I arrived at the hotel, she opened the door to her suite freshly bathed, wearing a terrycloth robe and smelling of expensive body cream.

We hugged in a friendly manner.

"How are you?" she asked. "And, C, how is she?"

"Good, good," I said. "Good, good," I repeated.

Why was I always nervous when confronted with her physically? Maybe I wasn't in the mood, after all.

"The suite is fantastic," she said. "And I've already ordered us room service. Hope you don't mind."

Shit. My cunt immediately moaned. God, I wished Rachel would tell me she'd become a born again, given her pussy to Jesus, so I wouldn't have to deal with this brushfire passion.

We sat on opposite ends of the couch, drinking wine, nibbling cheese and olives, almonds, popcorn shrimp (my favorite), and wending our way into comfort. I was convinced that if we were two gay men, our cocks would have been stiffly aimed at each other.

Even though I had just bathed (she'd insisted: *The tub is just too fantastic to pass up*), I was almost certain that Rachel could smell the steaming puddle between my legs. I was afraid I'd leave a telltale stain on the couch, but luckily, I'd layered myself in protective pajama gear: sweats, boxer shorts, a wife-beater, baggy old cashmere sweater, and thick socks.

The enormous bed loomed large behind us, sitting there like the elephant in the room no one wanted to acknowledge.

"Who are you seeing?" I asked. (Not: *Are you seeing anyone?* I shot straight from the hip. She was always fucking somebody—or bodies.)

"Clint," she answered. "He's a director. We met at the Sundance Film Festival. He's amazingly talented."

(*Amazingly talented?* Sooo L.A.)

"I showed him my favorite script of yours," she continued. "He really liked it."

(She was trying to hook me. Director. Script. Movie deal.)

"Right now, though, he's got so many projects in development."

"What's he like?" I asked.

"Sweet. Cocky. Uncompromising—in a good way. Charming. Gorgeous eyes."

A fist formed in my stomach. I was about to launch a solid offense and bring up my sexual escapades with Dia (amazingly talented painter, top galleries) or Joe (amazingly talented locksmith, father of two), but then I stopped myself. It was an old game between us and I was not playing. *We're just friends!*

"He sounds great. Hope I get to meet him," I said warmly, with tremendous affection and grace.

She leveled a gaze on me and smiled. "How many layers are you wearing?"

"As many as it takes."

I yawned on purpose. Enough of the game. I wanted to get in bed and go to sleep.

"Tired?" she asked.

"Yes."

"Okay. Remember, I'm taking us on a shopping spree tomorrow. Then lunch."

"Of course I remember. Why do you think I came?"

Rachel loved to buy me clothes. We shared the same dressing room, stripped and tried on countless outfits until she found *the one* that was perfect for each of us. Jewelry and watches, too. C didn't approve of these purchases, but I just reminded her that Rachel was Rachel. She did it for all her friends, which was not true. Only for me.

We settled into the bed, me with my layers, she wearing tiny panties and a sleeveless black T-shirt. I had taken a mild sleeping pill because I swore to myself that I would not break our oath: *Let's be friends but more, but without sex, only clear desire. Turned on, always turned on to each other. Let's not put our friendship in danger.*

I turned away from her, tried to find a soothing spot on the pillow to help me fall into dreams. That was when my cunt whispered this message to my belly button, who whispered to my nipples, who whispered to my ears: "Your cunt wants to know what exactly you intend to do with the throbbing ache between your legs?"

I sighed heavily.

My nips continued: "She asked, and we quote, 'Did you take a fucking pill for that!?'" (She was turbulent, my cunt.)

The oath! The oath, I reminded them.

These two words were passed down to the swelling mass between my legs, and I suddenly felt we'd struck an air pocket and were tumbling, falling, turning in my agitated cunt's wake.

(Writing partner: Help! Of course, you'd say, *just fuck her and get it over with.*)

Poor belly button, stuck in the middle, made a suggestion: "Ask her if *she's* turned on, too."

That question got my nipples' attention. The left, obviously feeling a bit drowsy, suddenly perked up. Both chirped in unison: "Yes! Yes! Ask her. Can't we stay up another hour, please?!"

My lips—not the bravest mounds of flesh, began to nibble each other. "Why do we always have to say the words?" they complained.

Belly button had another suggestion: "Why don't you just hammer your clit with your finger like you always do? That's fun. Then we can all get some rest."

"NO!" my nips cried.

I could not even tell you what my cunt had to say; it was way too vulgar for the written page.

I was half-expecting my nipples to join hands with my belly button. They could have grabbed my cunt, too, forcing her to join them. Then they could all start to sway and sing, "We shall overcome," plaintive, pleading. A rainbow coalition of sorts, perhaps my pubes would join in (it takes a village, a pubic village). It would be a peaceful demonstration, albeit simmering with buried rage.

So my lips, stalwart, shaky little warriors that they were, were about to whisper those words (*are you turned on, too?*), when suddenly Rachel's voice dripped into my ear, "I need to touch you."

(Stacey: Much better than *are you turned on, too?* And I was supposed to be the writer.)

I turned. She hovered above me, lips shimmering in the near-darkness of the room.

"I need to touch you," she whispered again.

She gently brushed those lips against my eyebrows, my nose, nearing my lips.

"It's okay, Elise, we need to touch." Her voice was a sigh against my face.

Without my permission, my arms reached out, hands grasping her waist and pulling her on top of me.

Her mouth met mine. "I need to touch you," her words landing on my tongue, allowing me to swallow them whole.

The warmth of her being pressing against mine was familiar and shocking at the same time. Our tongues carried traces of wine. Our cunts embraced, holding each other tight.

Rachel sat up. Her hands released her from her T-shirt with one glorious sweeping motion. I took her in with my eyes as if she were a masterpiece. Her delicate breasts were round and small with nipples like rubies. Her shoulders were muscled and her long arms lean from swimming every day.

Her hands moved to my waist and pulled at my sweater and wife-beater, deftly removing them and tossing them onto the floor. When our breasts met, a searing heat rippled through my body.

"I need to touch you," she repeated, like a chant, a prayer, a confession.

All I could do was moan as her tongue, once again, dipped into my mouth, matching the rhythm of her pelvis against my groin. Our hardening nipples danced against each other's.

My hands dived under her panties, exploring her soft ass cheeks. I rocked her harder against me, allowing my fingers to slip down and discover—as if for the first time—her hot liquid slit.

A low grunt echoed from her mouth into the cave of my own.

"I love you," escaped from my lips.

"I know." Her voice was hazy. It drugged me, lulled me like a lullaby.

What oath?

I had three fingers inside her molten fissure as her own fingers teased her fiery clit.

She offered me one ruby nipple, then the other. I suckled, nibbled, licked in just the way I'd learned from our history.

She rocked her hips faster and faster, squeezing the walls of her cunt as I released a fourth finger inside of her.

"Ohhhhh . . ." I heard, and the sound quivered within her chest, spilling, it seemed, from the nipple that still nestled between my lips. The sound glided down my throat, and I consumed her breast as if I'd never eaten before.

I could feel her orgasm before it arrived, that brief stillness prior to the quake. Her stomach trembled, her breathing harsh, and inside of her, my hand felt the growing vibrations.

I want my hand to always be right where it is.

Her body shook and shivered, and she grabbed my hand with her own, forcing it deeper, so deep it might have fallen off and disappeared. Maybe all of me would vanish forever into her cunt; perhaps I was meant to exist only there.

Her voice emitted a long, low lamenting cry, and she collapsed on top of me, aftershocks rolling through her flesh.

"I need to touch you," she whimpered over and over. I felt warm tears from her eyes dropping onto my face. Or were they mine?

We never did go shopping. We stayed in the hotel room, making love through the night, into the morning, until I had to leave. We slept for a few hours toward dawn. A sleep so deep it felt as if I was swathed in a watery cradle with other bottom dwellers in the dark belly of the ocean where no light would ever penetrate.

I entered a dream that was as big as another universe—not a dream at all, but another life, another planet I lived and breathed in. It was so real, so visceral, I was certain this place existed—out there, somewhere, and I didn't want to leave. I knew I couldn't describe this universe, couldn't pull it from where it existed and give it words, but I didn't know why.

Heading back to East Hampton on the Jitney, I curled up in my seat, holding my knees like a lover, realizing I couldn't think a coherent thought. My entire body thrummed with a sweet, painful ache. After an hour passed on the two-and-a-half-hour bus ride, the ache started to drain out of me. If I were a drunk, I'd have begun to tremble with the shakes.

I called Stacey. She wasn't home, probably at Jocko's being in love. I left a message: "I feel like roadkill. I'm spattered beyond recognition. Raccoon? Elise? Squirrel? Doesn't matter. Crow chow now."

I thought of what the conversation between us might have been like:

Elise: "I don't understand why I react this way. But I always have, suppose I always will."

Stacey: "Time to reframe, my fish-out-of-water friend. You have and always have had many lovers. That's all Rachel is—a lover. End of story."

Elise: "So why do I feel so empty? After her, always the agony of empty."

Stacey: "Elise, she's a vampire. She drinks your blood, takes you into ecstasy, then leaves you dry—saps the life force right out of you."

Elise: "That's it exactly."

Stacey: "Is it worth it?"

Elise: "I don't know."

Stacey: "You like misery."

Elise: "Fuck off."

Stacey: "That's better."

STACEY

Jocko and I had known each other for about three weeks. Strangely, it felt both shorter and longer than that at once. After our first night in the studio, we had made love every night since, in every room of his sprawling bachelor pad. Some nights we lay under the stars, the sweat gleaming on our bodies after a particularly rambunctious tryst, reveling in the last blistering days of summer.

During the day, he had accompanied *moi* to the ocean to photograph me surfing; I had joined him on several hikes through some of our nearby nature sanctuaries. Other than that, we had not ventured out into public. We had instead ventured *inside* to what felt like unusually immeasurable experiences.

On last night's date, I arrived at Jocko's house for what I thought was going to be yet another intimate evening together—just the two of us. But he had a surprise for me. I generally didn't like surprises, but Jocko's smooth, sultry words entered me like fine brandy on a fluffy, snowy night.

"Take off your clothes," Dark Eyes oozed. "I want to bathe you."

"But I already bathed," I responded.

"Do as I say, my love. You won't be disappointed." His hands rested on my shoulders, his eyes gazing into mine with a heat, a deep intensity, a virile universe that made my pussy swoon.

I leaned forward to kiss him. He resisted and instead turned me toward the steps that led to the bedroom suite.

"Take off your clothes. Get into the bath. Now." His words were clipped, stern.

(Note to writing bud: Had it been somebody else, I probably would have frozen at that moment, put up a fight, said *fuck off,* or tried to turn the tables, get control. Instead, I obeyed. Not only did I obey, but I felt something loosen inside me when I did, as if I'd released an anchor I didn't even know I was attached to. *I'm yours. Take me. I'll do whatever you want.* Is this love? Give it up, guppy. I need answers.)

Jocko had a sleek, old-fashioned claw-footed tub in the bedroom, a view of a canopy of oak and birch trees beyond the wall-sized window. The water, laced with lavender oil, was the perfect temperature. Music wafted in to accompany my watery submersion—an Italian aria, not one I was familiar with. Its melody was haunting, impassioned.

Jocko sauntered into the bedroom, an Armani shopping bag in each hand. He placed them on the bed before kneeling beside the tub. He rolled up his sleeves, began to wash my back with a warm, soapy wet cloth. He drizzled his fingers over my shoulders as he kissed me slowly, then dipped his arm into the water, gently greeting my handful with his open palm.

"And how is the bath?" he asked.

"Curious," I breathed. "And lovely."

"Curious that I asked you to take it?"

"Maybe," I said.

"Curious that you agreed?"

"Unexpected." His fingers rambled through the forest of my submerged nest.

"It is best," Jocko said, his voice soft as a cloud, "to live life without expectation. To delight in the surprise."

That voice, those eyes, his magnetic, masterful hand—all were making me shiver in the deepest parts of myself. Was this nerves? Love? One and the same?

"Open your legs for me," he commanded.

I spread them as far as the tub allowed. Two of his fingers sailed slowly into my harbor.

"Touch yourself," he said, as he rotated his hand slightly, pushing deep as could be, grazing languidly on my collarbone.

I reached between my legs, found my titilated, swollen clit, and sighed as my middle finger—intimate and knowing—drummed against it. It circled, then drummed again. My perfect rhythm was so precise, so personal. Jocko's eyes were fixed on my movements as if learning a new musical instrument.

"In this moment," he whispered, "you are the definition of delicate. So open, willing to go wherever I ask."

"Yes," I sighed. "Anywhere you want."

He smiled then, swiftly pulling his touch away from my inside world. I gasped as he gripped my wrist, urging my fingers away from my clit.

What was this? I was dizzy.

"Time to get out," he said softly, brushing my hair back from my eyes with one hand. He rested his palm on my cheek as his tender, searing eyes held me in their ineffable gaze.

"Stand up," he whispered.

I tried; he helped. We rose together. He stepped away and picked up a huge, soft bath towel to dry me off with. As he pressed the towel against my groin teasingly, my already insistent ache intensified.

He kissed my lips finally, deep tongue, deliberate. "In those bags," he finally said, "is your outfit for tonight. Everything you need. Get dressed, then come into the living room for a glass of wine before we go."

"Go?" I said, startled.

"Yes."

"Where?" I asked.

"Get dressed," he repeated, "then join me for a glass of wine."

He turned, taking my clothes—including my bra and panties—from the divan where I'd placed them, and disappeared from the bedroom.

He was dressing me? Curiosity coupled with trepidation teemed through me as I opened the bags. He had actually picked out an outfit that he wanted to see me in. This was uncharted territory for me.

What did I feel?

Inside the first bag was a black, classically tailored Armani suit. In the second bag lay an exquisite, to-die-for pair of black, high-heel pumps, black silk stockings, and two small jewelry boxes.

No bra. No panties. *Vroom vroom.*

The stockings felt luxurious, fit me perfectly. Next, the suit. The fabric was silken, covering me like a second skin. The neckline was low and just revealing enough. I opened the two boxes. A long, sterling silver necklace with a diamond tear-shaped pendant that came to rest between my breasts, clearly in existence just to hang there. A matching diamond bracelet caressed my wrist as if God had forgotten it was meant to be part of my arm.

I slipped on the black pumps and stared at myself in the mirror. I was gorgeous, radiant, exceptional. (Word swimmer: This isn't ego making up for the damaged parts. You should see me. You might start crying, my sentimental double guppy.) I had tears in my own eyes. Was this love?

As I stepped into the living room, Jocko was sitting on the couch, about to take a sip of wine. When he saw me, he lowered the glass, drinking me in instead.

"Bellissima." He bolted up, his voice infused with adoration, his gaze radiating absolute desire. I wanted to curl up inside of them, stay right there, perhaps, forever.

(Yo, Elise. You didn't hear me say *forever,* did you?)

I had grown up in a family that didn't value femininity—being a woman automatically meant that you were less valuable, less important. I rebelled against this drivel by relinquishing the aspects of myself that seemed too delicate, soft, vulnerable, believing that those qualities implied weakness. Standing in front of Jocko at this moment, however, I realized how sexy it was to express fragility, a yielding spirit. It made me feel both fierce and vital, and all of these qualities, I felt in my deepest self, were womanly and feminine.

To submit was to trust. To trust was to let go. Was this love?

I seemed to drift across the room toward Jocko. He took me in his arms just as the doorbell rang. It was Tomas, his driver.

We left the house, entered the Lincoln, and headed to our

destination—although Jocko still had not revealed where he was taking me.

"Unbutton your suit," he said a few minutes into our ride. "Show me your breasts."

Slowly and joyously, I obeyed. My cup runnethed over; I was overwhelmingly wet. A palpable, pulsing ache seemed permanently lodged inside of me, seeping even through my fingertips as I released the first buttonhole, then the second.

My breasts spilled forth.

Jocko leaned forward. "Tomas, please turn the backseat light on."

The dim light illumined us in a soft glow. As I looked down, I saw the sparkling diamond, nestled perfectly between the pillows of my exposed breasts.

"Tomas, do you like what you see?" Jocko inquired.

Hesitantly, I glanced up into the rearview mirror as Tomas stole a quick, nervous look.

"Oh, yes. *Muy bello, senorita.*"

I felt myself blush. How uncommon.

Jocko smiled. "Say, 'Thank you.'"

"Thank you, Tomas," I said quietly.

"Look at yourself, Stacey. Tell me what you see," Jocko continued.

I looked down at my breasts, my eyes grazing my own flesh in an oddly virginal way.

"Well, they're like a world unto themselves," I tried. "Like two planets . . . a source of life, pleasure. They've always been popular."

Jocko's sudden laugh filled the car. "Of course. Touch them," he whispered.

I caught my breath. What hold did he have over me? I felt like putty in his hands, a ball of clay he could re-form, sculpt, transform into whatever he desired.

"You can watch, too, Tomas," Jocko announced.

I did not hesitate at all. My clit thrummed slightly the moment my thumb and forefinger squeezed my right nipple as the rest of my hand cupped my warm globe. A small, eager sound escaped me.

Had my flesh always felt this supple, so velvety smooth? My nipple began to deepen in color, blossoming deep pink under my touch. The insistent ache between my legs spread through my thighs, and my entire body began to tremble from deep inside.

Tomas sighed. I looked up, meeting his gaze again in the mirror. A flash of heat rippled down my spine. I turned to Jocko who smiled a madly intoxicating smile. I felt drunk, happy, soaring.

I was holding both of my mounds now, flicking my nipples, bearing their delicious weight with each hand. I released one and lowered my hand to touch Jocko's prick, but he merely squeezed it softly before placing it back on my luscious tit. Then he unzipped my pants.

"Put your hand between your legs," he commanded. "Tell me what you feel."

I moaned, melting. My hand did as it was told. The drenched walls of my pussy contracted as if his voice were inside of me, probing ever deeper.

The silky, slippery liquid heat that met my fingers caused tears to well in my eyes. (Fish X two: Does this ever happen to you?) A low moan from my gut punched out into the air.

"Tell me," Jocko whispered.

I closed my eyes, reared back my head, my fingers curling

into my ravenous snatch, the palm of my hand kneading my in-flamed clit.

Ragged breaths punctuated the words that spilled out of me. "I'm yours . . . take me . . . everything. I love you. Love you . . ."

Gently, Jocko grasped my wrist and pulled my hand away from my swollen, swelling slit. A cry burst from my lips as he licked each of my fingers. Using his handkerchief, he wiped my hand dry. I couldn't have said a word if I'd wanted to. It was the most tender, overpowering moment in my life. I had told him that I loved him.

My face was nuzzled against Jocko's neck when we arrived at the Wölffer Estate Winery in Sagaponack. There were dozens and dozens of expensive cars pulling in along with Jocko's.

"Wine tasting?" I murmured.

"A benefit, and I want to show you off."

Normally, in this heightened state of arousal, I'd be disappointed, even angry that I couldn't be alone with Jocko and make love through the night. Yet, strangely, I was instead so utterly blissed out, entirely enraptured, that I would have done anything he wanted. I would have gone grocery shopping, pumped gas. Christ, I'd even have cooked. (Trusted co-author, you know how I am loathe to even fry an egg.) It felt so freeing not to have to make decisions, to release my will and surrender to Jocko's dictates.

We walked into the main room of the elegant winery with its marble floors and rich, dark wood walls. The expensive wines were displayed like precious jewels. The evening was a benefit for the Hampton Day School and the turnout was the typically wealthy, south-of-the-highway crowd mixed with well-known artists and writers, along with the usual wannabes.

Cary, my windsurfer squeeze, was there. He took one look at me—and my Italian stallion—and hightailed it to the far side of the room as if a stiff wind had just blown in. I winked at him; I hadn't heard from him since the summer. So much for Cary.

Preoccupied, Jocko ordered a pricey bottle of Pinot Noir for us. I leaned against him, a woozy smile on my face, feeling as though I didn't have a care in the world—and I never would again. The unrelenting throb between my legs only buoyed me as he introduced me to several people, but their faces and names dissolved quickly.

At that moment, life felt made up of only Jocko and I. We were encased, it seemed, in a sensual skin of togetherness. I noticed that both men and women looked at us, often smiling slightly, seductively. I must have leaked the scent of redolent sex while Jocko beamed the pride of the lustful lover.

At one point, he took my arm and led me along a hallway to the door at its end. He pulled out a key and unlocked it.

"Where'd you get that?" I asked.

"The owner owns two of my sculptures. We're good friends."

Closing the door behind us, Jocko held my hand as we climbed down a long, dark staircase. At the bottom, he flipped on a light switch. Several wall sconces lit up, revealing a path down a long, narrow passageway.

"Stay here," Jocko said, and he then proceeded down the hallway. Eventually I lost sight of him, but I was able to hear his footsteps echoing off the stone walls.

I heard the *click* of another light switch and at the farthest end of the hall, I saw Jocko's silhouette.

"Take off your clothes," he directed. His voice, deep and resonant, reverberated through my every nerve ending.

I slipped off my jacket, then my slacks. I still wore my high heels, stockings, and diamond jewelry.

"Now your stockings," he said.

I slipped out of my pumps, rolled off my hose, then put my high heels back on.

"Come to me," he said.

I strode forward. With every step my pussy beat a steady, unrelenting rhythm.

"Stop," Jocko commanded. He was about ten feet in front of me, still in the shadows. "Turn around."

I did.

"On your knees."

I knelt.

"Lift your ass toward me."

An unintelligible sound slid out of my throat as I obeyed.

"Exquisite," he whispered. "Spread your legs wider."

As I did, my body felt ignited from within, every pore a tiny bonfire. Between my legs, a raging blaze reigned.

"Are you wet?" he asked.

I dipped my fingers into the sea of myself and could not help but groan.

He moaned in response—we were a song together. "Slide your hand back to your tender hole, my beauty," he crooned.

My ass muscles contracted as my fingers, slick with hot juice, slipped across my favorite spot—the place Jocko had plumbed so expertly our first time together.

"But your pussy needs your attention right now."

I gasped, completely under his spell.

"Finger-fuck yourself, baby," he went on.

I groaned, my ass quivering, as I pressed one, two, three beautiful fingers deep into my scorching slit.

"Jocko." I writhed. "Fuck, I'm yours! All of me. Take me, now!"

For a moment, there was stillness. Then I heard the unmistakable sound of his zipper, and a thrilling wave catapulted through my entire body.

All at once, his arms lifted me from my knees. He turned me to face him, his majestic hands cupping my ass. He hoisted me up, his fat stiff cock slamming into my raw ravine. My legs wound around him as he punctured, pummeled, pierced my gash.

Ecstasy.

His tongue burst into my mouth and we both grunted—animal, primal. We were wild creatures, our sounds cascading from our bodies into each other's.

A feral, keening noise exploded between us, so loud the walls seemed to quake, the ground to tremble beneath us. Still holding me, he dropped to his knees. Our breathing rough and ragged, both of us gulped in air, our arms twined around each other as tight as could be, his prick still pulsing inside of me, my rhapsodic inner walls still squeezing against it.

"I love you," he said finally, kissing my eyelids, cheeks, neck, mouth.

Tears fell from my eyes as he gently lifted me in his arms and carried me through the passageway to where I'd abandoned my clothes. We were silent, no words shared as he dressed me.

We emerged back into the main room of the winery absolutely flushed, perhaps a bit disoriented. We sipped our Pinot Noir as the buzz of human voices filled the air, staring steadily into each other's eyes. Occasionally, we would speak a sentence or two to people around us. But we were still in our private thrall.

Eventually, his arm tight around my waist, Jocko walked us outside to where Tomas was waiting. We climbed into the car. My love held me close, as close as possible, my face resting against his chest, my ear listening to his heartbeat as if it were the most unutterably singular sound imaginable.

This had to be love.

ELISE

It was a relief for both of us when C finally left for her European exhibition. I'd been horrible to be around since I returned from my visit with Rachel. By this point in our relationship, C knew not to get into it with me about her. I'd become unreachable, surly, confused. However, without C, my erotic landscape had become a desert. No Joe. No Marisa. No C. Was this a sign I needed to stop having sex for a while? That was like unhooking me from life support. (All right, Stacey, a bit dramatic, but you'd feel the same way. Admit it!)

She could be wise, my writing partner, so I'd taken her advice: I'd been writing at least five hours a day. And exercising. *Indulging* (oh, how I wanted to slap Donovan for that) in no more than one hour-long crying jag per each twenty-four hour period. No phone calls or e-mails to Rachel. Not that she had tried to contact me since New York. That was her style: hit and run love. Out of sight, out of mind. It had been ten days. The hardest rule? I could only write one paragraph per day in my journal concerning Rachel. I didn't get to vomit up ten, twelve, twenty pages, as was my want:

September 24

I miss the beating slippery pulse of Rachel against my mouth, her taste, and the singular texture of her clit. I miss the slow drip of her juices after she comes, offering me sustenance. My body feels populated by a mass of tired cynics, demanding change. No more

*head buried in the sand, palms pressed over ears, eyes, lips, and
pussy for us!*

A few weeks went by. I both luxuriated and languished in my
newfound solitude. In the midst of my misery, I received a phone
call from Dia. She was showing the series of nudes she had
painted—all of me—at a gallery in Bridgehampton.

"Please come, Elise. I've missed seeing you."

I was into my fourth week of Rachel recovery and the idea of
seeing Dia and perhaps having another opportunity to make love
with her was tempting. I asked Stacey to invite Jocko so I could finally meet him, but she begged off, not ready to do the couple
thing in public yet.

Elise: What do you mean you won't come?

Stacey: We've only been together for a couple of weeks. It's
too soon.

Elise: Helloooo . . . it's been *seven* weeks. You must be forgetting
that you're a Double Scorpio. In that amount of time, you'd usually
have had at least two affairs.

Stacey: (dripping with attitude) Well, maybe this is not the *usual*
affair. Jocko likes us to be together—alone, if you get my drift.

Elise: Yeah, if you mean snowdrift.

Stacey: Brrr . . . that's chilly. Elisimo, if you really need me to be
there, say the word.

Elise: Okay, if I do I will.

Usually, I didn't like to attend those arty, narcissistic shoulder-
bumping, bad-wine events at all. But, truthfully, I'd had it with the
company I'd been keeping—namely me, myself, and dismal I. Al-

though once I knew Stacey would have come through if I needed her to, I was able to pull it together and wend my way westward of East Hampton.

The gallery was in an enormous white barn with huge windows and two floors, the second of which was an open loft space. There were at least seventy-five people in attendance when I arrived. There I was on the walls, dozens of me, naked, exposed, with two-thousand-dollar price tags typed under titles such as: *Nude #22.* Luckily, because of Dia's style, I was not recognizable. Well, not readily, anyway, unless you had committed my body to memory. C would know. Rachel, maybe. Others? I wasn't sure.

The drowsy, mid-October sun cast the space in soft pink and orange hues. The room buzzed with voices coming from huddled clusters of artists, patrons, and potential buyers. My eyes scanned for Dia, finally landing on her. She wore a low-cut blouse and tight black jeans. A hint of her lavender bra peeked out from beneath her shirt. She was radiant, not paint spattered as I had been accustomed to seeing her in her studio.

Four gushing fans surrounded her, and I felt a quick pulse of jealousy. A tall, handsome man stepped up behind her. He was bald in a hip way, wearing black-framed glasses and a casual black suit. His hand rested on the small of her back as he guided her politely away from the foursome and pulled her aside, whispering. That had to have been Nick, her live-in boyfriend who designed landscapes for high-end homeowners in the Hamptons. I vaguely remembered a framed photo of him in Dia's studio. They talked closely, somberly, and I could see Dia's shoulders tighten. She rolled her eyes and stepped away from him. He watched as she moved toward a couple in their fifties, obviously dripping with wealth.

I moved from one painting to the next, slowly, lingering, remembering the day or night I posed in each position. I was strangely detached from viewing myself naked. Occasionally, I focused on someone else staring at the paintings, how their eyes drifted across the canvas—evaluating, judging. Some smiled, obviously receiving pleasure from the indelible female form.

Finally I saw a moment of opportunity to approach Dia. I stepped up behind her. "Beautiful work," I whispered.

She turned, extended her hand to mine. "Thank you for coming," she said. Before I could blink, she moved on to someone else.

My legs felt like two cement blocks as another landed on my chest. A pressure built in my head and ears, my brain a drum being pummeled. I didn't know how—survival instinct?—but I made my way to the exit. As I passed by Nick I would swear the look he gave me was filled with venom.

I poured myself a deep glass of scotch at home, picked up the phone, and called Stacey. Big surprise, she wasn't there. I left a message: "Writer down. Emergency. Stat."

I picked up my journal, wrote my Rachel paragraph:

October 16

Touching you feels as necessary as heart chambers pumping blood. I can easily conjure up the ache of your fist exploding open my cunt, our eyes twined in a raw gaze, hushed murmurings from you, gentle as a drowsy puppy, "Breathe, let me in. It's okay. Relax, I'm right here." I offer all of me to you like a confession. The walls of my cunt expand, pulse against your tight ball of squeezed fingers on their snail-slow crawl inside of me. Fuck you. Fuck Dia.

As I wrote those words, a well of tears threatened to dampen the page, maybe even smudge the ink and render my words incomprehensible. Each salty drop was on an impossible mission (*this tape will self-destruct in ten seconds*). It was as if my tears were trying to protect me from putting it on paper, from the serrated vulnerability of knowing and exposure.

I waited for my writing partner to call me back, drank more scotch, tried to call C three times but couldn't get through on her cell phone. Finally, at two A.M., the phone rang.

"Stacey," I answered.

"No," the voice whispered. "It's me, Elise."

Dia. I was a little drunk—and stunned.

"I'm so sorry," she continued. "It was Nick. I told him about you. He's so angry about it."

"Why did you tell him?" I didn't understand people's apparent need to be honest at all costs. What happened to private thoughts, private acts, mystery? Coupledom should never erase individuality or privacy.

"It just happened. We were having a fight. I said it to hurt him."

"No wonder he looked at me the way he did," I said.

"He blames you, called you a predatory dyke."

Why was she telling me this? I didn't care what Nick thought. I didn't know him, and I was sure he'd spoken out of anger. She had made the first move, not me. Who cared?

"When I told him I invited you," she continued, "he went off."

I felt like I was being used as a weapon in their relationship, a tool to act out some ongoing drama, and I didn't like it.

"I have to go," I said.

"Wait, please." Her voice leaked desperation.

"Dia," I whispered, tired and defeated.

"He's going into the city this weekend. I want to see you. I can't stop thinking about . . . that night."

My clit pulsed. I was so fucking pathetic. Desire knocked, I answered.

"I'll think about," I said. (Of course I was going to see her.)

I hung up.

Our night together:

She had finished the last nude painting of me. It was late. Dark. We left her studio, walked together to our cars. She dropped her keys. We both bent to retrieve them. Our foreheads knocked. "Ow," we said. I found them, handed them to her. Our fingers twisted and curled around each other like tiny grasping legs and arms. Instinctively we both opened our palms, let the keys fall again, and as they jangled to the soft earth, she slid my hands across her ass and pulled me to her.

"I've wanted this for so long," she said.

She cupped my cheek, guided me to her lips. Her tongue—soft as a virgin's—snaked into my mouth with a longing that startled me. I caught my breath as her warm hand dipped between my legs and pushed hard against my jeans.

She was wearing soft cotton sweats, and I easily found my way to her curled pubes and liquid mass. I slid a finger inside of her, planted her on the hood of her car, and then released two more fingers into her wide-open damp cave.

I bent to find her clit with my mouth, and she lifted her hips, writhed beneath my mouth, squeezing my hand hard, pressing my drenched face against her clit. I could feel the pulsing madness of her body, the frenzy of every pore releasing, and I heaved my body on top of hers as she quaked and shivered for what seemed like an eternity. I licked her face, tasting the salt of her sweat, then suddenly craved a margarita.

We stayed on the hood of her car—I was startled by her hunger. As her clit spasmed for the fourth, fifth time, she wouldn't release my mouth, she demanded more, more, more. She was so not done.

Where the fuck was Stacey? I was having an erotic meltdown, and she was off somewhere happy-fucking-in-love with an Italian sculptor! Didn't she realize her writing partner was about to sign herself into a spa-slash-mental institution seeking drugs, massages, and drool spilling down her chin rather than real life? I didn't like Stacey in love; she was less available to me. Although—and I'd never admit this to her—the experience seemed so lovely, so endearing. Maybe I was just jealous. I missed C. Marisa was kaput. Joe was in Ronkonkoma. Rachel had sucked my blood. Dia was now knocking on the threshold of my desire. HELP!

STACEY

When the cell phone rang, I answered the call without bothering to check who might be trying to reach me. I just assumed it was Jocko, because on average he was calling me at least a half-dozen times a day. Quite out of character for my usually suspicious nature, I'd answer the phone from the gym, while perusing the vegetable aisle at the market, pulling into the gas station, driving on the highway (ah hah! The initial car-bent theme has returned yet again).

Vroom vroom, vroom vroom, there was no doubt that our hearts were beating pitter-patter in the love room.

So I could not have been more surprised when it was *her* voice, *the* voice, the very one that had buried me time and again, since our knowing of each other immemorial. The one, the only: *Gabrielle!*

"How are you, sweet pea?" she began.

"Uh, good, you know," I sputtered.

"I have something really serious to talk to you about. Is this a good time?" she queried.

"Hold on," I croaked, glancing around. Where was I?

Just hearing her voice had completely disoriented me. Oh, I was at Hampton Chutney Co. in Amagansett, waiting for my lunchtime *dosa*. I stepped outside, wandered over to an empty table in the relatively empty square, and sat down. I pressed each foot firmly against the ground.

"Yeah, I can talk," I finally said.

The truth was, I had not heard from G-spot since she'd left— nay, planted—her panties for me to find after her last visit. That was this past summer, when she'd obviously placed them in the bathroom's otherwise empty wire mesh wastebasket. Because she'd cleverly spirited away the rest of the trash elsewhere, hers was an overtly deliberate move. Let's be realistic; how would I *not* see them? Instinctively I felt I could judiciously surmise that she'd purposely left a part of herself behind. At least the part she'd wanted me to inhale, whiff, linger, cream, cry, paralyze, and possibly die over.

The memory of the black lace bikinis was suddenly over-whelming. G-spot's musky, slightly coppery scent flooded my senses. As I inhaled deeply it was as if my olfactory function launched into a spontaneous demonstration of its capacity to have stored the following aspects of what I'd sniffed on Gabrielle's soft cottony crotch almost two months ago: a tincture of garlic (from the pasta she had made for us their last night here); warm, slightly salted butter; droplets of Côtes du Rhône; damp hay.

Where the hay came from was anybody's guess. (Hello, my perspicacious minnow, your brilliant thoughts?)

The swirl of sensations within made her next words seem even more surprising.

"It's over," she announced.

"What is?" I asked.

"Me and him," she answered.

My brain spun in fast rewind. I could not even remember his name; *the cold, dead hand* was how I had always thought of him from the moment we had met at the Waldorf. Even then we had not actually met, just come into contact with each other's presence thanks to You-Know-Who. That was so her style, not even telling me they were married until that moment.

"What happened?" I asked.

Her sigh was so big, it toppled her. "Who cares? What matters is you—and me. I'm leaving him for you. We can finally be together."

My stunned silence.

"Are you there? Did you hear me?" she asked.

Leaving him for me?

"But I'm only doing it under one condition," she continued. Suddenly her tone changed to that of a meteorologist announcing the imminent arrival of an oncoming, catastrophic storm.

"Stacey, are you there?"

I was speechless. My heart slammed against my rib cage. My head felt like it had morphed into a missile, a moment from detonation.

"I . . . I'm here," I spluttered.

"Okay, baby. Here's the thing. I'll only do it if you commit to me one hundred percent. That means no more hanky-panky, just me and you. Monogamy. Fidelity. Posterity. What do you say?"

Posterity? The more meaningful question was, what *could* I say? The reality was, Gabrielle and I had not ever even been to bed together. It was possible—though I doubted it with every breath of my being—that we'd be lousy doing the dirty together. But besides that, the only person I'd made love to since I met Jocko—was, well, Jocko.

And I realized in that instant, Jocko was the only person to whom I wanted to make love to at all.

Plus, my snatch had not even vaguely responded to G-spot's words.

For Fate's sake, I was literally, undoubtedly, maniacally in love!

I felt my silence vibrating between us on the phone line.

"Stacey? Is it just too much all at once?" spilled out of her. "I thought about waiting to see you in person, but I'm leaving to-morrow for the Frankfurt Book Fair. I just didn't want to waste any more time. . . ."

"No," I interrupted, "it's not that. It's. . . ."

"Tell me, baby," she cooed. "Whatever it is."

I took a deep breath. "Gabrielle," I whispered, "I'm in love."

"I know, my love. Me, too."

That voice, telling me the very words I had waited so long to hear. Could I shut my ears? No, but I shut my eyes and kept talk-ing. "With someone else, I mean."

"What?" she shrieked. "You told me I was the only one!"

"You were," I blurted, "the only woman I've ever felt that way about. But I've fallen in love with a man. He's a—"

"I don't give a shit what he is! This is unbelievable. You must be kidding me. This is too fucked up for words. You know what? Fuck you!"

Click. She was gone.

I stared at the ground, my head heavy as if the world had rolled on top of it.

I was so fucked. Not only had I lost my Gabby, my one and only woman . . .

But I was in love.

I speed dialed Elise. No answer. The battery went dead on my phone.

ELISE

When I arrived at Dia's house, dozens of lit candles blazed everywhere I looked. They cast her home in a romantic haze with its darkpaneled walls, wood floors, rugs splashed with vibrant swatches of color, an eclectic mix of furniture and art all about. On the large square coffee table, our dinner plates sat side-by-side. That would force us to sit very close and face the fireplace, which was already ablaze.

"So happy you're here," she said, kissing me lightly on the cheek.

I did not know what to say.

She disappeared into the kitchen for a moment as I took in the scene. It was clear that she'd planned a reprise of our night on the hood of her car. What did I want? Why was I here?

I heard Stacey's voice: *Quit with the questions already. Dig that fire!*

Dia reappeared with a bottle of red wine. She seemed so at ease. I finally took her in: black leggings, sandals, an oversized cotton white men's shirt, her black bra slightly revealed. She handed me a glass of wine, held hers up to toast.

"Please forgive me," she said.

Our glasses touched. I believed her. I believed she felt genuinely badly at the way she had treated me.

She grazed my face with her hand. "You look amazing," she said, then dipped a finger into her wine and lifted it to my lips. I took it in—a salve, a balm, an offering.

(If my writing partner were anywhere on this planet, what I'd say to her was this: *I looked amazing? I had purposely dressed down, in baggy jeans (although my ass did look sweet in them, if I do say so myself), a long-sleeved tie-dyed T-shirt, and my favorite sneakers. I looked cute, slightly sexy, but amazing? Felt over the top. Why?* Stacey would ask. *Why can't you just take the compliment and move on? This might be exactly what you need: a night, a woman, a touch.*)

We sat on pillows in front of the fire, drinking our wine.

"I'd love to paint you in this light," Dia said. Her hands reached out and glided slowly up my calves to my thighs, which she gently massaged. Her translucent skin absorbed the flickering light, making it seem as if she glowed from the inside.

"If Nick knew you were here, he'd kill me," she said. Her lips curled into a wicked smile.

"Don't tell him," I said.

"He has affairs all the time," she responded. "Eventually he'll push them in my face. It's a sick dynamic, I know, but it's what we do."

(So, now I was part of their *sick dynamic*.)

"Why?" I asked.

"We're both . . . emotional sadists."

"So, you probably *will* tell him about tonight?" I was suddenly leery.

Dia laughed. "Probably."

I could have been anybody. She wanted me here only to hurt him. I put down my wineglass.

"I've gotta go," I said. "Sorry."

"What?"

I rose, moved to the door.

"Elise, wait!" There was a tinge of anger in her voice.

(What would Stacey say? *Run, fish girl, run!*)

My gut took over. *Leave,* it commanded. Normally, I'd wrestle a bit, search for reasons to ignore the insistent voice. Not this time. I would *not* be with Dia again. Period. I would not be a pawn in a game between sadists. Not my scene.

Once in my car, I felt relief. Often, our split-second perceptions were absolutely on the mark. Ignored, they came back to bite us in the ass. Oh what I needed was to be home, alone. Suddenly what I wanted more than anything was to reconnect with the me, myself, and I that wasn't so dismal and bereft. Maybe I'd play with my Magic Wand.

There would always be more lovers. (Right, Donovan? Please say yes. *No doubt, little swimmer.*)

STACEY

But would there be more lovers for me? It did not seem possible that I had turned Gabby down. And without a nanosecond of hesitation or doubt. She was the only woman I had ever had the hots for and those had cooked from my heart to begin with, not from my nether regions. From the instant I had met her so many years ago at the New York Book Fair, my life had changed. It was like a part of her had lived inside of me, always.

And yet.

Along came Jocko, my dark-eyed wonder. In my experience with him, I had already learned so much about love, about relinquishing the reins, discovered the paradoxical freedom of waving good-bye to control. Regardless, it didn't seem possible that I wanted to make love with him and him alone; I had never been that type of girl.

But now I was?

Life—even more than the little speck that comprised my own experience, mattering not even as much as a tiny eyelash on the face of the world—was incomprehensible.

ELISE

Ronkonkoma! I got a call from Ronkonkoma! Joe's wife and kids had gone to Disneyland and he was coming back here for the weekend.

"Are you free?" he asked.

"You have no idea," I responded.

After I hung up I shouted to Max, "GUESS WHO'S COMING? BUDDY AND JOE!"

Max wagged and barked along with me.

A fishing pal of Joe's offered his Montauk house for us to use all weekend. Max and I arrived at seven P.M. The second Joe opened the door, Max careened into the house and joined Buddy on a relay race through the rooms sniffing corners, furniture, and searching out potential food sources.

I hadn't seen Joe for over two months. He was thinner and obviously leaner from the brawny requirements of construction work. He wore jeans and a black sweater, appearing less working-class than usual. We didn't hug or kiss when I entered. Both of us acted nervous—like we had first-date jitters.

I glanced around the place. Perched above the Atlantic on Old Montauk Highway, the main room had floor-to-ceiling windows, a huge bed that faced the ocean, and an old-fashioned wood stove fireplace.

I walked slowly from room to room. Joe followed. The place was simple. Cozy. There was a small kitchen and fully stocked bar, along with an invitation from Joe's friend that we indulge in whatever we wanted.

"So," I said. "Your friend knows about us?"

"Bob," Joe answered. "Yes. He knows."

"Is he married?"

"Divorced."

"Why did you tell him?" I asked, turning slightly.

"He asked." Joe shrugged his broad shoulders. "Felt good to have someone to talk to about it."

I extended my hand behind me and found his. His palm was warm, and he squeezed with the gentle strength I longed for. I turned completely around.

"You look so good, Joe," I said, my eyes finally meeting his. "I've missed you."

His face flushed red. An adorable horniness gleamed in his eyes. "Me, too."

He pulled me hard against him, his arms winding around my back, his hands, insatiable, exploring, as his open mouth found mine. His hot tongue filled me, sucking with such intensity my knees went weak. He groaned, his hands holding my ass cheeks, pressing me into his simmering, hardening groin.

My cunt was churning, roaring, ocean wet, desire spilling out of me in wave upon wave. That delirious sensation of raw, physical need flowed through my body. Urgent. Vital.

My own hands greeted his newly muscled back, felt the flexibility and strength, the warm heat of his flesh under his sweater. My fingers celebrated the lack of softness, the brick solidity of Joe—a man, thank God, a man! It had been too long.

Still encased in his jeans, his escalating, hard-as-concrete cock seemed to complete the space between my legs as he lifted me easily, rocking my hips against his scorching crotch of explosive need. My clit ballooned against my own jeans. I wasn't wearing panties, and I could feel it ignite, a wet blaze as Joe kept rocking me against him. Our tongues were indiscernible—melted, fused together. Low, belly-deep moans from both of us filled the air.

Time didn't exist, seemed to stretch and extend beyond seconds, minutes, hours. How I missed this girth, the rough stubble of his cheek against mine, the raw power of his limbs. I could easily lift Dia onto the hood of her car as if she were a spirit. Joe could probably bench-press me above his head, twirl me around, and plant me wherever he wanted. He could overcome me, force me, fuck me with the sheer strength of his body compared to mine. This dominance ushered within me a kind of sweet submission. I welcomed it.

Lately I'd been under the emotional thumb of two women— Rachel and Dia. Sucked. Drained. Exhausted by too much feeling, too much internal wrestling, twisting within a tornado of painful longings, games, insecurities, insane projections. All of this was historical, psychological horseshit, if either of them wanted to know the truth. Men were simple. They were what they were. Sure, they had struggles, but bottom line, they answered to their biological urgings more easily than women did.

After pushing me onto the bed, Joe finally released his dick—a glimmering boulder engorged with life blood, the stuff that fueled this magnificent man. He pulled a condom from his back pocket. I'd already wriggled out of my jeans, and I grabbed the packet, tore it open with my teeth, slid out the nubby rubber, and glided it easily over his prick.

I dipped my hand into my throbbing, saturated pussy, rubbed my juices across his pulsing shaft, then flung wide my legs as he plunged inside of me.

The expression on his face was one of pure joy, rampant pleasure, careening ecstasy. I grabbed onto his back, bucking and writhing beneath him, our tongues stretching, sucking, probing as deeply as possible. I pulled off his sweater, dying to smell his sweat, slide my hands across the fleshy, muscled mass of this man.

We both cried out like tennis players grunting loudly with each strike of the ball. He rammed his stealth cock to the most subterranean depths of my wanting cunt. With each thrust I felt he was erasing the tainted remnants of Rachel and Dia. Cleansing me. Clearing the muddy, murky, messy paths they had traversed. I needed this fuck. My being needed this fuck. My psyche desperately needed this fuck. No hidden agendas. No games. No manipulations. Pure. Exquisite. Fucking.

I crushed my breasts against his rough chest, smashing my nipples as hard as possible against him. My own soft belly slapped against his ripped abs. His dick ploughed my cunt with a hunger, a fury, a raw need. I released my tongue from his mouth, seized his right nipple between my teeth and bore down. He screamed. I licked softly, sucked the nipple like a baby would, then bit again.

All at once, Joe's body spasmed, jerked, and he thrust as a surge of cum filled the condom. The heat of his liquid fuel seared my cunt, and I bucked—once, twice—then I orgasmed, meeting Joe's wailing moan with my own.

Max and Buddy, hearing our cries, suddenly appeared. They pounced on top of us in unison and began licking our faces and sweat-slicked bodies.

Stacey, I'm back. Your forlorn writing partner had a weekend of unmitigated fucking. No drama. No neurotic acting out. Two dogs. One man. A woman. The ocean, our canvas. Laughter and bodies shared. Good food and wine consumed. One college women's basketball playoff watched on ESPN. Simple. No complications. My thighs and pussy are sore. My lips are chapped. Nipples red and raw. What is it about a great bout of marathon sex that clears the synapses so swiftly? At times the brain feels like a dense jungle of gnarled trees, the air hot and heavy, each step labored through the swampy, muddy ground. Sex clears a path through that jungle, allows light in, lets you sail into the depths of the endless, rippling sea, offering a view of the horizon you feel you have never seen quite as clearly before.

So I'm ready, writing partner. I'm good to go. What's happening with you, lover girl?

STACEY

Did I die a little bit each time I made love? The *petite morte* we'd all heard about, the orgasm's "little death" was on my mind. With

Jocko, I'd experienced my orgasms as the earth-shattering, decibel-blowing, mythological beasts about which erotica writers had long written.

And when we climaxed together, what happened then? Did I lose another bit of myself in the merge?

Searching for meaning, this little Scorpio was. Wondering that if I was in fact losing myself each time I entered the libidinal world, why then did it feel so fucking good?

Too, I did not seem to be losing any weight, so I trusted I was not in danger of disappearing anytime soon.

(Elise: Let us vow *never* to ponder the topic of weight loss in our work. Boring, ridiculous, ultimately fattening subject.

And by the way, may I step off the scale and bring up Whitman again? It was *Leaves of Grass* I alluded to earlier—however mistakenly. My merging of those two magnificent examples of poetry was in no way intentionally derogatory, merely the result of a chaotic mind. [And I will confess only to you, a good stepping-off place into the paragraph that followed.]

Yet once I realized my faux pas [apparently I am in a French frame of mind. Would you like fries *avec* that, my hornyhead chub? That's a type of minnow—don't be so sensitive, Elisimo. I'll change it to comely shiner if you insist], I went back and read what I consider to be Whitman's masterpiece. If I had never pondered it in quite this way before, I think what I came to was that what he meant by *leaves of grass* was *everything*.

In other words, he suggests that when the *child* referred to in the poem entered the world, the first *object* he saw, he *became*. Thus when I see the grass I become it; when I see the streets, the village, the river, the horizon's edge, I become them. In a word, then, I become EVERYTHING.

What does this have to do with anything, you wonder? To my

mind, it refers back to my earlier questions about whether or not a part of me is lost each time I enter the cosmos of eros. Whitman, it would seem, is suggesting the opposite.

Which is a huge relief. First, because it means that leaving the house at all is a good thing. Second, it means that hooking up—if you ask me—is beyond immeasurable.)

I couldn't wait to talk to my Italian stallion about these ideas, reflecting upon them mightily as I pulled into his long, luscious tongue of a driveway. Those last few moments I suffered alone before finally basking in his presence always filled me with a certain savory edge.

(Writing partner, listen to me: *always,* like we had been together forever. Oops, there's that word again. Blush.)

When I walked in, suitcases abounded everywhere. Jocko was packing.

"Are we going somewhere?" I asked.

He laughed, that joyous, dark-eyed laugh of his.

"No, my darling. I am off to Venice in the morning."

"Venice? You're kidding. Why? Has something happened?"

"Just life. I need to see my family."

"Family?"

He touched my cheek. "You say it like you've never heard the word before. Yes, my family—my wife, my sons, my daughters."

His wife, his sons, his daughters? True, when we had met what now seemed so long ago, he had told me that his *family was from Venice.* Yet he'd been talking about his great-great-great grandfathers and who among them had been an artist, like himself.

So was he within bounds with this omission? Not by a fucking long shot. What a lying sack of disease. What a bleating coward. What a smidgeon of filth.

In an instant, I finally understood the roles we were playing: fucker and fuckee.

I was out of there in the time it took to turn around. Back in my car, barreling down that driveway. On my way to oblivion.

(Note to big fish: Scorpions are nocturnal, predatory animals. They feed on insects, spiders, leggy centipedes, *and* other scorpions. We know no bounds, you see. Our prey is located primarily by sensing vibrations, both airborne *and* from the ground. We are complex, you understand. After sex with her man, a female, on average, gives birth to between twenty-five and thirty-five young. Oh baby, they don't call us intense for nothing!

Plus, we got the sting. The venom of certain scorpions may produce pain and swelling at the site of our zap. Also numbness, frothing at the mouth [I can't tell you how many times I've seen that in my exes!], muscle twitches [that, too], breathing difficulties, and convulsions. DEATH by scorpion sting is the result of respiratory or heart failure—mere hours later.

You getting the picture? And don't forget I got it times two: Double Scorp that I am.

And something about Scorpios that you might not know? While they obviously represent the scorpion, they also represent the phoenix. A phoenix is a mythological female *firebird* that symbolizes immortality, resurrection, and life after death.

Are you with me here?

What all this translates into is the summer vacation I never took. I think it's time for a quick trip abroad to hmmm, let's say . . . Venice. And then, newly rejuvenated, I'll fuck my way through the rest of Italy.

When will I depart? When will I arrive? Love, I've come to realize, is all about that. First it comes, most often it goes.

But, to intentionally misquote Tennyson, It's better to have loved and lost than never to have lost at all.

Your thoughts, E?)

About the Authors

◆

Elise D'Haene is the author of the novel *Licking Our Wounds* (The Permanent Press), which was excerpted in *The Best American Erotica 1999* (Simon & Schuster). She has published several short stories including "Married," winner of the Hemingway Award for Best Short Fiction. Her film and television credits include Zalman King's *Red Shoe Diaries,* several erotic feature films (*A Place Called Truth; Black Sea 213; Shame, Shame, Shame*), Disney's *The Little Mermaid II,* and she was story editor for NBC's *Wind on Water.* Associate publisher of The Permanent Press, she lives in East Hampton, New York.

Stacey Donovan is the author of the novel *Dive* (Penguin Group), and co-author of the nonfiction work *Your Fate Is in Your Hands* (Pocket). The ghostwriter/editor of several other works of fiction and nonfiction, Donovan is also the author of two young adult novels, *Who I Am Keeps Happening,* and *The Last Four-Letter Word.* Consulting editor at Bridge Works Publishing, she lives in Amagansett, New York.